Distant Runner

A Novel by

Bruce Glikin

Library of Congress Number: 2005900854

ISBN Number: 0-9663458-2-7

Printed in the United States of America

FIRST EDITION

Bruce Glikin

Bruce Glikin is a writer and runner living in Houston, Texas.
He was a National Age Group Silver Medalist in the two-mile and the steeplechase. Seven of his twelve marathons were in the 2:40 range, with a personal best time of 2:39:11.His first running novel, Slinger Sanchez Running Gun, was initially published by Runner Triathlete News in 12 monthly segments, followed by a year's serialization in Missouri Runner. The book garnered strong critical acclaim from both athletes and journalists alike, and brisk worldwide sales followed. The novel, written in 1997 and published in 1998, was far ahead of the curve. It exposed and detailed a hidden drug culture that did not come to public light until almost seven years later.
Both 'Slinger' and Distant Runner, though works of fiction, are based on Mr. Glikin's life involvement in the sport, and his association with runners at every level from jogger to Olympian.

Acknowledgements

Both running and writing are solitary pursuits. Yet no runner or writer progresses without the nurturing and support of a cast of characters that is unfortunately too large to detail. Forgive me for the omissions, but here is a short list of those who stand out in my recent memory. Joe Fleming, who taught me more about distance running than any coach or book could ever have accomplished. Al Lawrence, one of the greatest competitors I ever had the luxury of having known and run with. Jim McLatchie, who was a coach unparalleled when it came to producing national and world class competitors. His wife Carol, a national class runner who early in a fabled career was a racing partner of mine until I could no longer match strides with her. Len Hilton, an Olympian, running companion, and great friend, whose untimely death with cancer broke the hearts of so many who knew him. The Rice University crew, a group that included a slew of sprinters, half-milers, milers, steeplechasers and sub 2:11 marathoners including Bobby May, Steve Straub, Jeff Wells, Marty Froehlich, Sean Wade, John Warren and Justin Chaston. Dr. Mark Scheid, another Rice product, whose encouragement kept me going as a fledgling writer. Hersh Levitt, for his years of loyalty. Dwayne Day and Andy McStay for bearing with me Monday through Friday mornings at our coffee club and offering me endless encouragement and counsel. George Stewart, who redefines selflessness and greatness. And special thanks to Jacquelyn Hopkins for her many hours of proofreading and suggestions. I thank her for the countless errors that she caught, perhaps making me look a bit less foolish than I truly am.

My most special thanks to my parents, who gave me life and a lust for living.

For the Munich 11

The kid peeled off a set of gray cotton sweats, garments that were in stark contrast to the colorful warm-ups, tights, and windbreakers worn by his competitors. It was slick and expensive gear that sported the logos and names of powerful athletic companies, multibillion-dollar concerns with operations that circumnavigated the globe.

His shorts were navy blue cotton with white stripes down the sides, a pair that had been issued in high school P.E. class. His racing singlet was a white tank top undershirt that was several sizes too large, making his birdlike arms and chest appear even thinner. This was a youngster who looked undernourished, a redhead pushing 5'10", who at most may have weighed 120-pounds soaking wet. He wore no socks, and his shoes were an ancient pair of leather racing spikes that almost fit. He'd picked them up at a garage sale for fifty cents, and was able to squeeze into them although they were at least a full size too small. But they clung snugly to his feet as he ran, and that was all that mattered to him. The black toenails and the blood blisters that they left behind were no more than inconveniences to him, conditions that he rationalized most track athletes suffered anyway.

As he folded his sweats and stuffed them into a nylon bag that held his training shoes, he ignored the snickers and condescending stares of some of his competitors. They were accomplished runners who knew everyone on the track scene. The kid was obviously a nobody, a wannabe runner out of his league in a town where track was a religion.

Almost every great American distance runner has run in Eugene, along with the world's elite from Europe, Asia, Africa, Australia, and New Zealand. It is a town that beats to a different drummer, a place where roses grow the size of plates, the Willamette Valley from the sky an emerald green that many compare to Ireland. It is the home of the University of Oregon, a place where hippie hangers-on from the Vietnam era and counterculture clones from the present meld with Oregonians of no-nonsense mentality. The disparate groups form an eclectic village, one where tolerance and indifference can be difficult to distinguish.

The mercury rarely goes to extremes in Eugene, the temperate climate making it an ideal place to live and train for track and field athletes and roadrunners. But even more alluring than the pristine landscape and the mild weather to the athletes who train in Eugene, is the town's appreciation for track and field, its fans more knowledgeable than any in the United States.

The Hayward Field Track on the University of Oregon campus fills its stands when just the hint of a great performance buzzes through the valley. It is unlike any other place in America in that regard, a country where track and field occupies a bottom rung in the plethora of sports that captures its fancy, some legitimate, many questionable.

As the kid stood, he ran his fingers through the thick shock of red hair blanketing his scalp. He looked all wrong, his ill-fitting shoes, cheap shorts, and tank top undershirt, obvious calling cards that he didn't belong. But if appearances can be misleading, the look in his steel blue eyes told a different story. They were killer eyes, possessing a calm that was disturbingly focused yet distantly detached. They were out of place on his baby face, the kind that belonged to an assassin assigned a hit.

As the runners completed their pre-race routines, the kid glanced up at the scoreboard, imagining finishing names, times, and places. The vision he conjured was etched vividly in his brain as the starter called for the 5,000- meter runners to line up.

He could sense the nervousness and anxiety of the competitors around him as they jockeyed into position at the start. The scent of their fear calmed him further. He was poised like a tiger ready to

2

pounce, camouflaged by a semicircle of unsuspecting prey. It was a scene that he had rehearsed in his mind since childhood, a vicious strike that in moments would become reality.

...

Five thousand meters is a distance of 3.1 miles, a race where the world's finest can frequently run world-class times for any distance from a half-mile up to the marathon. It is a contest of twelve and one half laps of a 400-meter oval track, an event that the Africans dominate just like every distance race that's run.

As the redheaded kid jogged to the starting area on the track — the 200-meter mark, or half the circumference of the synthetic surface -- he recalled record times and who had run them. The current world record for five kilometers was 12:39.36, a mark held by the Ethiopian Hale Gebreselassie, whom some track mavens considered the greatest distance runner who had ever run. It was a time that equated to about four minutes and five seconds a mile, a stunning accomplishment when put into record-setting perspective. Roger Bannister's breakthrough run of the first sub-four-minute mile in 1954 was an accomplishment that many thought would never happen. And now, a bit less than fifty years later, runners were approaching that pace for over three times that distance.

Bob Kennedy held the American 5,000 meter record in 12:58, and Jerry Lindgren had the longstanding high school record of 13:44. Oregon's legend, Steve Prefontaine, ran a high school best of 13:52. None of the aforementioned times or names intimidated the redheaded kid, a teenager who listed his age on the all-comers entry form as 17. He was beyond cocky, possessing a supreme confidence that the ancient Greeks labeled hubris.

As the runners lined up, the kid bent over and checked the laces on his spikes. Satisfied that the double knot would hold, he focused on a mark far down the track. As his eyes lasered in on the spot, his competitors checked their timing watches. Others breathed deeply as they attempted to soothe runaway nerves.

3

A puff of smoke and a crack followed as the gun went off. The redheaded kid sprinted away from the field, quickly putting distance on everyone. It was a suicidal tactic in a distance race where getting into oxygen debt early on was a certain recipe for failure. As he flew out, the seasoned runners in the field paid him little attention. They understood that an all-comers race was just that, a venue that attracted some accomplished runners and some who had done nothing. The skinny redheaded kid, who was out at a breakneck pace, was obviously the latter. He would possibly lead for a lap, or at the most two, before getting passed by the field on the third and dropping out on the fourth. It was the predictable pattern of nutty kids who tried to steal the limelight for a few minutes on Hayward Field Track, showboaters who rarely disrupted the pace of disciplined runners. The seasoned competitors would hang behind and run their own pace, confident that the front running pretender would quickly come back to them and die.

As the redhead made his way past the grandstand and the 200-meter mark, he was already far ahead of the field. None of the runners behind him paid him much attention, the kid oblivious to the electronic timer. His 200-meter split was 27 seconds, an asinine pace. He received equally less notice in the grandstands.

But a gaunt man with thinning hair studied him with hawklike eyes as he ran. He was unconcerned with the kid's split, or the ridiculous lead that he had put on the field. What did catch his attention was the youngster's graceful movement. He ran like a gazelle, his long, smooth strides consuming vast tracts of the fast tartan surface with no seeming effort or concern. He ran with his arms hanging loosely at his sides, the thumbs of his lightly closed hands brushing his hips as he moved. The arm action was in sync with his body, a study in fluidity with no wasted motion. His shoes kissed the tartan track with the deftness of ballet slippers, the foot strikes forward on the balls of his feet, the metal spikes flashing as time and distance blended in a lovely, flowing dance.

It was one of the most beautiful styles of distance running the man had ever observed, and his frame of reference was complete. He had spent the better part of his lifetime devoted to his craft, having viewed films of runners from the distant past; having competed against the cream of his era; and having stayed current, remaining closely plugged-in to the new generation of distance running greats. Like all world-class distance runners, the redhead's movement appeared effortless. To the untrained eye, the economy of motion belied his breakneck pace. The man noticed no sense of strain on the redhead's face. His jaw was relaxed and his lips were parted slightly, his breathing exhibiting no outward signs of labor.

The electronic clock showed 56 seconds as the kid crossed the race's start point at 400 meters. A tightly bunched pack of seasoned runners about 15 meters behind him, stared with increasing curiosity as he made his way around the curve. A dark-haired runner wedged in the middle turned his head slightly to the right.

"He'll be toast at 800," the man said.

His words were directed to a sandy-haired runner in a powder blue singlet.

The blonde nodded. "Sooner. He'll be gone at 600."

The kid was out of earshot of the conversation. But it wouldn't have mattered if he had heard. He was in his own world, frozen somewhere in the recesses of his mind, locked in a trancelike state. It was as if he was moving through time and space in a vacuum where the only awareness was self, a totally focused mindset where nothing else had meaning. It was a Zen-like state where the rest of the world had been shut out, a condition where there was no allowance for conflict or emotion. The man watching in the stands understood the look, having been there himself.

As the redhead crossed the 600-meter mark in front of the grandstands, the spot where the race would end, the man in the stands checked the liquid crystal display of his chronograph. He tapped the split button. The time was 1:27. He had captured the kid's splits at each 200-meter juncture, all three insanely quick efforts. It was a speed far in excess of a world record run, a breakneck rhythm that would equate to a 3:52 mile. It was a pace that was almost 13 seconds a mile faster than the current record.

After pressing the split button on his chronograph, the man's eyes refocused on the redhead. There was no discernible change in his form as he circled the track, no telltale signs on his face or in his body movements that spoke of distress, the precursor of eventual slowing and inevitable implosion.

A third lap passed with like results. The buzzing in the stands quieted as all eyes focused on the event unfolding. A veteran track and field reporter for a national magazine turned to a reporter for the Eugene Register-Guard. "Who is this kid?"

"I dunno. Never seen him."

He turned to his right, and then his left, and then to the row behind him, imploring a cast of regulars to the Eugene track scene.

"Anybody have a clue as to who this kid is?" he asked.

The response was shoulder shrugs, palms held up, and shaking heads.

"He'll die this lap," a silver-haired man said.

He didn't, and when he went through the mile in 3:52 a roar went through the crowd. Moments later the spectators were on their feet.

"Unbelievable!" the reporter from the track and field journal shouted. "Tell me this isn't a fantasy. Is he juiced, or what?"

"Who is this guy?" the reporter from the Eugene paper shouted. "Somebody's got to know."

"Pre's ghost!" a fan yelled.

"That's not a ghost," another bellowed. "That's a machine."

The gaunt man with the thinning hair touched the split button on his chronograph as the kid hit the mile mark. It was the fastest mile he had ever witnessed at Hayward Field and approached some of the greatest miles that he had competed in as a young man in international meets. The youngster, if indeed the 17-years-of-age that he had listed himself as on the entry form was accurate, was even more amazing. It was a performance so unlikely that it had mystical underpinnings, the stuff that dreams are made of but which rational minds rarely conjure.

As the youngster ran, the man with the thinning hair recalled his own youth, a time when joyful memories were outweighed by pain, a period when running was an escape from reality, a brief interlude into the world of fantasy. It was a solitary endeavor for him, and would have remained the same had it not been for fate. As he watched the redhead run, he wondered how fate had shaped his past, if the moment that he and a diehard group of track and field fans were now witnessing was the result of a carefully choreographed plan, or the whimsical magic of a child of serendipity.

As he studied the redhead's face, it spoke of a youth removed from his surroundings, a distant runner whose ability to bond and connect was missing. He understood the complex profile, as could only an individual who'd spent a youth battling like demons. As the man wondered about the redhead's past, his eyes widened. The kid broke stride and then came to a complete stop on the tartan track. A pin drop could be heard in the stands. The kid walked out to the sixth lane, sat down, and took off his left shoe. With no apparent sense of urgency, he began picking at his laces. A spectator in the stands with a pair of binoculars focused on the youngster. "Lace is broke," he pronounced loudly for all to hear.

"He's probably run out of gas," the reporter from the track and field journal proclaimed. "Quit!"

"Went out too damn fast," the reporter from the Eugene paper said. "But that was one hell of a mile!"

The man with the thinning hair studied the redhead who was sitting on the track. There were no signs of visible emotion in the youth's face. He worked deliberately, exhibiting no signs of panic, continuing methodically in an attempt to repair a pernicious shoelace that had frayed and broken. The redhead worked on the lace with a focus that was all consumptive, seemingly unconcerned as the once removed field closed the gap on him before passing.

The pack was a good 150 meters ahead of him before he slipped off his other shoe and stood. Gripping a shoe in each hand, he began running. His style did not change as he ran barefoot in the first lane, a hair's-breadth from the metal rail separating the track and the infield. The shoes moved in rhythm with his hands as he ran, arms hanging lightly at his sides.

As the kid passed the grandstand, the man with the thinning hair noticed that the kid clutched his track shoes with a viselike grip. The man understood why. It was obvious to him that the redhead hadn't tossed the shoes, only to retrieve them following the race, because of their value. The shoes were obviously precious to him, as were his school-issue gym shorts and frayed singlet. Though garments that were barely worthy of giveaway status, to the youngster they obviously meant much more. The man with the thinning hair understood the mentality, having grown up dirt poor himself.

"Wasting his time trying to catch up," the reporter from the track and field journal proclaimed. "He's finished. He'll never be able to make up that distance."

The reporter from the Eugene paper nodded. "Yup. Never make up that kind of a deficit."

The kid couldn't hear the cynics in the stands. If he had, it wouldn't have mattered. By two and a half miles he had worked his way back up to the lead pack.

"Maybe your proclamations of death were a bit premature," the man with the thinning hair said softly, making eye contact first with the journalist from the track and field journal, and then the reporter for the Eugene paper. Neither responded to him, treating him like a nonentity.

Screams of encouragement followed as the kid regained the lead 200 meters later. He moved with the same apparent ease as he had begun the race. Spectators in the stands were on their feet, clapping and cheering as he began his final lap. It was a small crowd, but its volume level resonated far out onto the University of Oregon's campus. The kid finished in 13:55, a good but not world-class time. But everyone in the stadium understood the significance of what they had just witnessed. His time was just a few seconds shy of what the immortal Steve Prefontaine had run as a teenager, and eight seconds short of Jerry Lindgren's high school American record. The shoe incident had cost him precious time, at least a minute or more, a finishing number that would have thrust him into world-class company.

As the reporter from the track and field magazine and the local writer from the Eugene paper made their way out of the stands toward the track, they moved too slowly. The redhead wasted no time as he stuffed his spiked shoes into his athletic bag and ran barefoot toward an exit at the far stands. The man with the thinning hair had a pleased grin on his face as he watched the redhead disappearing out of the stadium. The youth was an enigma, he thought. He knew about enigmas, having been labeled one also.

CHAPTER 1

DANNY MURRAY VANISHES

Danny Murray just disappeared one day, vanishing in the running world as mysteriously as he surfaced. He showed up out of nowhere, a puzzling if not shadowy figure, a painfully shy loner whose background had no definable beginning, middle, or end. He was a white boy with a reed-thin body and uncharacteristically long legs that moved like a gazelle. He could have easily been mistaken for a Kenyan save for his pale skin, a covering that sometimes reddened when he was angry or embarrassed. When it dappled rouge it mimicked the thick shock of silk that blanketed his scalp, luxuriant tresses that framed a lean and hungry face. He had shown up at a series of all-comers meets in Eugene, Oregon, and on a pleasantly cool summer night, the kind that distance runners crave and that Oregonians take for granted, run his final race of the summer in 12:36 for 5,000 meters, a world record.

It was a race that he had led from beginning to end. It was a stunning time in what had started as a minor event, a contest bereft of America's finest distance runners. The cream was already in Europe, honing their skills on a track circuit that aficionados pronounced an exercise in futility.

U.S. distance running had been declared dead, Americans, and most notably American Caucasians, having been declared genetically inferior to their African counterparts. One man had even written a book to back up that thesis, a poorly researched and highly manipulated tome that pronounced black athletes genetically superior to whites. It was a dollar-driven work, one with racist implications plain on its face to any well-thinking individual possessing even a smidgen of critical judgment.

But Danny Murray never seemed aware of or, if he was, concerned with any of that. He was just a kid who showed up one evening out of nowhere and waltzed through a series of world-class 5,000s in Eugene as if they were strolls in the park. Following the record race the kid dodged reporters' questions, leaving behind urine and blood samples that subsequently tested clean. It was indisputable proof that silenced cynics, the doubters that said that American youngsters didn't just show up out of nowhere and run world-class distance races. The naysayers said that didn't happen unless they were on the 'juice', shoptalk for a host of performance-enhancing drugs and blood treatments that could make a good runner great and a great runner a world recordholder.

Murray had not left a physical address on his entry forms of the all-comers meet, just a post office box and his age that he gave as 17. Only a handful of American runners had ever come even remotely near the times that Murray ran that summer, none as teenagers. The select group that had run respectable times on a world level were seasoned runners in their 20s and 30s, men who sported the scratch marks from international competition as badges of their mettle. And the only teenagers on the world scene that had ever approached the times that Murray had run were the Africans. And even those were suspect, the Kenyans in particular known to alter their ages like the weather. Documentation of their birth dates was generally as reliable as the permanence of footprints on windswept desert sands.

The rumors following Murray's runs were rampant. Some said they'd seen him camped along the Mackenzie River living out of an old beat-up Ford pickup truck. Others linked him to a trailer in the woods near Eugene. His past was equally as sketchy, whispers tying him to small towns in the Midwest. His youth was allegedly a series of moves from one foster home to another, an unwanted kid who logged endless miles over the prairie, the concrete and asphalt roads of the heartland. Some said it was an elixir for the hurt of being unwanted, the type of gnawing and ache that only an abandoned child can ever fully comprehend.

But the real story on Danny Murray remained a mystery. Reporters dug and they came up empty as he rewrote the book on American distance running. It was a summer that rekindled a fervor that had been ignited decades prior by a man named Steve Prefontaine, a runner whose charisma and charm were as dissimilar to Danny Murray's persona as oil was to water. It was a mystical summer, one in which American lovers of track and field regained hope. They waited with bated breath as their new hero set a world record at 5,000 meters, and appeared a lock for an Olympic gold medal.

But Danny Murray vanished into thin air following his spectacular performances, disappearing as astonishingly as he had surfaced. Allegations that the kid was a cold-blooded murderer followed, having raped and abused his younger sister whom he had allegedly kidnapped from her foster home. It left a confused track and field public disillusioned, empty, and angry. It was the heartbreak of unfulfilled promise, the hurt of what may have been.

Years passed before rumors buzzed in running circles that Danny Murray, a fugitive wanted for murder, had resurfaced.

CHAPTER 2

AMERICA, KANSAS
MAY 1994

America, Kansas is a small town that lies in the nation's heartland, a place smack-dab in the middle of a great prairie. It's a spot where rock solid citizens value hard work, love of country, and God, not necessarily in that order, and with varying degrees of conviction. It's a place where folks live and die off the land, where bone-chilling winters and blistering summers can scorch fertile fields into a barren wasteland; and where tornadoes can take everything else, whirring cyclones that buzz like the fury of a billion bees, and roar like a freight train as they pass. The black funnel clouds suck up farmhouses, livestock, and tractors as if they are plastic toys, before spitting them out with indifference miles from nowhere. Cows, cars, and kissing cousins are vacuumed up and go ballistic with egalitarian democracy, incongruous items mated in dark wombs of fury before being deposited to distant graveyards. They're dropped in places much like their origin, somewhere in the heartland of the oft- romanticized American prairie. Those with a more cynical view label it a vast wilderness, a desolate dust bowl where no-nonsense God-fearing Americans live and die following frequent desperate lives. It is the land of the free and the home of the brave, but can be an endless nightmare of predictable sameness and mind-numbing nothingness for those who dream of more.

Murray was a dreamer, and it was running that kept his dreams alive. For him it was his lifeblood, a distant cousin to those who ran to lower their cholesterol levels or trim their waistlines.

When Murray was five years old, he went for his first long run, a jaunt that took him down a Kansas farm-to-market dirt road and ended in a neighbor's barn. Murray covered himself in hay as he bedded down for the night, the child seething with anger and full of fear. Hot tears of hurt lumped with smoldering rage, scenes of the domestic violence he had just fled vivid in his mind.

His father was a drunk and his mother had followed. In later life Murray intellectualized that his mother's drinking was a feeble effort to appease her violent husband. He viewed it as her attempt to modify his behavior. He understood her flawed reasoning, that somehow by sharing a common activity with her husband, that she could grow closer to him and persuade him to quit. But Murray's father loved alcohol only. And when he drank, things predictably escalated into violence. They were savage outbursts, eruptions where Murray's mother Catherine became the victim of his wrath; times when horrors and unmentionables not fit for words were inflicted on her once soft face. But Murray only remembered his mother as pretty. His final vision of her was a romanticized notion; far removed from how she really looked the last time he saw her midway through his ninth year.

Danny Murray came home late on a Monday night, the third week in June. He had done that by plan, just like he always did; a coping mechanism to avoid his troubled household. When he wasn't playing ball or reading a book, somewhere away from home, he would log endless miles by bicycle or on foot across the prairie, often riding or running well into the night. That night he got off his bike in front of the small house that was his family's rented home, and carried it up to the front porch. As he set the kickstand, he could hear the unmistakable sounds of violence coming from inside.

He opened the screen and then the front door and, as he stepped inside, was met by the wails of his mother. He spotted her sitting hunched on the floor, back against a Sheetrock wall, arms encircling her knees, which were pressed to her chest. Her face was barely recognizable, eyes blackened and nose bloodied. Her eyes had a glazed look to them. It was as if she stared right through Danny, never really making contact or connecting. Slumped on a tattered cloth couch, smoking a cigarette and clutching a glass of cheap gin, was his father James. James Murray was a small man, about 5'6", dark hair and mean-looking little brown eyes.

"Come over here, boy," he said.

Danny froze.

"I said come over here."

Danny made a move toward his father. Then, with the swiftness and power of a cheetah, he bolted for his parents' bedroom. He locked the door and scurried to a lamp table where he picked up a telephone. He dialed the operator and she recognized his voice right away. "Tell the police to get here quick," he said. "This time is bad."

As he spoke, his father banged on the bedroom door. "Open it, Danny. Or I'm going to bust you up so bad you'll wish you was dead."

Danny moved like lightning to his father's closet and grabbed a 12-gauge shotgun that he knew was loaded. He released the safety and cradled the gun in both hands as his father pounded on the door. "Open up, Danny. Or I swear that by the time I'm finished with you, you'll wish you was dead."

Danny just held the gun steady as the door thundered from the hard fists of his wiry father. The doorframe cracked as his father drove his heel into the door. Four more kicks followed as wood shattered and the door swung open. Danny held the gun steady as he faced his enraged father, fear having been replaced by resolve, as he knew what he had to do. James Murray grinned as he watched his young son struggling with the oversized weapon. In the background Danny's mother's sobs were barely audible, the wails of his little sister Cindy strident from the bedroom he shared with her.

"What you going to do with that gun, boy?"

"Don't come any closer," Danny said. "I'll shoot."

"No you won't, boy. You don't have the guts."

James Murray moved forward as he spoke. Danny lowered the gun that had been pointing at his father's chest. James Murray was less than a body length away from Danny when the youngster pulled

15

the trigger. The boom of the shotgun reverberated in the small house like an explosion. The force of the blast lifted James Murray right off his feet. But it was the look of shock in the man's eyes that Danny would never forget. James Murray hit the floor on his back screaming in pain. The wails were bloodcurdling, his ankles shattered, fragments of flesh and bone spraying the air in a crimson geyser.

Danny stepped forward and shoved the barrel of the shotgun in his father's face. "Move and I'll kill you. Understand?"

James Murray just nodded as he wept in pain, certain that his young son wasn't bluffing.

The police came first and then the ambulance. James Murray would spend 18 months in Kansas prison before being released. He would never see his family again, drifting throughout the Lower 48 for the remainder of his short life, doing time in jails for everything from petty larceny to dealing drugs. He limped badly from the shotgun blasts, perhaps a poetic justice of sorts for an abused mother and her beloved son who ran like the wind.

...

Danny and his sister Cindy were split up following the shooting, the court sending them to separate foster homes. The caseworker told Danny that they were lucky, that not many kids got the chance they were getting. He explained that they were going to good homes, places where they could count on regular meals and a strong Christian upbringing. But Danny didn't feel so lucky the day that the caseworker visited him at his foster home, telling him that he would never get to see his mother again. He would later find out that Catherine Murray was found dead in a Kansas City flophouse, the victim of two fifths of cheap gin and a fistful of pills.

Catherine's body was returned to America, Kansas for a funeral, the town's lone church chipping in for a pine casket and a plot marked by a white wooden cross. The site was not far from the home where Danny and his sister Cindy were born. Danny held his sister's hand as the minister preached about life and death, explaining that only those

16

who accepted Jesus and God could go on to heaven. All others, he said, were doomed for hell. As Cindy wept, Danny comforted her, his arm around her as his mother's casket was lowered into the ground.

Danny wondered about the preacher's words as the pine box found its resting place in the cold ground. His mother had never said a word about accepting Jesus or God, and Danny would have bet his own life that she hadn't. Did that mean she would go to hell? Though she'd never said a word about Jesus or God, his mother always seemed like a good person to him, nothing more than the victim of a drunken wife-beater.

It wouldn't be until years later that Danny Murray would understand that his mother's death, a likely suicide, was an act of desperation. Catherine Murray had been forbidden to visit her children by a judge until she could prove herself clean and sober and with gainful employment. It was harsh terms, his mother having a grade school education, jobs few and far between in the small farming communities near America, Kansas.

The preacher's words had a nasty echo in Danny's young mind and he continued hearing them. It was inconceivable for him to imagine his mother in hell. He decided that the life that she had endured with her abusive husband was more than adequate punishment for any good person to bear, and if there was a hell, she had experienced it on earth in her own life. The sermon would flavor Danny for life in his contempt for religion.

Following the funeral, Danny and his sister were driven to their respective foster homes. When Danny was driven back to the home of Ben and Becky Smith that afternoon, he did his chores. The work followed one of Ben Smith's ever repeating lectures on the Godliness of hard work, one in which he likened idleness to Satan.

Dinners at the Smith house never changed. Other than the sounds of eating utensils tapping plates and the tinkling of glasses, resonance was limited to Mr. Smith's pre-meal prayer, along with what Danny would years later sardonically refer to as any 'pearls of wisdom'

17

that he saw fit to share with his captive nuclear family. It was a stultifying existence; one that Danny found suffocating.   His escape was reading and running. At night, after reading whatever book he'd checked out from his school's small library, he'd wait until he was certain Mr. and Mrs. Smith were both asleep. Then he would sneak out to run. Reading allowed him to escape to other worlds, while running served a dual function: a time to either let his fantasies run wild or to contemplate the turbulent events of his young life in an attempt to make some sense of them. Running and reading were his nurturers, two things in life he could count on for solace no matter how grim his reality.

The heartache of missing his sister Cindy would sometimes propel him to run nonstop in the darkness, long after the Smith's had gone to sleep for the night, to her foster home more than five miles away. Upon arrival he would tap on her bedroom window, all that was needed to arouse her from an anticipatory sleep. And then she would put on a bathrobe and slip out the window.

The two would sneak into the barn and often stay up all night. Danny would always bring along an illustrated children's book, whatever one he'd checked out of the library, and sit patiently as Cindy read out loud. He would continue to encourage her as she read, the child speaking in a soft voice, her rhythm slow as she traced her book's large-lettered words with her fingertips. When the reading sessions finished, Cindy told Danny of her fears, everything that troubled her, all things that he could relate to, having gone through similar crises. He would console her, reassuring her that everything was going to work out. And always reminded her that some day the two of them would have their own home and be a real family, a safe place protecting them from a world that had until then proven so hostile. It was a vision that Danny imagined clearly, himself with a loving wife and children, Cindy living with them as long as she chose.

Other than running, it was the only happy fantasy that Danny imagined. Before dawn he would run back to his foster home, sometimes slipping back into his bedroom without having had a moment's sleep. Even as a youngster Danny Murray had remarkable endurance, emphasis on the root word 'endure,' the ability to hold up under pain and fatigue without ever flinching. It was that endless supply of energy that drove him to make a better life for himself and his sister. When he ran he often had visions of himself circling a track, running like the wind as thousands in packed stands screamed, not unlike a scene he'd witnessed on television in the Olympics.

Intuitively, he knew that running was something that he would some day do well, though he'd never even seen a real track or even knew where one was located. It was the visions of a safe household with his sister and a livelihood secured by a running career that kept him going. Danny Murray had never had the luxury of experiencing childhood in his brief life, one where the source of his joy came from his ability to dream.

CHAPTER 3

WHISTLING WINDS, KANSAS
SEPTEMBER 1997

A series of court actions and moves had reunited Danny Murray and his sister Cindy, and they were now under the foster care of Tom Hornfield and his wife Camille. The Hornfields were a middle-aged couple with no children of their own, the fate of infertility having robbed them of their greatest wish. They were good-hearted people, firm but patient, and had treated Danny and Cindy better than any adults had in their young lives.

Danny had stunned Tom Hornfield with his razor-sharp mind, one where total recall was as natural to the boy as his fluid running. A number of incidents had proven to Hornfield that Danny had a gifted mind, but none more graphic than one that had occurred in the Hornfield home one evening not long after Danny and Cindy moved in.

Tom Hornfield watched Danny and Cindy as they read books in his living room -- Cindy, a school tome, Danny, Hemingway's The Sun Also Rises. What caught Hornfield's attention was the speed with which Danny flew through the pages. Convinced that the boy was just skimming and not reading, he walked up to Danny and gently took the open book from him, making note of the page.

"Are you reading your novel or skimming?" Hornfield asked.

"Reading," Danny said.

Hornfield flipped back three pages, and read out loud the first few sentences on the page.

"Can you tell me what happened after that?" Hornfield asked.

Danny proceeded to recite verbatim, word for word, everything that Hemingway had written. He went on that way for almost a page and a half before Hornfield stopped him. The middle-aged man was stunned at the youngster's brilliance.

Danny, when questioned, explained in a matter-of-fact tone that he had total recall. He further demonstrated his gift claiming that he had memorized the local phone directory. Hornfield brought in the directory, and Danny rattled off exact snapshots of every page, alphabetically reciting every name on random pages of the telephone book that Hornfield selected, including addresses and telephone numbers.

Stunned that the youngster had such a gifted mind, he never suspected the boy also possessed astonishing physical skills.

Tom Hornfield knew little about athletics and cared less, his focus a dry goods store that catered to the residents of the small Kansas town. So he was unaware that his foster son Danny had any innate talent as a runner; only that he spent a lot of time on his own running down asphalt and dirt roads and through farmlands, at all times of the day and night. He never attempted to stop or dissuade him, seeming to sense that running was the boy's lifeblood, an activity that was every bit as sustaining to him as the air he breathed.

On a Saturday afternoon, a few weeks following Danny's twelfth birthday Tom Hornfield and Danny picked up groceries in town. On their ride back to the house, Hornfield made a right turn and continued up the road to the school that Danny and Cindy attended.

Both the town and the small school in Whistling Wind were woefully short on amenities. So it made sense that the quarter-mile dirt track that the town's men had constructed circling the football field was decided on. The dollar amount for constructing the track was negligible; mostly the sweat equity of farmers, the use of their tractors, and an earth roller provided by a builder. Tom Hornfield would not have known the distance of the oval track had he not asked a friend. His interest had been piqued as Danny watched the television with big eyes, viewing a mile race that was being rebroadcast from a Big 8 track meet from the University of Kansas campus. It was apparent that Danny drank in every word that came out of the announcers' mouths, and undoubtedly stored every fact in his clear mind that he would call on at some later time.

Tom Hornfield knew little about track races or the mile, only reasonably sure that a time of around four minutes or under was considered respectable if not good. The number 'four' had come from something that he had either read about or heard in the past, the four-minute mile having a resonance that sounded familiar. As Hornfield shut off the engine of his Chevy truck, he turned to Danny. "Son, do you have any idea how fast you can run a mile?"

"No. I've never owned a watch."

"Would you like to try?"

"Sure."

"I'll time you."

"Okay."

Danny and Tom Hornfield got out of the truck and walked out onto the track. Danny was clad in blue jeans, a pair of canvas sneakers, and a t-shirt.

"You need to do anything before you start, Danny?"

"I'd like to warm up, if it's okay."

"Go ahead, son."

He waited as Danny jogged two laps of the track before stretching. Then he did a series of 100-yard sprints, emulating the routine he'd seen on television that other distance runners went through before their races. When he was finished warming up, he jogged up to Tom Hornfield.

"Ready?"

"Yes."

"I'll say, 'On your mark, get set, go!'"

"Okay."

Danny lined up at the start point on the track, preparing to run in a counterclockwise direction just as he'd seen the runners on television do. Tom Hornfield eyed his wristwatch as the sweep hand approached straight up. He glanced at Danny whose eyes were focused ahead on the track. His foster son had a look in his piercing blue eyes that spoke of total concentration and calm, like he was in a vacuum, oblivious to everything but the task ahead. "On your mark..."

Danny leaned forward.

"Set..."

Danny froze.

"Go!"

Danny accelerated smoothly, his running style so effortless that it belied his speed. Tom Hornfield checked his watch as Danny finished the first lap in less than 70 seconds. It was a time that Hornfield knew as neither good nor bad for a 12-year-old boy.

When he ran the second lap in almost the identical split, Hornfield knew that Danny was consistent, a trait that he equated with good character. Though it was apparent to Hornfield early on that Danny was highly suspicious of adults, if not afraid--and with good reason in light of what he and his sister had gone through in their turbulent young lives--he also realized that the youngster had a sense of resolve and work ethic that was far advanced for 12-year-olds.

At three laps Danny crossed the start point in three minutes and twenty-seven seconds. Hornfield studied the youngster, whose form had not changed from the start, clicking off subsequent laps with metronomelike consistency.

When Danny approached the last curve of the final lap, Tom Hornfield assessed the boy's style. No changes were apparent in his form, and it remained constant as he navigated the final straightaway of the dirt track.

Tom Hornfield checked his watch, attempting to be as accurate as possible as Danny reached the finish. He crossed the line in four minutes and thirty-six seconds, a time that meant nothing to Tom Hornfield concerning Danny's performance in relation to other 12-year-olds. He did not know that his foster son might have run the fastest mile that any 12-year-old had ever run. But he did realize that it fell short of the time of four minutes or under, a time that he assumed was

23

good by mile standards. Danny continued jogging, and did another lap before stopping in front of his foster father.

"Are you alright, son?"

"Yes sir."

"Your time was about four minutes and thirty-six seconds."

Danny just nodded.

"I suspect you'll need to make a lot of progress before you'll be considered an accomplished runner."

"Yes sir."

"Would you like me to drive you home, or would you prefer to run?"

"I'll run."

"Very well. I suspect when you get home that Mrs. Hornfield will have a list of chores for you."

"Yes sir."

"Be careful on the roads."

Danny nodded.

Tom Hornfield went back to his truck and started the engine as Danny ran back toward the house. It was the last time that he would ever talk to Danny about his running.

...

At a parent-teacher meeting Monday evening, Tom Hornfield and his wife Camille met Danny's teacher, Mary Henderson. She was a plain-looking woman with closely cropped brown hair and steel-framed glasses. There were rumors around town that Mary, a Berkeley graduate, was an agnostic with left wing political leanings. Some said she was a Communist, others a closet lesbian. But she had gotten along well with Danny, and his report cards reflected that with the high marks he was receiving.

After introducing herself to the Hornfields, Mary Henderson said, "There are some things I'd like to discuss with you about Danny."

"Has he been a problem?" Tom Hornfield asked. "You know he's a foster child and has had a difficult background."

"No. Not hardly. On the contrary, he's been very cooperative. And I'm well aware of his past. Indeed, he's had a troubled childhood up until now. Danny speaks highly of both you and Mrs. Hornfield."

The words brought a smile to Camille Hornfield's lips, but her husband Tom still looked concerned. "What did you want to discuss about Danny?" he asked.

"Mr. Hornfield, when I did my graduate studies at Berkeley, I did my thesis on gifted children. It became apparent to me early on that Danny has a photographic memory and that he was reading at a much higher level than anyone in his class. For that matter, I'd be willing to wager, anybody in this school, which is quite remarkable considering his age."

"That's heartening," Tom Hornfield said. "Danny most certainly does have an affinity for reading. That and running. When the boy isn't out running, you can generally find him with his nose buried in a book."

"Yes, he is a voracious reader. And his tastes are quite mature. He also has a remarkable gift for crafting words. I can assure you that his papers are very adult in structure and tone."

"Are we talking things of an inappropriate nature?" Hornfield asked.

"No," Mary Henderson said smiling. "I'm talking about mature in the sense of highly developed thought. When I first read one of Danny's essays, it became clearer to me that he was a gifted child. Recently that was borne out by an I.Q. test that I gave him. Danny is very bright, Mr. and Mrs. Hornfield. He has a genius I.Q. It is the highest of any child I have ever tested."

Both Mary and Tom Hornfield nodded, neither of their expressions exhibiting shock. "I assume you both recognized the fact Danny was bright?"

The two looked at each other and nodded.

Tom Hornfield gazed at Mary Henderson and said "What is the problem?"

"There's not a problem per se here. But Danny has special needs that cannot be properly addressed at this school. I'm doing my best to design a curriculum to meet his needs. But--and I say this without trying to be self-serving--I fear that as he advances at this school that the resources of instructors that he will encounter in the future will fall woefully short of what he'll need to keep him challenged."

"What do you suggest we do? You know we are of limited means," Camille Hornfield asked.

"I think the first step is just recognizing that Danny has special needs. And since you are both aware of his gift, we can progress from there. I have some contacts in other places that may be able to help. There is one school in particular where I know staff. They accept gifted children purely on ability. Scholarships are generally available to fund them if financial need is warranted."

"Are you talking about contacts from your college? Berkeley? And a children's school in that area?" Tom Hornfield asked.

"Yes," Mary Henderson said. "I know educators in the Bay Area who I'm certain can help us."

Tom Hornfield shook his head. "No, Miss Henderson. Danny will do fine right here in Kansas. Berkeley, California, is not the type of atmosphere where we would wish to send Danny. Whistling Winds is the type of decent place where a child like Danny should be raised, and will be raised. I know he is in good hands with you, as I feel certain he will be in the future."

"Mr. and Mrs. Hornfield, I don't know if you're familiar with I.Q. numbers, but Danny's is exceedingly high. His is a gift that is extremely rare. The type of education that he has received up until now, mostly through his own reading, can only go so far. He should be allowed to flower to his maximum, not be held back. He deserves that chance. I hope in the future that you can keep your minds open to a change and that we can have more talks concerning Danny."

Tom Hornfield shook his head. "No, Ms. Henderson. Both my wife and I are pleased that you have taken an interest in Danny and thankful that he has been receptive to you. But that is where it must stop. Danny is living here in Kansas, and that is where he is destined to stay. Kansas is a very fine state and has produced more than its share of fine human beings. I am not sure we can say the same for those in Northern California."

Mary Henderson just nodded, understanding that her words were being spoken to deaf ears.

...

The following Sunday afternoon, Danny and his little sister Cindy were riding their bikes down a country road less than a half-mile from the Hornfield's small tract home. Mrs. Hornfield would serve dinner in less than an hour, the post-church meal, a feed that predictably consisted of either meatloaf, chicken, or ham, along with produce from Mrs. Hornfield's garden, biscuits made with lard, and peach cobbler for dessert. It was unpretentious food prepared without seasoning, fare that bordered on institutional blandness. But the meals were better than Danny and Cindy were ever served in their former households, and the knowledge that they would be served with clockwork regularity spoke volumes of their significance. Storm clouds and light rain began to fall when Danny sensed that dinnertime was nearing. He said to Cindy "Let's head back."

As they turned their bikes around and pedaled toward the Hornfield's small wooden home, Danny saw a sight to his left that froze his blood. A funnel shaped cloud that was darkening the sky was heading toward them and the Hornfield house like a whirling black twister. Danny didn't hesitate. "Get off your bike, Cindy."

She did, and he took his sister by the hand and led her to the edge of a cornfield. "Lay down," he said.

She lay beside him, and he pressed her to him, his arms wrapped around her, her head buried in his chest. As he held her, it was apparent to him that she had wet herself.

27

"I'm scared," she said.

"Close your eyes."

"Why?"

"Do what I say," he said in a firm but gentle tone.

She did, and the air was electric with the earsplitting fury of what sounded like a billion buzzing bees, as the tornado approached. Danny's eyes widened as he watched the black funnel cloud spinning madly above, everything gut black, the buzzing at a fever pitch that threatened to shatter his eardrums. Cindy clung to him with viselike intensity. "Are we going to die?" she asked.

"No. But be still until it passes."

The two remained entwined in a deathlike clutch, Cindy's body red hot, as the tornado roared like a freight train. An eternity seemed to pass before the black funnel cloud spun past them. Danny held on to Cindy for a lengthy period after the storm cloud had passed, not letting go of her until he was certain it was safe. Cindy was sobbing softly when he released her and said, "It's okay. You can get up now."

"I'm scared," she repeated.

"It's okay now. I promise."

As the two of them stood, Danny could see the black funnel cloud spinning across the prairie, knifing out swaths of crop and earth with impunity, bearing naked a path of destruction, sucking up and spitting out everything from its black jaws like an enraged monster.

When Danny and Cindy made it to the Hornfield homesite, everything was gone; house, fence, trees, and yard. All that remained was the slab and the storm cellar that was shut. Cindy waited on her bicycle as Danny checked out the storm cellar that he found uninhabited. In a coffee can hidden under a cot in the cellar, one that Danny had seen Mr. Hornfield remove on a number of occasions to check its contents, he found five hundred and eighteen dollars in cash. Danny stuffed the money in his jeans. When he came back out, Cindy said, "Mr. and Mrs. Hornfield are dead, aren't they?"

Danny just nodded, knowing that the couple was gone, and that all they had left behind after a lifetime of struggle was tucked in his jeans. He wondered what the future held for him and his little sister.

CHAPTER 4

STILLWATER, OKLAHOMA
DECEMBER 1967

"Next one's yours, Seward."

Gabe Seward jogged to the front of the pack, a group of eight runners that comprised the Oklahoma State cross-country team. Seward was the lone freshman who had made the squad, a California product from the Bay Area.

He had bounced from one foster home to another as a youth and had several minor scrapes with authorities before turning things around in his junior year of high school. The about-face was attributable to a high school math teacher, Terry Prescott, a runner with a passion for the sport who coached cross-country as a sideline. In Gabe Seward he recognized a youngster with talent, but more importantly a kid with a work ethic that he described to his running buddies as 'boundless.' And it was apparent to the coach right from the beginning, that Seward was a natural teacher, always assisting the younger runners and providing words of help and encouragement.

Prescott's only conflict with Seward was convincing him to back off training, the rail-thin kid with hollow cheeks and sunken eyes, always pushing the envelope on both mileage and intensity. Seward's persistence paid off as he developed quickly into one of California's top schoolboy distance runners, no small feat in a state that cranked out track and field talent that was arguably the most fertile in the nation.

As Seward jogged to the front of the pack, he measured his words, his tone soft spoken. "Let's go the maximum on this one. Ten minutes."

Groans followed his words, and then curses. Seward's choice for his section of the speed workout was predictably the worst. He always opted for the longest possible effort. The workout, one of Coach Tubby Edward's favorites, was comprised of ten-minute segments broken down into intervals. Each runner in the group was allowed control of one ten-minute session. The break period following each effort could be no more than one half the time of the running segment. For instance, if the runner in charge chose to break down his ten-minute segment into 5x2 minutes, the maximum allowed rest between efforts could not exceed one minute. When it came time for Gabe Seward to make his choice, it was a given that he would opt for the full ten minutes of running nonstop, probably at a pace of five and a half minutes a mile or faster.

"You're going to pay for this one, Seward," Tommy Darwin said. "Straight into a frigging headwind."

A slight grin curled Gabe's lips. "This will be a piece of cake," he responded. "Let's go."

He adjusted his glasses, wire-framed generic specs that accentuated his gauntness and gave him an owlish look.

"California crazy," Rubin Gomez muttered. He was a Hispanic kid from Houston's North Side, Gabe's roommate, and had become his closest friend since enrolling at the college in September.

Gabe took off running hard into the teeth of a nasty headwind, an exercise that no distance runner in his right mind would want to attempt. Running out in front was a distinct disadvantage, magnified in a headwind, the runners who worked off each other's backs able to draft. It was the same principle that applied to bicycle and automobile racing, drafting dramatically reducing the workload of the object tucked in the slipstream. Gabe pushed into the teeth of the Oklahoma wind, not intimidated by the ten minutes of nonstop hammering that would be pure hell for the rest of the eight-man squad.

For everyone but Gabe, long distance intervals were likened to pulling teeth without anesthetic. Seward's dream was to become a great miler, the quest of almost every American distance runner in 1967. And his coach believed that he indeed could reach elite status in the mile. But he felt that Seward's best events would ultimately be in the long distances, races that included anything from the three thousand meter steeplechase up to the marathon. His reasoning came from the gut, intuition stemming from Gabe's makeup.

Seward loved running long distances all on his own, and it never mattered when or where, time of day and scenery largely irrelevant for a kid who could get lost in his thoughts. And when it came to running intervals, the speed portion of runs that most loathed, Gabe would pick the grueling, long, repetitions over the shorter ones any time he had the choice. Any distance under a half-mile at top speed was agony for him. But turn him loose on a twenty-mile run, with a series of varying efforts that often approached or surpassed race pace, and he was a happy runner.

His leg lift was closer to the ground than the greatest milers; those whose high knee-lift epitomized record setting middle distance runners. Seward's style was more akin to the skimming motion of the Kenyans, the Africans who were virtually untouchable at all the long distances.

As Gabe ran, the cold Oklahoma wind cut through his gray sweat top chilling him to the bone. He balled his fingers in the tube socks that covered his hands as makeshift mittens, and yanked the wool ski cap further down his ears. The action barely blunted the sound of howling wind.

It was the week after Thanksgiving, the cusp of winter, the first snowstorm of the season likely no more than a blue norther or two away. Gabe had been warned of Oklahoma's extreme weather, conditions that were far removed from the temperate climate of his northern California home. There it rarely got too hot or too cold, Pacific breezes mellowing the fertile coast in dreamy puffs; the blow enchanting a vineland that yielded succulent fat grapes, blushing red fruit nourished by the warm California sun.

But harsh weather had proven to have little effect on Gabe's psyche. He had been a child of tough times, and it would take a lot more than frigid winters or blistering summers to dampen his spirits. The running had given him a new lease on life; a bright path through what had been a dark forest of dysfunctional family life and abuse. Now he had a paid college education to look forward to, a career, and the chance to excel at a sport that came as natural to him as the air that he breathed.

It became quickly apparent to Rubin Gomez that Gabe was cut from a different bolt of cloth than his teammates. While they pursued careers insuring financial success, Gabe talked about joining the Peace Corps upon graduation, working as a counselor in the toughest inner city neighborhoods and inside prisons with hardened criminals. He felt comfortable with the disenfranchised, and they with him, a mutual understanding that they shared from like childhoods.

When Gabe first showed up in the dorm room that he would share with Gomez, Rubin's eyes focused on the lone tattered canvas bag that Gabe carried. It proved to hold all of his worldly possessions, mainly t-shirts, underwear, socks, and threadbare jeans.

The thin mattress bunk beds with the squeaking box springs-- standard issue for the cinder block dorm rooms that housed Gabe and his teammates--was a constant source of complaint by the collegians that came from more affluent homes. To Gabe, his bed was a luxury, a bonus to a young man who had spent a good part of his formative years sleeping on floors and in automobiles, often with no more than a blanket for both cushion and cover. When on road trips with his roommates he was the first to volunteer to crash on the ground, content to curl up in a sleeping bag when motel beds were filled. And the Student Union food, notorious for its wretchedness, was almost always okay with him. Having gone to bed so many nights as a child with an empty stomach had made him that way.

Other than the sounds of heavy breathing and training shoe bottoms striking the asphalt road, all was quiet as the team of runners followed Seward straight into the teeth of the howling headwind. Gomez cursed silently as he worked off Seward's back, the thin man's frail frame providing woefully inadequate draft in the relentless blow. As the wind whistled in his ears, Gomez pulled his wool ski cap down tighter, only his face exposed to the elements. His eyes clouded with water as he pushed, and he could feel his hamstrings tightening.

Seward was the final runner of the group, and when he finished so would the session, followed by a relaxed jog back to campus. It was a torturous workout, one where the speed merchants had punctuated their sections of the workout with burner bursts of speed, efforts that flooded muscles with lactic acid as if shot from a syringe.

Gomez glanced at his watch as he pushed. Five minutes had elapsed since Seward's effort had begun. Rubin's hamstring ache had deepened and his calves were tightening. His legs were stiffening and he knew it wasn't just him. The sounds of his teammates' training flats striking the asphalt were more pronounced, and their breathing was more labored. Everyone was dog-tired, their legs turning to stone.

Gomez focused on Seward, whose head and shoulders remained steady as he knifed through the headwind like a sleek racecar. He was crazy, Gomez thought, a certified nut, both driven to run like a madman and sublimate his needs to others. It was a motivation that Gomez came to learn had no religious roots, just the internal workings of a complex man who was a born caregiver. He figured that Seward would take the shirt off his back for a stranger, or hand him his last morsel of bread if he were hungry. The selflessness coupled with what Rubin viewed as an almost pacifist attitude, Gabe always the peacemaker. In Gomez's eyes, he doubted that Gabe could inflict harm on another human being. Yet he knew that Seward possessed another facet to his personality, namely fearlessness. It was that aspect of his persona that enabled him to take risks in places and situations that Gomez would avoid at all costs. Gomez came to trust Seward implicitly, understanding that he couldn't have chosen a more loyal friend. But when it came to serious racing, as opposed to training runs, Gomez watched Seward change dramatically. The thin man took no quarter in competition, stretching every fiber of his being with a deathlike urgency to finish a step ahead of his competition.

It was as if Gabe had pent-up demons that surfaced just during races, only to disappear immediately following their conclusion. He saw his competitors as a source of energy, the concept of viewing them as the enemy foreign to his makeup.

At awards ceremonies following races, Seward had a knack for disappearing. So Gomez would pick up Gabe's medals and trophies, items that never went on display in their dorm room.

Curious as to what happened to the mysteriously disappearing awards, Gomez clandestinely followed Seward one Saturday afternoon after their morning run. The journey led him to a poor part of town. There, Gomez watched in hiding as Gabe conducted a series of short races he'd organized for a group of poor kids, the youngsters watching him with wide eyes as he spoke.

Following the races' completion, Gomez felt his heart kick in his chest as Gabe unzipped his canvas bag. Seward called forward each youngster one at a time, saying a few words, before shaking their hands and handing them one of the medals, trophies, or certificates that he had never claimed as his own. Gomez returned to his dorm visibly shaken, his eyes clouded with water, the event having shaken him.

As he pushed through the headwind, drafting the best he could on Seward's back, he tried to put aside the immediate anger that he felt for his roommate. Gabe was a temporarily possessed demon, he reasoned, a running machine that was dragging him and his teammates through hell. The fleeting notion even crossed his mind that Seward was attempting to punish them, perhaps for lacking the humility that he possessed. But he laid that quickly to rest, understanding that oxygen deprivation and fatigue were responsible for his irrational thoughts. As the session ended, the breathing of the runners, who now jogged in a tight group, was heavy.

As Gomez and Seward approached their dorm, Rubin said "Why are you pushing so hard, Gabe?"

The two were walking as Gabe massaged his chin with his thumb and forefinger, a pensive look in his grayish-blue eyes. "Rubin, when I feel good, I like to run hard."

Gomez shook his head. "You're always feeling good, Seward. It's unnatural for a person to always be as positive as you. You know the only thing harder than being a saint is living with one."

Seward grinned. "I will try and remember that, amigo."

"So what are you going to do for fun this afternoon? Walk on hot coals or lay on a bed of nails?"

"Actually, I'm going to make some peanut butter and jelly sandwiches, and then I'm going to open a nice can of sardines." Gabe rubbed his hands and licked his lips, like a gourmet anticipating a meal by a world-class chef.

"Yuck," Gomez said, his stomach turning. It was Seward's form of supreme indulgence, making peanut butter and jelly sandwiches on day-old bread he'd purchased at the market, followed by a tin of nasty-looking cheap sardines swimming in oil.

"Delicious," Seward said. "And there's plenty extra for you too."

"No, man. I'll pass on that. I'm boogying to McDonald's. Want to go shoot some pool when I get back?"

"Let me take a rain check on that. I've got a few things to attend to."

Gomez just nodded, knowing where Gabe was headed. He was going straight to the worst neighborhood in town to see the kids that he was mentoring. Rubin worried that one of these days Seward would not return, to be eventually found in a dumpster, or somewhere in a back alley, with his throat slashed. But Gabe never had those fears, Rubin understood. He was incapable of thinking that way. Crazy guy, Gomez thought; Gabe was the eternal optimist and bleeding-heart liberal. But he tolerated his roommate's sensibilities because he kept them to himself. Gabe didn't proselytize, and he didn't make value judgments.

In Rubin's eyes, Seward was removed from the peace-love phoniness patter that well-heeled students were preaching during this Aquarian age; kids of privilege who let their hair grow long and spent a lot of money on hippie clothing and drugs in an attempt to be cool. They talked a good game as a war raged on in Southeast Asia, blasting American policy, when their real motive was nothing more than saving their own hides, Rubin thought. Gomez figured most of them would end up just like the parents they despised. But that wouldn't include Gabe Seward, whom he'd bet would never change.

CHAPTER 5

CLAY, KANSAS
APRIL 1999

Danny Murray felt uneasy about Darrell and Tammy Quick right from the get-go. But the child welfare people weren't overly concerned with the opinion of children when it came to determining their own fate. So when the court awarded foster care of Danny and Cindy to the Quicks, there was nothing that Danny could do to stop it. Danny's insecurities heightened when the Quicks drove him and his sister Cindy back to their new home, a normal-looking tract house not far from town.

Upon arrival they were introduced to the Quicks' biological children, Melvin and Faye, teenagers with ferret eyes that had a milky blue tint. Melvin's left eye was lazy, just like his father Darrell's. The Quicks all bordered on obesity, in stark contrast to Danny and Cindy who were reed thin.

Darrell Quick worked for the Internal Revenue Service, while Tammy had a job at a local funeral parlor. Danny felt uneasy as Melvin stared at his little sister, an almost identical probing look that mimicked the gaze that Darrell had scrutinized her with in their first meeting. The stare was a red flag to Danny, an omen that his sister was at risk of some danger that he couldn't define. Upon entering the living room, Darrell Quick said "This is Danny and Cindy Murray, and they will be here for as long as I see fit. They will obey the rules of this household. If they do not, the two of you will report to me immediately. Is that understood?"

Both Melvin and Faye nodded. Danny's ears reddened as Darrell turned to him and Cindy. "We have rules in this household, and you will follow them or pay a price. Do both of you understand that?"

Cindy nodded while Danny remained still. "Do you understand me, boy?" Darrell bellowed as he hovered over Danny.

Without making eye contact with Darrell, Danny said, "Yes."

"Look in my eyes when you talk to me, son!"

Danny stared directly into Darrell Quick's lazy eye, the intensity of his glare as hard as stone. Quick moved back reflexively, fearful of what he saw.

"I hear you," Danny said in a shockingly deep adult tone.

Quick turned his head to avoid Danny's penetrating eyes. His voice was noticeably shaking as he said, "Take them to their rooms, Tammy."

...

On a Wednesday afternoon at about half past three, Danny pulled up to the Quick home on his bicycle. Darrell and Tammy were still at work, while Faye had stayed after school for band practice. Danny spotted Melvin Quick's bicycle standing in the driveway, a discomforting thought as he realized the teenager was at home alone with his little sister Cindy.

As Danny stepped into the house, he sensed something was wrong. He walked to Cindy's room and opened the door. The little girl was undressed, lying on her bed weeping, Melvin on top of her fondling her.

Danny ran into his room and grabbed a baseball bat. Then he bolted out of the house after Melvin who was moving toward his bicycle in the driveway. Melvin was already on his bike and pedaling as Danny intercepted him. Danny swung the bat, the force of the blow striking the wheel of the bike and knocking Melvin off. As Melvin hit the pavement, Danny struck him in his stomach with the bat. Repeated blows knocked the wind out of him. As Melvin lay still, Danny hovered angrily above him clutching the bat, only the rising and falling of Melvin's stomach assuring him that he wasn't dead. When Melvin came to, his body convulsed and he coughed. Danny, still above him and wielding the bat, said, "You want to live or die?"

Melvin wheezed and whimpered as he begged for his life.

"If you want to live, then you do exactly as I tell you," Danny said. He gripped the bat so tightly his knuckles were white. "And if you don't, I swear that someday I will come back and kill you."

Less than ten minutes later, Danny and Cindy Murray left the Quick house. They got on their bicycles carrying their belongings, the five hundred and eighteen dollars that Danny found in the Hornfield's storm cellar, still tucked in his jeans. It was seed money that he'd earmarked for a new life for him and Cindy.

CHAPTER 6

LONELY GHOST, NEW MEXICO
THREE DAYS LATER

Thomas Tribblehorn was half Sioux, half black, and a hundred percent loner. He eked out an existence from his social security check and by renting out the shed that adjoined his cabin. The cabin was isolated in a thick forest in the Quick Silver Mountains, about a thirty-minute drive from Lonely Ghost.

Danny and Cindy had just gotten off a Greyhound Bus and ambled over to a Taco Bell when Tribblehorn spotted them. Over a breakfast of burritos and coffee, Tribblehorn overheard Danny's conversation with Cindy. The boy discussed the difficulties they may encounter renting because of their ages, even though he had cash. Tribblehorn's ears perked up when he heard cash. He got up, balancing himself on a cane, and limped toward their table on his wooden leg.

Tribblehorn stopped in front of Danny. "Looking for a place to stay?"

Danny studied Tribblehorn's dark eyes. "Maybe."

"I've got one up on the mountain," Tribblehorn said. "There's a room attached. It's not much, but there's running water and a flush toilet. You pay me a $125 a-month cash and the place is yours, no questions asked."

"How can I get into town?" Danny asked. "I have to find work and my sister has to go to school."

"Bus comes by every morning at 5:30 on a road not far from my place. Comes back in the evening too."

Danny stroked his chin as he studied Tribblehorn's face. The man looked rough, but seemed honest. Murray knew he had to make a quick decision. If he chose to go along with Tribblehorn, he would risk being turned in with Cindy to authorities and being transported back to Kansas. There he could face all sorts of problems, perhaps even battery and assault, not knowing what type of injury he had inflicted on Melvin Quick. But Tribblehorn's offer to Danny of a place to stay, with no questions asked were the right words. He knew that there would be dealings with any adult, anywhere that he tried to find shelter for Cindy and him. His gut told him that Tribblehorn was worth a gamble. "I'll give you $100 a month for your place," Danny said. "But you have to swear that you don't tell anybody we're with you. And if anybody in town were to somehow find out that we were living with you, then I want you to tell them that we're your nephew and niece, that our parents died and you're our uncle looking out for us."

Tribblehorn looked at Danny and grinned. "Not likely anybody's going to believe that story. You and your sister are as white as damn store milk."

Danny thought in silence. "Supposing your brother or sister had adopted children? And we were them?"

Tribblehorn grinned again. "That's a stretch, White Meat. You've got a real fertile imagination and a real sharp mind. Pretty damn smart for a kid of your age. Okay. I don't give a damn. You give me a month's rent and I'll play your little game."

Danny looked at Cindy whose eyes were suspicious. "You'll come into town with me every day," Danny told her. "I won't leave you alone."

Cindy whispered to Danny. "He smells bad."

"Don't worry," Danny whispered back. "That doesn't mean a thing. He'll be okay. Trust me."

Cindy said, "Okay."

Danny made eye contact with Tribblehorn. "A hundred bucks a month and you've got a deal," Danny said.

"White Meat's going to negotiate," Tribblehorn said. He grinned, displaying empty tooth sockets and brown stumps. "Okay. You've got a deal. Show me the money."

Danny said, "Just a minute."

He took Cindy by the hand and they walked back into the Taco Bell. "Wait for me here," Danny said.

He proceeded into the men's room, slipped into a stall which he locked, and retrieved $100 from his jeans. With the money tucked in his fisted palm, he came out. Cindy followed him outside and, when he reached Tribblehorn, he handed him the money. Tribblehorn took it and counted it out slowly. He nodded, stuffed it in his jeans, and said, "Follow me."

Cindy and Danny tagged behind him as he limped his way to an old, beaten up Ford pickup. The paint was mostly gone, major portions of the rusted frame gaping with pitted holes. The three sat in silence as Tribblehorn drove them up the mountains to his isolated cabin. The air was clean and cold as they climbed; the thick forest of trees in stark contrast to the desert-like setting from where they had started.

Danny felt a sense of comfort as they ascended, his instincts telling him that he had made a good choice. The mountains were unlike anything he had experienced in the Midwest, giving him a feeling inside that was indescribable. He felt both a sense of peace and power as they ascended; a far cry from the isolating, and sometimes depressing, emotions that gripped him in the barren prairie from which they had escaped. He felt like they had entered a new world, a place like the magical kingdoms he had read about in books from the school libraries back in Kansas. He put his arm around Cindy's shoulder and whispered in her ear. "Everything's going to be okay. I promise."

Cindy just nodded, trusting her older brother who was all that she had in the world to trust.

...

Danny got a job at a diner in town washing dishes and doing janitorial work, employed by a woman who paid him sub-minimum wage. Though it was apparent to her that Murray was underage, she could also sense that he was desperate to work and exceedingly bright. She took advantage of him, paying him a paltry, off-the-books salary, in cash. A second job at a car wash with like arrangements provided him with barely enough money to pay for rent, food, clothing, and money for Cindy's school supplies. Still, out of each paycheck he managed to save a few dollars, his sense of survival heightened by the tough times he and his sister had survived.

Tribblehorn was far exceeding the limited expectations that Danny had of him, the man with the rough-looking exterior and shadowy past proving to be reliable and nonjudgmental. Tribblehorn arranged to share food costs with Danny, and welcomed the youngster and his sister into his cabin to take their meals.

The crippled man's most prized possessions were a collection of dog-eared paperbacks, tomes stuffed in unfinished pine bookcases that covered all the cabin's walls. They were works that ranged from novels to histories and thick biographies, an eclectic mix with no apparent bias for author or subject. Tribblehorn had only a third-grade education but, through incessant reading and an insatiable appetite for knowledge, had become a learned man.

It quickly became apparent to him that Danny was brilliant and shared his passion for reading. Knowing that the youngster would not have the luxury of attending school and a formal education, he seized the opportunity to feed a quick and fertile mind. It was an intelligence that was far more advanced than Tribblehorn had ever dreamt. He assumed the teen was gifted, Danny's memory photographic as he could play back books, even the difficult classics, almost word by word after reading.

Tribblehorn's mentoring was low-key, generally no more than the two discussing an author's work after reading. In those discussions Tribblehorn was shocked at the adultlike grasp that Danny had of each work. He would then hand him a new one, and the process would continue.

The communication between the rough-looking man and the youth was largely visceral, verbal communication sparing. Tribblehorn assumed that Danny would reveal bits and pieces of his troubled childhood at his own pace. With the building of trust, that happened.

The threesome spent most of their nights in the cabin reading, Danny and Tribblehorn for self-knowledge, Cindy for school. Each night after Cindy was tucked into bed, Danny would leave the shed. Inhaling the sweet mountain air freshened by scented pines, he would jog along a dirt path that led away from Tribblehorn's cabin, accelerating to a run as he climbed or descended the asphalt road that crisscrossed the mountain.

Tribblehorn often watched through his window with curiosity as the thin redheaded youngster took off. The running appeared natural to him, Tribblehorn thought; as native as the adult like instincts that compelled him to care for his little sister Cindy; impulses that drove him to look after her like she was his own child.

CHAPTER 7

A ROAD RACE IN LONELY GHOST

On a Saturday morning in May, Danny and Cindy caught a bus into town. They walked from the bus station to a flea market in the town square, a place where artists rented out stalls to sell their creations and merchants hawked their wares.

Danny helped Cindy pick out some resale clothing, worn garments that would serve her until she grew out of them. He also purchased her a pair of silver-plated earrings, a present for her birthday which she was celebrating that day. They meandered around from stall to stall until almost noon before Danny took Cindy to a McDonald's facing the square. He bought her a Kid's Meal, and a Coke for himself, a purchase that would leave them enough money for a return bus ride back up the mountain if Thomas Tribblehorn didn't show up.

In a field, about a ten-minute walk from the square, they met Thomas Tribblehorn. The reclusive man was making one of his rare appearances in town for anything other than the purchase of groceries or dry goods. The event that brought him down from the mountain in his old pickup truck was Lonely Ghost's annual spring balloon fest, an affair that widened Cindy's eyes like saucers. As the trio sat on a frayed wool blanket that Tribblehorn had brought from the cabin, Danny saw a sight that captured his attention. A gaunt-looking man with a white beard and white hair, clad in black jogging tights and a white shell nylon windbreaker, was erecting a running race finish line chute with the help of several volunteers.

The structure consisted of ropes tethered to metal posts that were being driven into the ground. At the end of the chute they set a digital clock, unlike any that Danny had ever seen. Within the next hour more runners appeared, and soon the grounds were teeming with bodies. Some ran fast while others jogged, and some did calisthenics while others stretched. Curiosity got the best of Danny as he watched the sea of bodies. "I'm going over there," he said to Tribblehorn.

The old man nodded.

Danny said to Cindy, "I'll be right back."

Then he jogged over to the chute area, looking out of place in his faded jeans, sweatshirt, and beat-up sneakers. At a table where runners had congregated, Danny picked up a printed sheet. It was an entry form to a run that was being held in conjunction with the balloon fest, a ten-mile race that was scheduled to start in just minutes. The entry fee to the contest was $15, a price that was out of reach for Danny. He laid the form back on the table, and then he jogged back to Tribblehorn and Cindy. "They're having a race," he said to Tribblehorn. "Can you take care of Cindy while I run?"

Tribblehorn nodded.

Danny placed his hand on Cindy's shoulder. "You be good. I'll see you when I'm through running. Tonight Mr. Tribblehorn and I have a surprise for you back at the cabin."

Cindy nodded with a smile on her face, suspecting that the box her brother had brought back to the cabin the previous day contained a birthday cake.

"Is there an entry fee for the race?" Tribblehorn asked.

Danny nodded. "Yup." He shed his sweatshirt as he spoke, exposing a white t-shirt with holes, before dropping the sweatshirt on the blanket.

"What are you going to do?"

"I'm going to start at the back of the race after everyone's off and running. When I finish, I won't go through the chute."

Tribblehorn grinned. "I saw the Boston Marathon one year when I was working up there at a fish market. There's always runners in that race that don't pay and run without numbers. They're called bandits."

47

"They can call me whatever they want," Danny said. "I don't care. I am a free man and I run. Nobody will ever control my running."

"Then go, free man!" Tribblehorn exclaimed. "Go and kick some butt!"

Danny jogged toward the starting area where runners were already lining up. He slipped in at the back, looking out of place in his jeans and t-shirt, most of the other racers clad in expensive running gear. The race would be new ground for Danny, his first contest, and his first time to run a measured road distance. He had no idea how long ten miles was or how long it would take him to finish. In the past, all he had ever done was gone out and run. Sometimes he would run for an hour and others up to two or three, courses unmeasured. He ran by feel, intuition his guide.

As Danny gazed at the runners packed into the herd in front of him, he noticed they were of all shapes and sizes. Most were clad in running gear that looked expensive and recently purchased. They were a curious sight to him, some smelling strongly of deep-heating balms and liniments. Many shone with the gloss of Vaseline, the viscous jelly applied liberally to every imaginable body area that could possibly chafe.

Some sucked fluids from plastic squeeze bottles, containers holding water or energy replacement concoctions. Others chewed on candy-bar shaped health bars that were touted to do the same, while others ate paste from tubes guaranteed to maximize results. Some sported fanny packs that held everything imaginable from toilet paper to aspirin; gear in total that Danny figured could equip a small pharmacy.

The outfits of runners varied greatly, from those clad in full jogging suits--garments that Danny was certain would be too cumbersome and warm to run in once the race began—to those stripped down to the minimum, bare-chested males in shorts, their female counterparts in jog bras and shorts. It was a sight that Danny had never witnessed, a whole new world to a youngster who rarely had

48

experienced runners in his formative years. The bulk of his runs had been done on isolated prairie roads, and recently mountain trails, places where he rarely crossed paths with fellow runners. Danny's main frame of reference for runners still came from the television snippets he viewed as a child. There he had seen college meets from Kansas and the Olympics. Both were venues where the athletes looked nothing like the group he viewed at the back of the pack.

Murray stared up at a man next to him, his curiosity piquing as the man breathed loudly through his mouth. It was a harsh sound, a consumptive wheeze with a deathlike rattle. In an area to the left of the start, runners stood in line in front of portable toilets that had been brought in for the event. A high-pitched squeal amplified by loudspeakers was followed by a man's voice. Following a lengthy prayer, one that Danny managed to largely block out by a Zen-like visualization of the upcoming race, he took a deep measured breath and tried to relax his body.

As the starter's gun cracked he remained in place, patiently waiting until all the runners in the race were ahead of him before starting. He felt uneasy as he began, running as a bandit who had not paid the required entry fee. He was certain that fact would be obvious to anyone who noticed him, he being the lone competitor in the race not sporting a race number pinned to his clothing. He wondered what type of action, if any race officials would take if he were caught. And if he were caught, he wondered if there would be repercussions concerning him and Cindy.

He felt certain that Thomas Tribblehorn would vouch for himself and his little sister as their uncle and guardian. But he feared that authorities wouldn't buy that story. His experience with child welfare people in both Kansas and Oklahoma, ever since he had shot his father and his mother had been declared unfit to care for him and Cindy, had been horrific. They had never listened to anything that he had told them, not when selecting foster homes for him and Cindy, or anything else. And he had no illusions that things would be any different in New Mexico if confronting the same arbiters of public authority.

That chilling knowledge, coupled with the reality that he and Cindy had fled Kansas and their foster home illegally, exacerbated his fears. And the fact that he had struck Melvin Quick in the stomach with a baseball bat magnified his angst. He imagined himself being jailed, with Cindy being placed in another foster home. The scene of her in the process of being molested by Melvin Quick flashed vividly in his mind, as he contemplated the helplessness of not being able to look after her. But his paranoia eased dramatically as he got into the flow of his run, his thoughts centering on the race.

There were many separate races going on, he thought, all levels of runners strung out on a desert-and-mountain course that would test their individual levels of resolve. As he moved past the joggers and walkers in the rear of the pack, they observed him with curiosity. He was a frail-looking kid running in faded jeans, tattered t-shirt, and frayed tennis sneakers. He looked badly out of place in an event which most of its competitors considered a serious competition.

Moving with a fluidity and grace far removed from those around him--a style that, years later, running aficionados would liken to gliding--Danny wended his way through and around slower runners. They were weekend athletes who ground out every painful step, many fantasizing faster running times that they would never achieve. They wheezed as they struggled for oxygen, Danny's breathing not detectable as he floated down the road. The laboring runners were unconcerned with Danny's street clothes or his effortless movement. They were too preoccupied with their own struggles, navigating a challenging course that would crisscross the foothills, an up- and downhill race, the difficulty of which was compounded by altitude.

When Murray had first begun running from Thomas Tribblehorn's home high on the mountain, he had noticed an immediate difference in effort from the flatland runs he took across the prairies of Kansas and Oklahoma. The rarefied mountain air made breathing a chore, nothing like the Midwest from where he had come. But in a short period of time, he had adapted to altitude training, and was already prospering from its benefits. Racing now in the foothills, at a significantly lower altitude than of Thomas Tribblehorn's home in the mountains, was much easier.

He was unaware of the benefits of altitude training, not knowing that his oxygen transport system, which was already highly advanced, had become even more so in the rarefied mountain air. His musculature had benefited greatly also. The labor of moving up steep grades at a measured pace, followed by running downhill at speeds that were sometimes breakneck, developed muscle groups that could not be worked the same way on the flats of the Kansas and Oklahoma prairies. Since moving in with Thomas Tribblehorn, Danny was unknowingly training in the preferred method that world-class distance runners did.

Two miles into the race, Murray spotted the first of five aid stations that he would encounter. It was a place where volunteers manned tables laden with paper cups. Some were filled with water, others with sport replacement drinks. As runners veered toward the aid station table, Danny watched as they grabbed cups of fluid. Some stopped and drank, while others picked up the cups on the run, drinking as they moved. He continued running, avoiding the fluids table, wary of taking anything. He was keenly aware that he was running as a bandit, an illegal entrant who had not paid his fee.

He cautiously increased the tempo of his pace. At five miles he heard his split time, just a few seconds over thirty minutes. The pace of six minutes a mile meant nothing to him. But he calculated that doubling the effort would bring him in at about an hour, a time well short of many of the nighttime jaunts that he took alone high up the mountain. As he calculated, he reasoned that the remaining distance would be easy for him to negotiate, especially at this lower altitude where it was so much easier to breathe. He increased his pace the next mile, and just past the six-mile point had worked his way up to a pack of runners who were moving quickly. They were the second pack, trailing only a group of elite runners, a trio of Africans who were far out of sight and could not be caught. Among them were two Kenyans and a Moroccan, world-class runners who had been invited to the race. For them it was a good day's pay with little spent effort, a negotiable drive from their American residence near Albuquerque.

The pack that Danny worked his way into included nine other runners, men ranging in ages from their late teens to early 40s. It was apparent to Danny by their physical stature and movement that they were of a different breed than the legions of runners he had passed leading up to them.

Danny tucked himself into the back of the pack, trying his best not to draw attention to himself. But the inevitable happened, and soon he was sucked into the middle of the pack. He stuck out noticeably, a scrawny redheaded kid in blue jeans, moving effortlessly in the midst of top local-class runners. A man with shoulder-length salt-and-pepper hair and a pitted face covered by a like beard peered down at Danny with angry eyes.

"This is a race, you bloody little wanker," he said in an accent unfamiliar to Danny. "Bugger off."

The strange speech pattern was Australian, a country that Danny could locate on an atlas but one in which he had never met a native.

Danny remained silent, averting eye contact, moving without flinching.

"I said piss off you little poofter," the Aussie bellowed. "You don't bloody well belong here."

"Why don't you shut up and run, Hughes? He's not bothering you." The man responding was Darren Stone, a man who had just turned 40, a slender athlete with wide shoulders and honest dark eyes.

"Bloody hell he's not!" Hughes shot back. "The little carrot-topped bugger. He trods on me and I'll shove an eleven Nike straight up his skanky little ass."

"Shut up, Hughes. I'm about to lose my sense of humor."

"Piss off, Stone," Hughes hissed. "This little redheaded wanker is a bleeding bandit. He's got no bloody race number."

Hughes turned to Danny to vent his vitriol. "Where'd you jump in the race, you little redheaded faggot? The six-mile mark? Hiding in the scrub, were you?"

"Shut the hell up, Hughes," another Aussie voice chimed in. "I've known you too long. You're nothing but Victorian track trash."

"Piss off, Campbell."

Michael Campbell, a good four inches and thirty pounds less than Hughes balled up his fist. "Let's get it on, Hughes. Right now. I'll kick your ass on this bloody blacktop road, just like I did in Australia."

The two Aussies had competed on the international track scene as half-milers years before, Campbell the superior runner, having represented Australia in the Commonwealth Games and World Championships.

"Go dip your eye in shit," Hughes spit, his voice shaking.

Danny could sense the fear in the larger man's tone, Campbell having sent out a warning that Hughes perceived as real. Murray continued running, flanked by Campbell and Stone, the three matching strides. By seven miles they had pulled away from Hughes and the pack. At eight miles a split time of 46:38 was called. Danny had run miles three through eight at a shade over a 5:30 mile pace, a stunning feat for a runner his age. Stone eyed Danny as the split was called, watching the youngster move effortlessly in his blue jeans and tattered sneakers.

"What's your name, son?" Stone asked.

Danny didn't answer.

"Okay," Stone said. "None of my business. But I'm curious. Did you run this whole race? Just a nod will do."

Danny nodded yes, a response that both men he ran with had no difficulty believing. It was apparent to them--both veteran runners that had devoted the better part of their lives to running-- that Danny was for real. The trio remained even as they approached the finishing chute. With less than a hundred meters to go they began to sprint. But just before the chute, Danny veered wide, avoiding the finish chute as Stone and Campbell completed their race.

Their finishing time was 57:29, maintaining the same pace that they had since Danny hooked on with them at the six-mile point. Stone's eyes remained fixed on Danny as the youngster ran across the field toward Tribblehorn and Cindy. It was obvious to Stone that Danny was very young. He had run a stunning race, one of epic proportion for a kid. Stone wondered who he was and where he came from.

He jogged to his van, and from the back grabbed a box of new training shoes. They were sevens, an estimate of Danny's shoe size. Then he jogged across the field toward the blanket where Danny was speaking with Tribblehorn and Cindy. As he jogged, Danny spotted him and turned, and took off running. He ran toward a mountain road north of the city, moving quickly as he headed north.

Stone continued jogging toward Tribblehorn and Cindy who were now standing, about to begin their trek back to Tribblehorn's truck. Stone was slightly winded as he approached Tribblehorn and stopped. His breathing was quick as he said, "I'm Darren Stone. And I've got something to give to the young fellow that I ran with. Can you tell me his name?"

Tribblehorn didn't answer.

"Okay," Stone said. "It's none of my business. It doesn't matter. But tell the kid these shoes are his. He would have won his age group in the race, and he deserves them." He handed the box to Tribblehorn. "Tell him I own Stone's Running Store and I'd like to meet him. I'm there Monday through Saturdays. Maybe he'd like to run with us sometime."

Tribblehorn nodded.

"Thanks," Stone said. Then he turned and jogged back toward the race finish area where runners were still coming in. Intuitively, Stone felt that the kid and the old man were hiding something, a secret that could damage them. But he doubted that they had done anything criminal, feeling that their obvious distrust of outsiders was likely rooted in experience.

It was apparent to Stone that the redheaded youngster was fearful of strangers, but at the same time gutsy, his running speaking for itself in that department. It was conflict that he reasoned could drive the running phenomenon to levels beyond the imagination of only a handful, but could also lead to his undoing. If the boy was indeed in the tender age range that he suspected, he was without doubt the most gifted child runner that he had ever witnessed or read about. As Stone recalled Danny's run, he imagined the possibilities of what the youngster could achieve with a good support system and proper coaching. He was a once-in-a-lifetime talent, the kind that dreams are made of for those who still can.

CHAPTER 8

LONELY GHOST
JULY, 1999

On the second Sunday in July, Thomas Tribblehorn had taken Danny and Cindy into town to shop for groceries. It had been one of the hottest and driest summers that Tribblehorn had ever remembered in the thirty-plus years since he had purchased his parcel of land and built his cabin. Creeks and rivers had dried up and there was dust everywhere. Swaths of parched earth had fissured and cracked, and foliage that was traditionally green had withered and browned. Hungry deer and bear had become more brazen as they'd come closer to the cabin foraging for food, trees and mountainsides barren of the berries and grains that sustained them.

As Tribblehorn and Murray loaded groceries into the truck, Tribblehorn gazed up the mountain. A plume of dark smoke on the clear blue horizon made him uneasy. "Do I still get my ice cream?" Cindy asked.

"Yup," Danny said. "Just like I promised.

Tribblehorn's eyes were still locked on the horizon, the puff of smoke seeming to have darkened. "I promised to take Cindy for ice cream," Danny said. "Can we stop by Dairy Queen?"

Tibblehorn said, "Okay," a worried look in his dark eyes as he studied the acrylic blue New Mexico sky, free of clouds but for the puff of smoke lolling on the horizon.

As Cindy and Danny walked out of the Dairy Queen eating ice cream, Danny sensed that Tribblehorn was uneasy. The man's focus was intently locked on the horizon, up toward the mountain where the three lived in his cabin. Danny's eyes found the area Tribblehorn was

56

watching, focusing on the dark cloud that seemed to be widening. "What is it?" Danny asked.

"Not sure," Tribblehorn said. "Looks like a fire. But hard to tell where it's coming from."

Danny intuitively fingered the hip pocket of his jeans, his total life savings sewn inside, along with a few dollars and change in his outer pocket. It was money that he never left off his person, not even when he went out to run.

As the three climbed the mountain in Thomas Tribblehorn's truck, the air thickened with smoke.

"Goddamn fire," Tribblehorn said as they drove, his face ashen. "Mountain will go up like tinder."

About halfway up the mountainside they stopped, the road having been cordoned off by New Mexico state troopers. Danny's pulse quickened as several highway patrolmen approached their truck. He turned toward Cindy. "Don't say anything," he said to her.

She nodded.

Tribblehorn put his truck in neutral and stepped on the parking brake as a trooper approached. He stuck his head outside his window that was rolled down.

"Fire up on the mountain, sir." The trooper began. "Sorry, but the area's closed. You'll need to head back down until it's safe to come back up."

"I live up here," Tribblehorn said. "Been living here for over thirty years. My cabin's less than a half-mile from here. Everything I own is in there."

"Sorry," the trooper said. "But we've got orders not to allow anybody past this point. The fire is quickly burning out of control. This whole forest is like a powder keg ready to explode."

"I know my way around this land like the back of my hand. I'll come back down if things don't look right."

The trooper adjusted his mirrored sunglasses and adjusted his hat. "Can't help you, sir. Please turn around and go back down the mountain. Stay tuned to a local radio station. They'll let you know when it's safe to come back up."

Danny felt ill at ease, knowing that if Tribblehorn got hostile to authorities, he and Cindy would be in dire straits, their identities sure to be questioned.

Following a lengthy pause, Tribblehorn nodded, turned his truck around, and headed back down the mountain. When they were out of sight of the patrolmen, Tribblehorn turned his truck hard to the left, driving toward a fire trail in the woods that Danny had run on many times before.

"What are you doing?" Danny asked.

"Going back to the cabin," Tribblehorn said. "Grab what things we can."

As he spoke the truck shimmied and shook, the terrain rugged as the old pickup navigated the chopped dirt road that snaked up the mountain. Less than a quarter of a mile later, the smoke had thickened to the point where visibility was difficult. Danny said, "This isn't safe. We need to go back down the mountain."

Tribblehorn shook his head. "Nope. Got my whole life invested in that cabin."

"Then let us out," Danny said defiantly. "I'm not going to risk Cindy's life."

Tribblehorn stepped on his brake. He turned toward Danny. "I'm going up to the cabin. What you do is your choice. You want to get out here, that's okay."

"Yeah," Danny said. "Let us out."

He opened the door for Cindy, and as she got out and he closed it, Tribblehorn pushed back up the mountain. Danny took Cindy's hand and the two began walking down the mountain, the smoke not as dense as they descended. But soon Cindy tired, and Danny raised her on his shoulders. He walked that way all the way down the mountain back into town, the fire quickly incinerating everything in its path on the other side. At the diner where Danny worked he found refuge with

Cindy, and the two sat and watched the news along with locals, the only story that of the fire that was burning out of control in the Quick Silver Mountains.

He learned that wildfires live and die by the land and fuel and weather that they encompass, and that with the right combination can rage into runaway infernos. And with current conditions, anything in the fire's path would ignite — trees, shrubs, grass, peat, and humus. The key, he learned to stop the fire, was to rob it of its fuel, so areas dense with dry trees were the worst potential problems for firefighters.

The fire had apparently, like most fires, started low on the other side of the mountain from where Danny had come, and spread upward rapidly, heat transference accelerating with flora for fodder located above the inferno. The blazing midday heat, when the fire was reported to have started, brought the fuel closer to its ignition point, and the low humidity exacerbated the blaze, ripe conditions for the plant life on the mountain to give up more of its moisture to the atmosphere.

The strong and unpredictable winds that swept the mountain range made the firefighter's job even more treacherous, the rapidly moving winds pushing flames toward fresh fuel and providing a constant source of oxygen which boosted the blaze's intensity. And as the fire increased, it actually began to create its own intense wind systems.

The blaze was fought as helicopters and planes continuously sprayed retardant water in front of the fire, slowing it down but doing little else. Soon after the flames were spotted, an initial attack team carried in by helicopters descended upon the scene, the staging area, or anchor point, a safe distance behind the blaze. There a crew of firefighters attempted to gain ground on the blaze by surrounding it with trenches, while hand crews set backfires around the fire line to exhaust flammable foliage. But the backfires were risky ventures, apt to burn out of control, while changing wind conditions could also push flames away from such traps. The command post for the fire was set up in Lonely Ghost, near the car wash where Danny worked his second job.

Within five days the fire had consumed about 15,000 acres, with over a thousand firefighters working the blaze. They came from different parts of the country to assist the New Mexico crew, working exhausting shifts of twelve hours and up on the fire lines.

A large tent city mushroomed in the staging area lower on the mountain where firefighters ate and slept. Slurry bombers and helicopters continued to dump retardant water on the blaze throughout the weekend, bombers dropping thousands of gallons of red slurry with each pass. But the slurry operation was suspended on days when thirty-mile-an-hour-plus winds made flying too dangerous, the winds whipping flames in speeds in excess of twenty miles an hour.

The fire produced smoke that was visible over thirty miles away. Danny learned later in the week that a drifter with a long history of mental illness was being held with suspicion of having started the blaze.

The two slept on the floor of the diner for the fire's duration before it finally burnt itself out.

On a Monday morning Danny walked into Stone's Running Store, and Darren Stone recognized him immediately.

"How are you, son? " Stone asked.

"Been better," Danny said.

Stone looked over Danny. It was apparent to him that the teen's clothes were not clean and that he hadn't bathed.

"What's up?" Stone asked.

"I think I've lost my home," Danny said. "I was wondering if you could give me a ride up the mountain to check?"

"Sure," Stone said. "Just give me a minute."

He went into the back of the store and another worker came out, a young man in his early 20s who looked to Danny like a runner. "I should be back early in the afternoon," Stone said.

"No problem," the young man said.

"Come on," Stone said to Danny.

Murray followed Stone out to his truck and the two were soon driving up the mountain.

As they headed up, Danny was not prepared for the devastation that he witnessed. Everything was blackened, the scorched earth and remnants of once magnificent trees reduced to charred waste. The fire had consumed and blackened thousands of acres of tranquil forest with a finality of Armageddon-like fury.

Danny felt certain that the cabin he and Cindy had shared with Thomas Tribblehorn, and the man himself, had been consumed by the blaze. The part black, part brown Native American man with whom Danny had bonded had undoubtedly been engulfed by the blaze trying to save his cabin and belongings. Familiar landmarks and trees were gone, vanquished by flames and turned to ashes. As they crested the mountain Danny said, "You can turn back. There's nothing left."

On the way back down the mountain Darren Stone said, "Why don't you and your sister come over to my place? My wife will be glad to have you stay with us until you can get back on your feet."

Danny eyed Stone suspiciously. At the moment he had few options, and Cindy needed a decent place to sleep.

"Okay," Danny said.

The two stayed with the Stones for five days, and Danny purchased clothing and essentials for himself and his sister. He'd managed to save enough money to pay for the goods, without having had to tap into the sum that he'd been carrying with him since recovering Tom Hornfield's life savings from his storm cellar.

At night Danny could overhear Stone arguing with his wife Julie. When he heard her say that the best thing the two of them could do was to turn Danny and Cindy over to child welfare authorities, Danny quietly gathered his belongings and Cindy's, and stuffed them into a secondhand backpack he'd purchased at the town flea market. Before dawn he roused Cindy, and they sneaked away to the local bus station where they caught the first bus out of town. It was heading west; a direction that Danny thought best-suited him and his little sister.

CHAPTER 9

OLYMPIC NATIONAL PARK–
SUMMER 1968

On a Saturday morning, the second week in June, Gabe Seward and his friend Robert Rojas jogged on a soft dirt trail. It wound through a thick dark forest, snaking up lush foothills, angling upwards to pure vertical, as it climbed toward majestic mountain peaks that seemed to kiss the sky. Gabe breathed deeply, the scent of fresh pine inebriating as the Pacific Ocean crashed below. It was one of earth's last unspoiled treasures, a slice of virgin acreage preserved in Olympic National Park.

He rubbed his hands as he ran, the morning air brisk, a bit colder than he preferred. Both men were wearing tights and sweatshirts, their training shoes touching the trail lightly as they ran. They moved without speaking, a scene reminiscent of centuries past, time when Native Americans lived in harmony with the sacred forest they called their home. The forty-mile stretch of secluded park was known as Kalaloch, an Indian name pronounced 'clay-lock.' It was a setting as close to Eden as Seward had ever experienced, the two weeks that he and Robert had camped and trained there were some of the best days of his life. The forest was so thick with trees and green with flora that shrubs seemed to grow on top of and out of each other.

In the Olympic Mountain range hovering high above, thick-chested elk and big buck deer roamed freely. They were clear-eyed animals with majestic racks, healthy specimens that would never grace the trophy rooms of well-heeled hunters. They seemed to pose for photo opportunities on snowcapped mountain ridges, set in billowing clouds hovering far above the madness of city life.

The occasional fiery-eyed eagle, jealously guarding his territory above, seemed to warn potential interlopers that this was sacred land; that violators would be dealt with swiftly and harshly. Below them the Pacific teemed with activity, salmon and whales sharing the icy blue waters with a vast array of rich marine life.

The big-shouldered beach outlining the water was of luxuriant, clean sand, a scented powder free of the signs of civilization. Driftwood in its natural state made passage across the sands difficult in places, one of nature's few remaining woodsheds that man would never plunder.

The two had broken down life to its simplest form--running, eating, and sleeping--consuming the most basic of foods with minimal preparation. Their free time was spent exploring the forest, mountains, and beaches of the park, and reading the used paperbacks that they'd loaded in Robert's ancient Volkswagen van. They were books that were purchased for pennies on the dollar at garage sales and library clearances, novels, biographies, and histories with frayed covers and pages that belied the treasures inside. They were words that further stoked the two runners' lust to know more and come to some better understanding of a life that was often so brutal yet dear.

As Gabe ran, he reflected on his childhood. His father was a drunkard who was constantly in and out of trouble with the law. He was ultimately convicted of drug dealing and spent eight years in prison before being released and disappearing. Gabe had not seen him since he was in grade school and was content with the reality that he would never see him again. His mother had developed a drinking problem too, and did what she could to hold on to her children whom she eventually yielded to the state.

As Gabe ran, he thought about the foster homes that he had been raised in and of the difficulties he encountered. But he recalled the good as well, optimistic that the remainder of his life would hold much joy. It took the interest of just one man, a high school math teacher with a passion for running, to turn his life around. Gabe understood that it had been running that had given him optimism, a new lease on life. Through time he'd come to understand that his ability as a runner was a gift, one that he'd vowed to himself to nurture and bring to full fruition.

Following the hour-long morning run on the trail, the two returned to their campground and ate a breakfast of cereal and bananas. They dozed and read all afternoon, and ran again that evening before eating a light dinner and retiring early.

The next morning they got into Robert's van and drove south. About twenty minutes later they pulled into a parking lot where a host of other runners had gathered. It was a thirty-kilometer race that the two had planned to use as a training run, one that was being touted as a Northern Washington championship. As they warmed up, it became apparent that it was a major race, and they learned that $500 in cash would be awarded to the winner. It was a sum that was large to both Gabe and Robert who survived on hobo budgets. Neither discussed the prize money as they warmed up, the two unaware of what level of competition would show up to race.

As they lined up at the start area, they looked around for familiar faces and saw none. There were no Africans in the field, a condition that greatly increased their chances of being competitive.

As the gun went off, Gabe and Robert ran side-by-side, running comfortably with a lead pack of about twenty runners. By five miles the pack had dwindled in half, and by ten halved again. At twelve miles Gabe said to Robert, "How are you feeling, my friend?"

"Good," Robert answered, his tone convincing.

"Hard half?" Gabe asked quietly, almost a whisper.

"You bet," Robert said.

The two men accelerated in sync and threw in a blazing half-mile, opening up a lengthy lead over the remaining pack of three runners who could not respond.

A mile later Gabe and Robert were running free of the field, the two quickly coming to the realization that one of them would take the top prize. As they worked in tandem, they communicated without talking, taking turns drafting off each other's shoulders, both content to work together as opposed to alone. With less than two miles to go, Robert bent forward and grabbed his side. Gabe could see the pain etched on Robert's face, a look as if something was stabbing at his gut.

"What's wrong, amigo?" Gabe asked.

"Got a bad stitch," Robert said. "I'm going to walk."

Robert stopped running, as did Gabe.

"What are you doing, Seward?" Robert asked as he walked, holding his side, trying to pull out and knead the crippling stitch.

"Same as you, amigo. I'm walking."

"Seward, get your skinny ass in gear and run."

"No. We'll do this together."

"Damn it, Seward. I don't want any sympathy. Run!"

"I am walking, Robert. And enjoying this beautiful day."

"You idiot, Seward. There's five hundred bucks up for grabs."

"Robert, both of us are living quite well right now. I can't honestly say that five hundred dollars will have any significant difference in improving the quality of our lives."

"Seward, you run or I'm going to kick your ass."

"Amigo, if you have enough energy to do that, then you should run."

The two walked for what seemed to Robert like a lengthy time, before he began jogging again. The stitch left Robert's side as mysteriously as it had appeared, and the two men were soon running again at full pace. Less than a quarter of a mile later, Gabe's face had a desperate look as he searched the forest on the side of the road.

"What's wrong?" Robert asked.

"Amigo, I believe I must have eaten something that didn't agree with me. Maybe the same culprit that gave you a stitch. Nature is calling and I'll see you later."

Gabe ran off the road and into the woods, disappearing in the shadows. When he got back to the road and resumed running, he searched for Robert who was out of sight.

"Betcha thought I was going to leave you, didn't you Seward?" Robert said.

Gabe turned his head. Behind him was Robert, running off his shoulder.

"I figured you were up the road, Robert."

"I knew that's what you'd think. I couldn't do it. I waited for you behind a tree. Just wanted to see what kind of reaction you'd have when I came up on you."

"Why didn't you keep on running?"

"Obvious reasons. I know I'd have never heard the end of it if I had taken off and left you. You think I'd have done that after you waited for me?"

"This is just a training run for us. We're not treating this as a race. What difference does it make?"

"Five hundred bucks, dingbat."

"I've already told you. . ."

"I don't want to hear it, Seward. No more. Now that we know we're not going to cut each other's throats, we better put the hammer down. Look behind you."

Gabe turned his head back to see two runners who were no more than twenty-five yards behind them and gaining rapidly.

As Gabe's head turned forward, a thin smile parted his lips. "We have one of two choices, Robert. We can either bury these two gentlemen right now, by running a blistering last mile, or have a little fun with them."

"What are you talking about?"

"You have a fertile mind. Use your imagination."

"You're a sick man, Seward."

"So you opt for choice number two?"

"Okay, Gabe. We'll play your game. But if we don't have that $500 in our hands tonight, I am going to kick your skinny ass."

"That's a strong incentive for a win. Now let's let these gentlemen catch up with us and have a little fun."

Gabe and Robert ran a measured pace as the two runners behind them pulled up to their shoulders with a little less than a mile to go. As they tucked in behind, it was apparent to both Robert and Gabe that the pair had worked extremely hard to make their way up to them, their breathing quick and heavy.

"Glorious day, isn't it gentlemen?" Gabe asked without missing a beat.

Neither answered, Seward speaking easily as the runners behind them breathed frantically.

"We have been having the time of our lives here camped in the park," Gabe continued. "Where are you two gentlemen from?"

"Why don't you shut up?" the taller of the two runners behind them said, gasping for breath as he spoke.

"My, that's not very neighborly", Gabe said.

"Shut up, asshole," the other one chimed in.

Gabe glanced at Robert who was grinning. They read each other's minds through their eyes. They gradually picked up the pace, not so fast that the two runners behind couldn't keep up, but fast enough to tax them. The breathing of the two runners behind them got even louder.

"Robert, I have a feeling we are going to eat steak this evening," Gabe said quietly.

"And a bottle of really righteous fine wine," Robert said.

Gabe ran his hands together. "And apple pie for dessert."

"Why don't you shut up and run, assholes," the shorter man said.

"Sorry," Gabe said. "I didn't mean to break your concentration."

He and Robert cranked it up another notch, and soon the breathing of the two runners on their shoulders became distant grunts as they increased their pace and pulled away.

With less than a half mile to go, Gabe said, "That was too easy, Robert. I think we should have a bit more fun with those rude young men. Are you up for it?"

"You're crazy, Seward. Let's not screw with this. We need that $500."

"Robert, I never knew you were so mercenary."

"What the hell you have in mind, Seward?"

"I think much of the same."

Robert pointed his forefinger menacingly at Seward. "We lose this race and I'm going to dump all your gear in the ocean and leave your sorry ass behind."

Seward smiled. "I have had worse happen. But I can assure you, we won't lose."

Robert was sweating bullets as he and Gabe allowed the two runners whom they'd already disposed of to come back to them. It was not a smart thing to do, he thought. You never knew for sure what a runner could do when given a new lease on life. Robert became increasingly anxious as Gabe bantered on enthusiastically, extolling the beauty of the landscape and nature in general, the angry runners right behind breathing like freight trains. With less than a hundred yards to go, the smaller of the two runners behind them took off like a sprinter. He breezed past them like they were standing still.

"Damn it, Seward!" Robert hissed. "Now look what you've gotten us into."

Gabe glanced at Robert for a brief moment, and then the two responded. Their knee lift was high as their stride length lengthened dramatically and their turnover quickened. They sprinted with everything they had as they fought to bring back the runner they'd so foolishly given multiple chances. They passed him with less than twenty meters to go, finishing ahead by just a few steps. As Gabe and

Robert crossed the finish line, they clasped hands, a symbolic gesture indicating they were tying.

On the drive through the forest back to their campsite, Robert said to Gabe, "We almost got our asses kicked today because of you."

Gabe smiled. "Almost doesn't count."

"What made you so cocksure we could beat those worthless little s.o.b.'s, Seward?"

"Because, Robert, it was apparent that those two young men were up against competitors who were out of their class."

Robert didn't respond. Following a lengthy silence he said, "Seward, you really didn't care about the $500, did you?"

"That is correct. I didn't."

Robert turned his head toward him. "You're crazy, man."

Gabe grinned. "Perhaps."

"You know that I'd have been pissed off if we hadn't won that $500," Robert said.

"Yes. I'm certain you would have."

Following another long silence Robert said, "Steaks and wine tonight?"

Gabe rubbed his hands and licked his lips. He patted Robert on the shoulder. "Sounds wonderful to me, amigo. But first we check some local haunts to find a couple of lovely young senoritas to join us for dinner, and an evening communing with nature."

"You really are out of your mind, Seward. The chances of us scoring two chicks are slim and none. We haven't had a hot shower in a week, and our clothes suck."

Seward smiled. "You should not be so negative, Robert. I see two lovelies in our future this evening. And it is a very clear vision."

Robert shook his head. "You're nuts, Seward. Off the wall."

Seward didn't answer, a Cheshire grin lighting his sunken face.

CHAPTER 10

HOUSTON, TEXAS
JUNE, 1976

When Gabe Seward settled in Houston upon completion of a Master's Degree from Oklahoma State in 1976, he had a broad view of the world. He'd qualified and run in the U.S. Olympic Trials in 1972 and 1976, done a three-year tour of duty in the Army that took him all through Europe and parts of Africa, and coached track and field at his alma mater. That, along with a sometime turbulent childhood, grounded him in reality.

In Houston, he hooked up with a group of men and women he'd been friendly with in the Bay Area around San Francisco. It was an eclectic group, the common thread that bound them: their desire to effect change by positive action. That entailed eschewing the corporate world, pursuing instead low-paying careers in social work and teaching, places where their mentorship of disadvantaged children would reward them in a way no paycheck could.

They rented an ancient house in the Heights, content to crash on its creaky wood floors in sleeping bags and blankets until they could afford box springs and mattresses. Their meals were basic, consisting mostly of rice, beans, and pasta. And their entertainment was reading and lengthy, sometimes all-night, discussions that frequently got passionate and heated. Political systems and economics were the most common topics of debate, with some roommates more fervent than others in their convictions as to what courses of action would most positively effect change in a world of glaring imbalances.

Gabe mostly listened, experience having shaped his thoughts as opposed to theory. Every 'ism' that he'd studied and experienced had merit, but downsides as well. He'd come to conclude that the U.S.

system, though deeply flawed, was still the model that the rest of the world looked to and envied. That thought was deeply tested when he moved to Houston, a boomtown where haves and have-nots was a stark reminder of the wonders and horrors of a free market system. Houston's oil-driven economy was booming in the mid-'70s, a situation that was unlike much of the U.S. that was mired in recession.

Visible wealth in the city was unremarkably common, opulent homes, flashy cars, expensive jewelry, and designer clothing the order of the day. It was a city of plastic surgery and trendy restaurants and clubs, a place where petroleum profits fed every hunger and desire known to its denizens. It was a town where immense fortunes could be made overnight, where the worn cliché of 'It's not what you know but who you know' was a reality etched in stone.

Banks and savings and loans were issuing signed blank checks for the lucky insiders, mainly white males who collateralized their loans with thinly veiled fictional balance sheets that rarely got scrutiny. They would be living in apartment projects one day and building them the next, along with subdivisions and high-rises, or whatever proposal they tossed on the receptive desks of the good-old-boy banking network.

The real estate market and the city's business infrastructure as a whole would continue to climb dramatically through the '70s as the oil-based economy raced ahead. It would not be until the early '80s when energy crashed, that the house of cards known as Houston came down along with it.

Houston's booming economy brought along with it immense opportunity for those at the upper end of the food chain, but it also introduced a whole new set of problems for those at the bottom.

As Gabe found employment at Houston's Wellsley House, a North Side community center funded by private money, his area of concern became the neighborhood's largely Hispanic makeup and their unique problems. The neighborhood had a disproportionate number of illegal aliens, men and women who had risked everything in getting into the U.S., uneducated people who spoke little or no English

72

in a land that was light years away from going multilingual. With the deck so heavily stacked against them, their chances of finding employment were slim; and when they did, they were frequently off-the-books jobs that paid below minimum wage.

Employers frequently took advantage of them as they fostered slave labor, rarely to be caught by agencies monitoring those activities. And when they were exposed, they were generally hit with monetary fines that were no more than hand slaps. Without health care, insurance, or any of the amenities that most American workers took for granted, the Hispanics that became Gabe's extended family struggled to survive in a culture that was perhaps more receptive to them than the one they had escaped. But it was a far cry from what he viewed as equitable in a land that touted the sanctity of inalienable rights.

On a Friday afternoon, Gabe walked back to his office shaking his head. It had been a tough day at the community center, with oppressive summer heat the likely culprit for the kids' bad behavior. He'd broken up several fights, a nasty cat-scratch brawl among some adolescent girls, and an even worse poolroom explosion that erupted in the community center's recreation room among some teenage boys.

Dispirited by their behavior, Seward had closed down the billiard room and sent the kids home early. As he entered his office, he stared at his athletic bag before slumping into his chair. It would be good to get out and run, he thought. He wished more of the kids ran, an activity that worked magically to lower their anger levels. He already had several of the kids running, shuttling them back and forth to Memorial Park in community center vans several evenings a week. But it was a slow process convincing them to run, most of them preferring to play on one of the many team sports he coached them in, especially softball and soccer.

Gabe leaned back in his chair and propped his feet up on his desk. He pulled on his San Francisco Giants hat and cracked his knuckles. His thoughts turned to a girl in college whom he had fallen in love with and who had ultimately broken his heart. As he recalled the painful memory, he heard a banging on his door.

"Come in."

The door opened and a Hispanic little boy, about 10 years old, stared at Gabe with frightened dark eyes.

"What's up, Rodolfo?" Gabe said.

"Coach, you got to come with me. Right now."

Gabe studied the child who looked petrified.

"What's wrong, Rodolfo?"

"Daddy's gonna' kill Angelina if Momma don't come back."

Gabe's face turned an ugly shade of gray. "Let's go," Gabe said.

He followed Rodolfo and the two ran back to Rodolfo's house that was three blocks from the center.

When Gabe and Rodolfo got to the home, police cars had fronted it. Gabe recognized several of the cops in the yard, men and women whom he came in regular contact with in the neighborhood. The cop in charge of the beat, Johnny Martinez, was standing outside the front of the house as Gabe approached. Gabe stopped and turned to Rodolfo. "Rodolfo, you'll need to stay here."

Rodolfo said, "Okay," eyes wide as he remained near the curb by a police car. Gabe then proceeded toward the house.

"What's happening, Johnny?" Gabe asked.

Johnny's face showed the obvious strain of a tense situation.

"Apparently Angel's flipped out," Johnny said. "He's holding his four-year-old daughter Angelina as hostage, and threatening to kill her and himself unless his wife comes back. According to him, she's run off with some guy."

"I know Angel," Gabe said. "Can I talk to him?"

Johnny studied Gabe. "I don't think so, Gabe. Angel could end up killing you too. Then my ass is on the line downtown."

"Angel will listen to me," Gabe said. "I know him."

"What the hell you think you can tell him that will get that little girl out of there in one piece?"

74

"I'll come up with something, Johnny. Just give me a chance."

Johnny shook his head. "I don't know, Gabe. My inclination is to storm him and take him out."

"Then you may end up with two needless deaths."

Johnny stared at Gabe. He rubbed his chin. He checked his watch. "I let you go in there and things don't turn out right, that's the end of my career."

"What's worth more, Johnny? Your career or the lives of a four-year-old little girl and her father?"

Johnny stroked his chin. "The father, I don't care about. It's the little girl I'm thinking of."

"There's a little boy involved in this too," Gabe said, his gaze shifting toward Rodolfo who was still near the street with several cops by their squad car. "He loses his father and sister, what do you think his life will be like?"

Johnny just shook his head. "Christ, Gabe. This situation ain't damn tough enough, and you lay that guilt trip on me too? Damn..." Johnny stood silent for a lengthy period of time, just scratching his head. And then he said, "Okay, Gabe. You see what you can do. But I can't make you any promises. If we hear anything going on in there, we're going to storm and start shooting. If you get taken out by accident, I can't do anything about that."

Gabe nodded. "I understand, Johnny. But please give me some time. I think time is the key here. If we don't rush this thing, I think Angel will come around to his senses. As far as I know he's not a drinker and he doesn't use drugs. So I think we have a good shot at being able to talk him out of this."

Johnny just nodded. "Okay, Gabe. Go for it."

Seward nodded and walked to the front door that was unlocked. He took a deep breath and opened the door.

"Angel, it's Gabe Seward. I'd like to talk to you."

"Go away," Angel said. "I don't wanna talk."

Gabe continued inside. There in the living room, Angel was sitting on a vinyl-covered couch with his little girl who was asleep in his lap. In his right hand he cradled a revolver, the barrel of which was resting on the child's shoulder pointed at her head.

Gabe continued toward Angel and sat down on a chair facing him and the little girl.

"I haven't seen you in a while, Angel. What's happening, my friend?"

"Gabe, I don't want to talk to you. I don't have no beef with you. Why don't you go? If you stick around I'm going to have to hurt you too."

"Angel, I know you've been doing a good job with Rodolfo. He's become a hell of a little soccer player. And you know, I have a sneaking suspicion that someday he could develop into a very fine distance runner too."

Angel's eyes opened widely. "Yeah. He's a good little kid. But I don't know if this world is a fit place for him to live in."

"I can understand that, Angel. There are times when I think that way also."

"You do?"

"Sure, Angel. Lots of times I'll get down."

Angel studied Gabe, stroking the little girl's head gently with his fingertips, the gun pointed at her head. "What you got to be down about, Gabe? You're a white boy. You ain't married and got no kids to take care of. What you got to be down about?"

"Angel, all sorts of things bother me. But I do my best to deal with them."

"What could bother you, Gabe?"

"Lots of things, Angel. In fact, right before I came over here I was bothered by the thought of a woman."

"You got a woman bothering you, Coach?"

"The thought of a woman, Angel."

76

"What happened?" Angel's eyes had widened and his tone softened.

"When I was in college I met a young woman that I fell in love with. And I thought that she was in love with me too. I bought her an engagement ring and we'd planned to be married. She was all I could think about. I'd made all these plans in my head as to how we would have a beautiful life together, raising kids and the whole bit."

"What happened to her? Did she die?"

"No. She left me."

"Fucking bitch. I been there. Bet you wanted to kill her."

"No. I was just very sad. And then to make matters worse, I found that she had become involved with a very good friend of mine."

"Puta," Angel spat. "You shoulda cut his fucking throat."

"Where would that have gotten me, Angel?"

"Woulda got you even."

"Maybe. But for sure it would have gotten me a ticket to prison to be executed."

As Gabe spoke, the little girl woke up. She rubbed her eyes and buried her head into Angel's chest, obviously unaware of the danger she was facing.

"Rodolfo tell you what's gone down?" Angel asked.

"He did."

Angel nodded his head. "That's what I like about you, Gabe. You don't b.s."

"Thank you, Angel. I appreciate that."

"How much he tell you?"

"It was brief. Just that your wife had left and you were angry."

"Fucking bitch ran off with a goddamn drug dealer," Angel said. "Sorry mother selling drugs to kids in the 'hood."

"That's low, Angel."

Angel nodded, and then he began weeping. Tears streamed down his eyes and his whole body shook as he wept. "I never did nothing bad to Elena. Nothing. I never fooled around on her or nothing.

77

Worked two jobs most of the time, and gave her every paycheck I made. I never drank, or did drugs, or hit her, or any of that shit. I was good to her, Gabe. I swear to God."

Gabe nodded. "I believe you, Angel. I have every reason to believe you."

The little girl squirmed in Angel's lap. He smoothed her sweaty hair with the palm of his free hand. The heat in the room was oppressive. "Why did she do that to me, Gabe? Why?"

"I don't know, Angel. Sometimes people do things for no good reason at all. But you can't beat yourself up over that."

"I don't want to beat myself up. I want to beat her up and her boyfriend up."

Gabe nodded. "I understand. If I were you, I'd be angry too."

As Angel stroked the little girl's hair, his eyes shifted and locked on Gabe's. "I don't want this child to live in a world like this. A world like this ain't worth living in."

Following a lengthy silence, Gabe said, "Angel, I know you love Angelina. How would you feel if your wife's boyfriend were to come in here and threaten to harm your little girl?"

"I'd kill the son of a bitch."

"To protect Angelina?"

"Damn right."

"Then why would you hurt her?"

"That's different, Coach."

Gabe shook his head and said softly, "I think it's the same thing, Angel. If your little girl is hurt, what difference does it make who hurts her? Look at your beautiful little girl, Angel. You know you don't want to hurt her. Not anybody else or you. Look how sweet and innocent she is, my friend. She is truly an angel from heaven. I know you too well. You don't want to harm her. You are just hurt and angry because of your wife's bad behavior."

At that Angel broke down and started sobbing heavily. As he sobbed the little girl began crying too. Gabe got up and walked to

Angel. He gently laid his hand on his shoulder. "Let me have the gun, Angel."

Angel shook his head, no.

Gabe breathed deeply. "Okay, Angel. If I can't have the gun, let me have the child."

"You'll take care of her?" Angel asked.

"I will make sure she is well cared for," Gabe said.

Angel continued stroking the little girl's scalp, tears still streaming from his eyes. His body shook as he lowered the gun and handed the child to Gabe. Gabe took the child in his arms and said, "Come on Angel. Let's go outside. Everything is going to be alright."

"No!" Angel said angrily. "Take her and leave, Gabe. Or I take both of you down with me."

Gabe studied Angel's eyes and knew what he had to do. "Okay, Angel. But I'll be waiting outside the door for you when you change your mind."

Gabe carried the crying child from the room and walked out the door of the house where police met him.

"You gentlemen..." Gabe started.

His words were interrupted by the blast of gunfire. His body jolted. The little girl hugged him in a deathlike vise, her body red-hot. She wailed loudly as police rushed inside the house, Gabe continuing to walk with her in his arms.

"Blew his freaking brains out," he heard a cop yell. Gabe made his way with the sobbing child toward Rodolfo who was still standing in the yard near the street with the policemen by their squad cars.

As Gabe studied Rodolfo's eyes, it was readily apparent to him the youngster sensed that something tragic had occurred inside the house. What could be worse, he thought, than explaining to a youngster that his father had put a gun in his mouth and blown his brains out?

CHAPTER 11

EUGENE, OREGON—HAYWARD FIELD
JUNE 2002
THE NIGHT OF DANNY'S FIRST TRACK RACE

By the time Seward got to his pickup truck, the light Oregon mist that clotted the air had thickened to a steady rain. The temperature had also dropped quickly, unseasonably cold weather for Gabe who had grown accustomed to Houston's boiling hot and humid summers. The Bayou City was a place where temperatures in the 90s with matching humidity was standard for six months of the year, the winters no more than a series of brief Canadian fronts that rarely brought the mercury below freezing.

It had taken him time to make the adjustment from the Northern California weather that he had grown up with as a child, to living in the tropics. The San Francisco Bay Area had a climate that was often chilly and rainy, far removed from Houston's sultry climes. But now that Seward was past 50, he was thankful to be living nearer the equator. He found the hot weather easier on his running body, a machine that had long passed 100,000 miles. It was a mechanism with an engine that hadn't lost a beat, but a chassis that had endured its share of scrapes and dings.

The miles of pounding had stiffened his legs and joints, conditions that were exacerbated in the cold and wet. It made slow and careful stretching a necessity, an exercise that he rarely needed to employ in Houston's sweltering heat and humidity. As Gabe's windshield wipers squeaked, he anticipated the cold and wet run that he was about to endure. A few miles outside of Eugene, he pulled his pickup into a roadside rest area and killed the engine. He reached for a pair of tights that were resting on the passenger seat beside him on top of training shoes, windbreaker, and hat. In the darkness he got out of his street clothes and into his running togs.

Minutes later he was out of his truck jogging, moving on the other side of the road against traffic, heading steadily away from Eugene. The traffic was light that evening, and he'd run for twenty minutes, what he estimated to be about three miles, when he saw a pickup truck that appeared to be stranded on the other side of the road. As Seward got closer a car passed, its headlights lighting the stranded vehicle. In the light he recognized the figure of Danny Murray, the kid he'd watched run the astounding race that evening at the all-comers meet at Hayward Field on the University of Oregon campus.

Murray was standing in front of a beat-up truck, gazing into an open hood. Seward approached cautiously, his run slowing to a jog before walking. As Danny backed away from his pickup and spotted Gabe, the lights of a passing car lit his face. It was a cautious look, maybe even fearful, Seward thought.

"Hey partner," Gabe said in an upbeat tone as he approached. "Run into a little problem?"

Gabe stopped several feet away from Danny. Murray studied the thin man in his running clothes, the expression on his face full of caution. "My truck broke down," Danny said.

Danny's anxiety level rose, the truck he had purchased under an assumed name along with a fake driver's license.

Gabe stroked his chin. "Know what the problem is?"

Danny shook his head. "I'm not sure. I think it's my distributor."

"Mind if I have a look?"

Danny, his face still etched in mistrust, paused. "Okay," he said.

Gabe walked over and peered under the hood of the open truck. His knowledgeable hands groped around. After having Danny turn on his lights and attempt to crank the engine, he determined that the problem wasn't his battery.

"I'm not sure what we've got here," Gabe said. "But I think you're right. I think your distributor's gone. I've got some tools in my pickup back up the road, and there's a gas station open back there. Why don't we jog back to my truck, and see what we can do?"

Danny continued studying Seward cautiously. "What do you want?"

"To help you," Seward said.

"Why?"

"Why not?"

"I could think of a lot of reasons. How do I know you're not weird?" Danny asked.

Gabe grinned. "You don't."

Following a lengthy silence Danny said, "I watched you coming down the road. You were moving pretty fast. Do you run a lot?"

"I've been known to."

"Around here?"

"Not much."

"Where?"

"Right now in Houston, Texas. Though I've done a bit of running in other places too."

"Where?"

"The Bay Area of California where I grew up. Oklahoma State where I went to school. The other Big 8 schools where there were track meets. And even a little bit on Hayward Field track right here in Oregon."

"You went to Oklahoma State?" Danny asked. His eyes had widened.

"Yup."

"Ever run in Kansas?"

"Sure did. Meets at U.K. and K. State."

"What's your name?"

"Gabe Seward."

"I've never heard of you."

"I'm not exactly a household name. And it's been a while since I ran there. I would reckon before you were even a thought."

A thin smile curled Danny's lips. "Were you any good?"

Seward shrugged his shoulders. "It's all relative."

"What was your event?"

"In college I ran the mile and the 5,000. When I got out, I stuck mostly to the 5,000."

"How come?"

"Too many fast milers out there. I didn't have the talent to compete with them in the mile."

"What was your 5,000 best?" Danny asked.

"I ran 13:30," Seward said.

Danny studied Seward. "I'm a runner too. I ran my first 5,000 this evening."

Seward just nodded.

"How much are you going to charge me for helping me?"

"Not a thing."

"Why are you doing this?"

"Because you need help. And being a runner doesn't hurt your case either."

"You'd just help me for no reason?"

Gabe shrugged his shoulders. "Why not?"

"Lots of reasons," Danny said. "I wouldn't."

Gabe stroked his chin. "You're not too trusting, are you?"

"No. And with good reason."

Gabe nodded. "I can understand that."

After another lengthy pause Danny said, "Okay, I'll run back to your truck with you. But you try anything, and you'll be sorry. I promise."

Gabe held his palms up as if intimidated by the youth's warning. "Hey, I understand. I don't think you're a man to be messed with."

Danny shut the hood of his pickup truck and locked the cab.

"Okay, then. Let's go."

They ran back into the teeth of a headwind and a hard rain, and by the time they got to Seward's pickup, they were soaked. They looked like two thin, drowned rats as they got inside Gabe's vehicle, both shaking from the rain and cold. Gabe started the engine of his old truck and put on the heater. From his athletic bag that was behind him, he pulled out two large towels. He handed one to Danny, and took the other himself. The windshield clouded up as they dried themselves, steam escaping from their bodies. "I don't have enough money with me to buy a distributor," Danny said. "But I've got it back at my trailer. Want to go back there first?"

"No, I trust you," Seward said. He put on his defroster and waited for the windshield to clear before turning around his pickup and making his way back to a service station.

As they drove back to the service station, Danny said, "My little sister is by herself back at my trailer. She'll be scared and worried that I haven't come back. Can we go get her after we get the distributor and bring her with us while we work on the truck?"

Gabe nodded. "No problem, big guy."

At the service station Seward purchased a reconditioned distributor that he knew would fit Danny's pickup, a part that Danny again promised to pay for once he got back to his trailer home.

Seward turned around at the service station. He drove with Danny past the broken down pickup that was still on the side of the road before coming to Murray's trailer site. It was a remote locale in the woods, a place with water and electrical outlets housing several dozen other trailers. Danny's trailer was small and beaten up, the worst looking one on the lot.

"Be right out," Danny said. He opened the door of the pickup and a cold rush of wet air made Seward shiver. Gabe watched the youngster as he approached his trailer and fitted a key into the metal door.

Several minutes later Murray came out of the trailer, accompanied by a painfully thin redheaded girl who looked like a younger version of him.

She got into the truck, keeping a cautious distance from Seward, clad in ill fitting, threadbare clothes. Danny got in next to her and shut the passenger door. "This is Mr. Seward," he said to Cindy. "He's a runner too. He's going to help me with my truck."

Cindy just stared at Gabe suspiciously.

"How are you?" Gabe asked.

Cindy didn't answer. "She doesn't talk much to strangers," Danny said.

Gabe nodded and said, "We're going to get your brother's pickup fixed up, and the two of you will be back home in no time as snug as two bugs in a rug."

A small grin curled Cindy's lips as Gabe drove on through the rain.

When they got back to the truck, the rain had let up, and Seward pulled out his tools and went to work. With Danny's help the distributor was installed quickly. As Danny cranked up his engine, Seward smiled.

"I forgot to give you your money for the distributor," Danny said. "Follow me back to my trailer."

Gabe followed the two back to their trailer, and Danny held the door for Cindy and Gabe as they stepped inside. The inside of Murray's trailer was Spartan but clean, housing two small beds and a kitchen table with three chairs. "Did you eat yet, Cindy?"

She shook her head no.

"How about you, Mr. Seward?"

"Call me Gabe."

"Gabe."

"No, I haven't."

"Want to eat with us?"

"Sure," Seward said, his curiosity piqued concerning the boy.

Danny boiled up a big pot of pasta, and with it served a loaf of day-old white bread that he'd purchased at a grocery store in Eugene. The three attacked the food ravenously, all three starved after a long day.

After dinner, Cindy crawled into her bed with her clothes on and pulled the covers over her. She shut her eyes and fell into a deep sleep as Gabe and Danny sat at the kitchen table.

"I've got a little admission to make, Danny," Gabe said.

"What's that?"

"I saw you run this evening at the all-comers meet in Eugene."

"You did?"

"Yes."

"It was my first official track meet," Danny said.

"I'd say you did pretty well."

"I wish my shoe hadn't given me trouble. I had a good one going."

Gabe nodded. "You did. I've had things like that happen myself, too. But I never came back the way you did. That was courageous."

Danny shrugged his shoulders. "There was no competition for me in that meet."

"There were some fine runners on that track, Danny. Some pretty well-known local names."

"Nobody that can hold a candle to me. No one has a clue as to what I'm capable of doing. But they're going to find out really soon. I'm going to be the greatest distance runner that ever lived. And I'll be running times that will airmail anything that's currently in the record books."

Gabe stroked his chin, grinned slightly, and nodded. "I would have no problem accepting that."

"I'm going to make more money as a distance runner than any runner ever has before me. And with it I'm going to give my little sister everything she's never had. My running will be a vehicle for us to have a decent life. We've gone through some hard times."

Gabe nodded. "I can understand hard times. And putting your sister's needs first is a noble gesture."

"Do you believe me?"

"Yes, I do."

"How do I know you're not just flattering me?"

"I've been running for a lifetime and I've never seen a performance like yours tonight. I have a pretty good idea of what type of time you could have run if your shoe hadn't given you trouble. I'm certain you had at least another minute in you."

"A lot more than a minute. I wasn't going to show all my cards the first time. Now there's a buzz. Everybody is going to wait for my next race. And I'll give it to them. That's when you'll really start getting an idea of what I can do. But it's going to be a slow process. I'll be running records for years to come."

"I have no reason to doubt you."

Danny searched Seward's eyes. "So you ran at Hayward Field? When? And how come?"

Gabe nodded, and told him about his forays on the fabled track, including his two Olympic Trials runs.

"How many years have you been running?"

"Almost 40."

"Who's the best distance runner you've ever seen?"

"Talentwise? Or what they accomplished?"

"Both."

"Of what they accomplished, I'd probably say Emil Zatopek."

"I read about him. His times weren't all that great."

"Not by today's standards, but you have to realize he dominated his peers in a time when training methods were very unsophisticated. Plus, he trained in Czechoslovakia, and that didn't make matters any easier. Zatopek had the heart of a lion and the soul of a saint."

"I've read that." Following a lengthy silence Danny said, "As far as raw talent, who was the greatest distance runner you ever watched?" Murray asked.

"There were a lot of them that I had the pleasure of watching. Off the top of my head, Viren, Rono, Lopes, Yifter, Shorter, Aouita, Morcelli, Gebrselassie, El G." Gabe stopped and stroked his chin. His voice became almost inaudible as he said, "But I suspect I may be sitting right across from the most talented distance runner ever, staring him straight in the eye," Seward said.

Danny didn't flinch. "You have that right. I am going to destroy their records and accomplishments."

Seward nodded.

"If you say that you can do something that you can't, that's bragging," Danny said. "But if you're sure of what you can do, say it, and then you go out and do it, that's fact. I'm going to run faster than any distance runner that's ever run, from the half-mile to the marathon."

Gabe nodded. "I suspect you know your capabilities."

"Yes, I do. And no coach will ever advise or control me. Everything that I've learned about running has been on my own, by running and reading. I don't need some glib coach telling me what to do so he can get the credit. I've read too much about that. I'm not going to be any man's mule. I'm going to do it all on my own."

"Self-knowledge is the greatest teacher, Danny. But sometimes you can pick things up when in the company of experienced runners. I'm talking about the ones who have reached the top and know what they're talking about."

"Maybe. But it's not for me. Did you ever have anybody coach you?" Danny said.

"Sure. In high school and college. But the adviser that helped me the most wasn't actually my coach. Not in the traditional coach-runner relationship. He was an active competitor too, and we trained together and learned from each other's successes and mistakes."

"I don't need anybody else," Danny said.

Gabe nodded.

"How did you get started running?" Danny asked.

Seward told Danny about his life, the youngster's eyes wide as Gabe replayed a condensed version of his life story. It was apparent to Seward that the youngster sucked in his every word like a sponge, bonding to him in a way that was obviously a rare, if not first, occurrence for the youth. When Seward finished his narrative, Danny told his story. Gabe maintained an expression that didn't change as he listened. Silently, he empathized with the young man who had endured so much adversity and travail, a street-smart, savvy survivor, as tough as any youth he'd ever encountered in a lifetime of dealing with troubled youngsters.

When Danny finished, Gabe said, "I'm going to be around here for a while before I head back to the Bay Area to see my family. Do you have a pencil and paper?"

Danny went into the small kitchen area and came back with a wire notebook and a yellow pencil. He handed them to Gabe who was quiet as he wrote. "I've printed out my name, address, and telephone number in Houston, Danny, just in case for some reason I don't make it to your next meet. I want you to know that if you ever need anything, or I can help you in any way, contact me."

He handed the pencil and notebook to Danny who studied the print.

"I've got to go now, amigo," Gabe said as he got up. "It's been a pleasure meeting you, and I wish you luck with your running."

"Just a second," Danny said.

Murray went to his bed and reached under the mattress. Then he came back with a fistful of bills. He counted out a sum of money. "This should cover the distributor," he said, as he handed the bills toward Seward.

"No, thanks, Danny. This one is on me."

Murray shook his head. "No. I don't take charity. You helped me and I'm paying."

"Forget it, my friend. Use the money to get Cindy a jacket. She's going to get sick without one."

Danny shook his head. "I don't accept charity. I'd rather steal first."

Gabe grinned. "That's fine. Then I'll take an i.o.u. on your future winnings."

Danny said, "You sure about that?"

"Absolutely." Seward then stuck out his hand that Danny took.

"You still do track work?" Danny asked.

"I've been known to."

"I've got a session planned two nights from tonight. Will you still be around?"

"Yes."

" Want to run part of it with me?"

"I'd love to," Seward said. "But there's no way I could run even a small portion with you. Age has caught up with me and I'm too slow. But I'd be honored to come out and watch you. Or even put a clock on your intervals if you'd like."

Danny nodded. "Yeah. That would be fine. I get off work late. And by the time I put Cindy to bed and jog to the track, it will be past ten. Can you make it that late?"

"No problem," Gabe said.

"Good," Danny said. "You know where the high school track is, down the road we came in on?"

"Sure do."

"Well, I'll meet you there around ten."

"Sounds great."

As Gabe pulled out of the trailer park and back onto the road, he thought of Murray and his little sister and their struggle to survive. He wondered if Danny could somehow pull off the miracle of raising Cindy while continuing to grow as a distance runner. It bothered him that the bright young man would probably never have the opportunity of going to college, facing a lifetime of low-paying jobs with little or no benefits. It was a cycle he was all too familiar with, having spent a lifetime in the company of troubled youths.

Maybe running would be Murray's salvation, Gabe thought. But he knew through experience it was unlikely; that the odds of Danny Murray attaining financial security through a running career were slim at best. Few ever did, the nasty specter of injury and burnout often taking their toll, especially on runners as young as Danny. As he drove through the thick Oregon forest, Gabe Seward wondered what twists and turns Danny Murray's life would take. He suspected that the kid had a potential world record in him, and with a few breaks could run to the top. Life was like that, Gabe thought as he drove. Sometimes all it took was a break.

CHAPTER 12

Two nights later, Danny Murray left his trailer and ran out of the lot toward the road leading to the high school track where he did his interval training. He left Cindy behind by herself, a condition that was unsettling to him, but one that he'd coped with since fleeing the child welfare system.

The two had been fending for themselves since he was 14 and she was 9, underage runaways who had managed to survive against heavy odds. Leaving Cindy alone as a latchkey kid in a trailer park was unnerving to Danny, far removed from entrusting her to Thomas Tribblehorn, a man whom he'd come to understand and rely on.

Danny was uneasy with the cast of characters who inhabited his trailer park, largely transients and the habitually unemployed, people that he tried to shield Cindy from the best that he could. But he understood that his sister was lonely, especially for the companionship of other children. So when she befriended another little girl at the trailer park who was her same age, he cautiously allowed the friendship to blossom.

He permitted Cindy to play with her friend in the trailer park courtyard, or inside his trailer when he was there. But entering the little girl's trailer was off-limits, as was bringing her or her mother into his trailer when he was gone.

His caution was rooted in his suspicion of the little girl's mother, a woman Danny estimated to be in her early 30s. She was a hardened figure with stiffly sprayed platinum hair and shifty little eyes. Whenever Danny spotted her in the trailer court, she was wearing a mottled white terry cloth bathrobe and shower thongs. Her hair was generally

92

wrapped in a towel, an ever-present cigarette dangling from her lips, her right hand clutching a block glass tumbler. The glass held ice and fluid that Danny suspected was largely gin. The few occasions that he'd had brief conversation with the woman, she reeked of the same stench he remembered from his father and mother. They were both drunks, gin drinkers.

When she left the trailer at night she was heavily made-up, clad in cheap-looking, revealing outfits. She told Danny that she worked at a restaurant in Eugene as a waitress, but he knew better. He'd seen her in town on several occasions, leaving a topless club that was a front for prostitution. And on numerous occasions, he'd witnessed a sea of rough-looking characters entering or leaving her trailer. It was generally late at night when he saw the men, times when he was either going out on, or returning from, a run. Danny wondered how she shielded her little girl from the obvious sex trade that was going down in her trailer.

One character in particular bothered Murray. He was a Hispanic man with a droopy black mustache, mid- to late 40s, who sported an angry red scar that outlined the right side of his face. The slash had puffed and cured as salmon-colored tissue, swelling from a razor that had sliced his face and disfigured his lips. His droopy black mustache was weak cover for the distended flaps, providing little camouflage for matching slabs of cleaved red meat. He drove a silver Porsche 911 with California plates.

When Danny first made eye contact with the man, he sensed immediately that he was cold-blooded, a potential threat to his sister. Living among lowlife was another negative in Murray's life, one that heightened his desire to become the world's premier runner. It was a title that he envisioned culminating in fabulous wealth, a condition that would provide him and his sister with the means to escape their wretched surroundings.

He dreamt of the day when Cindy would have a decent home, and he'd never have to be concerned with her safety. Murray knew he was on the cusp of that dream, and could almost taste the fruits of his labors that would soon be rightfully his. But reality tied him to the moment; a hard truth that left him limited options in choosing a home.

His paycheck mired him in low-rent trailer parks, places that attracted tenants who were predictably trouble. They were places he loathed living with Cindy but, with limited alternatives, were the best he could muster.

Keeping a low profile and remaining anonymous was critical to his existence, circumstances that would limit his chances of being caught by authorities. He was still underage and understood only too well how the child welfare system worked. If he were exposed, they would snatch Cindy away from him in a heartbeat.

Danny jogged over to the high school track about five miles from his trailer and was relieved to find it uninhabited. He knew if he were spotted by anyone who had watched him run in the all-comers meet in Eugene, it would be a hassle. But he was actually looking forward to Gabe Seward showing, feeling a sense of trust in the man that was rare for him. Murray was a youth who was hardened and generally suspicious of everyone, experience being his advising professor in the school of hard knocks.

Danny sat on the tartan track and stretched, and then he removed his training shoes. He slipped into his spikes that he'd carried with him, and placed his training shoes on the starting stripe of the inside lane. He stood up and breathed deeply. As he stretched, he saw Gabe Seward enter the facility and jog toward him. The thin man with the gaunt face was clad in black tights, matching windbreaker, and a Giants baseball cap. Gabe continued to Danny and, when he reached him, extended his hand.

"How are you, amigo?"

"Okay."

"And Cindy?"

"Fine."

"That's good," Gabe said. "Have you recovered from your race yet?"

"Oh yeah."

"Any problems afterwards?"

"No. That was an easy effort."

A small smile curled Seward's lips, wondering if perhaps there was a bit of bravado in Danny's assessment. Seward knew that Murray had run a very taxing race, and that any runner, regardless of talent level, would be feeling its effects just days later. Gabe remembered how his legs felt in his younger days following a race. They came back fairly quickly, but there was always soreness until the lactic acid that had built up in the muscles was flushed out.

Seward had found that his racing formula, for runners under 40, held up well over the years. The recipe was one day of rest for each mile of the race, before attempting another race or race-simulated workout. Danny had just raced 5,000 meters, or 3.1 miles, meaning it would take him a minimum of three days to fully recover. Only then would he be running at optimal levels with minimal muscle fatigue. But that was under normal racing conditions, Seward thought. Danny had run a race that must have extracted much more.

Following a broken shoelace, he had made up a tremendous amount of lost distance, catching the field and winning in a remarkable time. The effort must have taken a huge toll on him, Seward   thought.

As Gabe recalled Danny's stunning race, he reminisced and longed for the days of his youth. Running hard then on a regular basis was something he never thought about, his legs generally recovering quickly with a night's sleep. But ever since he had past 40, his recovery period was much longer. Now at 53, he was thankful any time he went on a run when his legs came around, a condition that almost always took a lengthy, slow warm up.

If age and experience had taught Seward anything about distance running, it was the knowledge that the sport was the sum product of a lifetime of work. The process couldn't be rushed, and every runner progressed at a different pace. But Seward also realized that there were differences in runners' native abilities, and training and patience could only take them so far. In order to reach elite status, there had to be a genetic component involved also. Obviously, Murray had picked the right set of parents to become a world-class runner. It was a rare phenomenon, one that occurred in many cultures and every race.

"You warmed up?"

"Yup," Danny said. "And ready to go."

"What kind of workout do you have planned?"

"I'm going to do four times a half with a three-minute rest. Then three times a mile with a four-minute rest. Then a two-mile, followed by a quarter jog. And then a set of hundreds, probably about eight, with jog back recoveries after each one."

Gabe nodded his head, his pulse elevating as he contemplated Danny's workout. Murray was attempting a session that he and his college teammates called the 'ball buster.' It would be seven and a half miles of top-end running compressed into a short period of time, a workout of epic dimensions. It was a session that would tax any distance runner to the max, regardless of skill level. If the kid was able to pull it off and run fast times, Gabe felt confident he'd have the ability to run with anyone.

He reasoned that the workout that Danny had chosen would be a more accurate gauge of how fast he could run 5,000 meters than the actual race he'd done at the all-comers meet in Eugene. The fact that Danny had stopped in the middle of the race, and then come back to catch the field and win in a startling time, made the predictability of an uninterrupted effort difficult. The downside of the conundrum was that the forced rest he had taken, due to a broken shoelace, might have prevented him from imploding later in the contest. But the upside was that the interruption, more likely, might have added a minute or more to his finishing time. Gabe's interest was piqued as he studied Danny, whose eyes were clear and showed no signs of anxiety or fear.

"Ready?" Gabe said.

"Whenever."

"You start, and I'll get you," Seward said.

Danny toed the start line, leaned forward, and ran. He moved lightly on his toes, his motion effortless as he skimmed toward 200 meters. He continued running with no seeming toil as he ran the curve, and negotiated the final straight toward Gabe. As he crossed the 400-meter mark where Seward stood with his stopwatch. "56.7," Gabe yelled.

It was blazing speed, top-end effort for most runners that Murray made look easy, in the first full lap of his ambitious workout. Danny's form remained unchanged as he sped back around the oval. He appeared to be hovering above the ground as he approached Seward for the second revolution. As he hit the line, Gabe called out "1:53.3."

It was a lightning fast time for 800 meters, within a few seconds of a finishing number that would win open 800s in many meets. Murray nodded as he heard his split, and he continued jogging slowly. He moved counterclockwise on the track before turning back and heading toward Gabe. Seward checked his watch as Danny approached. "Another minute, big guy."

Murray nodded. A two-minute interval had elapsed since his effort, and there was about a minute remaining until his next one.

As Danny approached Gabe for his next effort, Seward said, "Thirty seconds."

"I'm ready now," Murray said.

Danny's assertion meant he was cutting his rest period short, making his coming effort more difficult. The shorter the rest interval between efforts, the less time it allowed the cardiovascular system to recover. Seward felt Murray was making a mistake by cutting his allotted rest time down. He would likely go into oxygen debt much sooner than he would have with a full recovery, and pay for it badly later in the workout. It was no different from runners who went out too quickly in races and then died badly later on. It was a phenomenon that could most simply be described in terms of a tank of oxygen. If that tank is depleted too quickly, all systems shut down.

The runner that judiciously uses his allotted reserve, a measure that is determined by the volume of oxygen mass that his cardiovascular system can process, will run his best effort or race. But Gabe offered no advice, just nodding and pressing the start button on his chronograph as Danny's foot hit the start line for his second 800, and the redheaded gazelle lifted off.

Seward studied the youngster's movement as he navigated the first curve of his second effort, and sped down the straightaway toward the 200-meter mark. There was no visible change in his form, his running as smooth as silk. Murray's face showed no sign of distress as he approached Gabe for the first lap of his second effort, and as he hit the 400-meter mark, Seward yelled, "56 flat."

Danny acknowledged him with his eyes and a brief nod, his look focused yet serene. The form remained constant as Murray turned the corner at 600 meters. As he approached Gabe for the completion of his second repetition, Seward waited until he crossed the start line and yelled "1:52.1."

Murray nodded again, continuing to jog counterclockwise. Less than a minute later he'd returned, his breathing not even audible. No more than thirty seconds had elapsed before he said, "Let's go."

Gabe quickly punched his chronograph as Danny started his third effort. He'd cut almost a minute and a half off his intended break time, action that Seward thought suicidal. Murray's workout had barely begun, and he was already pushing the envelope by having significantly reduced his rest time for his first two efforts. He had a long way to go in his workout, Gabe thought, and it was inevitable he would pay for it badly toward the end. But as Danny approached Seward for the first lap of his third 800, Gabe could still not detect any visible changes in Murray's face or form. And the youngster's breathing was almost unascertainable as he passed him, completing the first lap.

"54.8," Gabe yelled.

Danny just nodded, and continued speeding around the track.

As Murray reached the 600 mark, it was difficult for Gabe to tell in the moonlight, but it seemed to him that Danny was switching into a higher gear as he came home. His stride had lengthened slightly, his turnover seeming to have quickened, and his elevation having heightened. His hands that had been grazing his hips were a bit higher, and his arms were pulling more strongly. Gabe glanced at his watch and shouted "1:49.2."

Danny acknowledged him again by a brief nod and continued jogging.

The effort stunned Gabe. Murray had run a hand-timed second lap of 54.4. And he had done it with ease, the third of three incredible 800s with very short intervals in between each. The kid was better than he ever could have imagined, Seward thought. But there was no way he could continue his breakneck pace. Gabe had watched his share of world-class runners, including the Africans, run high-powered workouts, but not in the manner that this kid was doing. There was no frigging way this kid could continue his relentless pace, Seward thought; no frigging way.

Danny took almost the full three-minute rest following his third 800, and as he approached Seward, said, "This one's going to be quick."

"Lordy mercy," Gabe whispered to himself, shaking his head in disbelief. Seward pulled off his glasses that had fogged, blew on them, and wiped them off. He put them back on and said, "Go for it, buddy."

Danny took off like a rocket on his fourth 800. Gabe was so stunned by the power and grace of his movement, that he forgot to check Murray's split as he hit the 200-meter mark. He was still mesmerized by the youngster's form, and forgot to check his watch or call Danny's split as he reached the 400-meter mark also.

By the time Seward realized his mistake, Murray was already a hundred meters into his second lap. But as Danny passed Gabe, it was apparent to Seward that the look in Murray's eyes was different. It was not a distressed look, but one that spoke of cold and calculated focus.

It was a maniacal yet controlled look, the kind that he'd seen before with the psychopaths that he'd visited in prison when doing research in his criminal psychology studies.   As Danny hit what Gabe estimated to be the 600-meter mark, Seward glanced at his chronograph. It read 1:20. "No frigging way," Gabe said out loud. He focused on Danny, whose running style mesmerized him. There was no way Murray could have run 600 meters that quickly; not after his first set of 800s which were all balls-to-the-wall efforts. As Seward studied Danny in the moonlight, the youngster appeared to elevate even higher. He looked like a low-flying jet as he roared down the final 100-meter straight of tartan, streaking home toward Gabe with power and grace. Seward punched his chronograph, a shrill beep following as Danny crossed the line. Murray continued jogging past him and around the track oval, his hands on his hips, his breathing finally audible.

Gabe checked the numbers on his chronograph. "My God!" he exclaimed. He didn't realize how loudly he'd spoken.

Danny heard the words from a distance and grinned. He knew the effort had been quick, and had a good idea as to his time. He had run so many intervals since coming to Oregon that it had reached the point where he could usually predict within a second or two of how fast he had run.

Murray turned and jogged back toward Seward, who looked visibly shaken. "1:45.6," Gabe said in a hushed, if not reverential, tone. Danny nodded and continued jogging.

It was apparent to Murray that Seward was visibly shaken. And he was right. Gabe had never witnessed a session like Danny had just completed, not by the Africans or anyone else. The 1:45.6 was world-class time, the kind that could win a World Championship or Olympic final.   Seward pinched himself and jumped up and down. He took off his Giants cap and roughed his scalp. He was awake. He wasn't dreaming. This kid was a genius, beyond anything he ever could have imagined. There was no question he could run a near-world-record time at 800 meters under race conditions. But the longer distances were still up in the air.

The remainder of Murray's workout would be revealing, providing a clearer window into what he could do at longer distances. Gabe could not imagine Danny continuing the kind of all-out effort he'd managed, surely not for the remainder of the session that he'd planned. It was too much for a kid of 17 to pull off. It was too much for a runner of any age to pull off.

Murray took the full three-minute break that he'd allotted, and began his first of three one-mile repeats, with a four-minute rest interval in between. The session began nine meters behind the start line, the added-on distance necessary to make a complete mile for four revolutions of the 400-meter track.

Danny appeared to be almost jogging as he came through the first 400-meters in 64 seconds. His form hadn't changed as he glided through 800 meters in 2:07, 1,200 meters in 3:10, and the mile in 4:13. Gabe just shook his head in disbelief as he yelled out the final split. Murray appeared to have completely recovered from his blazing set of 800s, and had just run a fast mile in an effortless fashion.

With a little less than three minutes elapsed in his break, Danny jogged back to Seward and said, "Hit it now."

Gabe tapped his chronograph and Murray took off, the youngster again trimming a large measure of precious rest time off his first repetition. Gabe studied his style that hadn't appeared to change a bit, and when he came through the first 400 in sixty-one seconds, Seward's pupils were dilated ink black. The 800-meter split was 2:02, and as he called it out, Danny noticeably got higher on his toes.

"Whoa!" Gabe exclaimed, as Murray approached the third lap. Seward looked at his chronograph and yelled, "3:00 flat," as Danny buzzed by. Surely the fourth lap would get Murray, Gabe thought. There was no way he could continue his relentless pace. But when he hit the finish line and Seward yelled out "3:59," the middle-aged man was visibly shaken. How much more could the kid have left?

Danny took the full four-minute rest following his second mile, and as he approached Gabe for his third- and final-effort mile, he said, "Let's push the envelope on this one."

Seward, too shaken to speak, just nodded.

This was all too much, he thought. He didn't do drugs, he didn't drink, and he sure as hell didn't have visions. If there was ever an event in his life that had approached the supernatural, this was it. Things like this weren't supposed to happen. He squeezed himself again to reconfirm that he wasn't dreaming, and then he scratched his arm. Either this was real, or he had completely lost his marbles and gone off into another world.

Danny shot out like a heat-seeking missile as Seward tapped his chronograph. No splits on this one, Gabe thought. He wouldn't look at his watch or call out anything to Murray. Seward wasn't certain why he'd made that decision. But something told him that it didn't matter to Murray, who was locked in a trancelike state, Gabe's splits irrelevant to him at this point. As Danny approached Gabe for the first lap, Gabe just clapped his hands and said, "Looking great, big guy."

Danny barely nodded. His focus was hard as he jetted laps two and three. His form remained unchanged on his final lap, and as he smoked toward Gabe and the finish, Seward's chronograph squealed loudly as Murray touched the line. Gabe never looked at his chronograph as Danny turned the corner of the track. Less than a minute later he returned and stopped in front of Seward.

"What did you get me in?" Danny asked.

"Haven't looked. What's your guess?"

"3:56," Danny said without hesitation.

Gabe showed his chronograph to Murray. Danny just nodded, no change in his expression as he said, "Pretty close."

He continued jogging in a clockwise manner, before turning back to Seward for the start of his two-mile. Gabe waited a lengthy time before checking the digital numbers on his running watch. They read 3:55.8. Gabe's heart thumped in his chest like a kicking mule as he tried to make some sense of it all. "What else can he do?" he asked himself.

The two-mile began another nine meters behind the mile start, and Gabe walked down to the new start point as Danny approached. He studied Murray's body as the redhead jogged. There were no signs of stiffness in his movement, none of the visible signs of distress that he'd come to associate with pain or fatigue. If anything, Murray looked even more fluid and relaxed than when he'd begun the workout.

He appeared to be jogging as he went through the first mile in 4:12. His form never changed as he ran an almost duplicate second mile, finishing the effort in 8:23.7 Gabe yelled out the time to Danny who just nodded.

Murray did a long cool down jog, and then a set of 100 sprints that Seward didn't time. The sprints didn't matter. The workout was over. It was the greatest workout that Gabe had ever witnessed, perhaps the greatest workout that anyone had ever witnessed. He was so stunned it left him speechless as Danny returned to the infield. He sat, slipped out of his spikes and into his training shoes.

As he stood up, he said, "I know that in order to get an official record and a qualifying time for the Olympic Trials, I have to join the United States Track and Field Federation. The idea of doing that makes me sick inside. Why should I have to join some organization to get a record? What have they ever done to help me? And what will they ever do? I think it's total bullshit. I have to pay some bureaucrats so I can run. It's absurd. And they're corrupt. They've refused to release the names of athletes who have tested positive for drugs, hiding under the defense that the American justice system doesn't work that way. The rest of the world despises them for that."

Gabe grinned. "I'm sure they have done nothing to help you up until now. And likely won't in the future, other than, as you say, try to control you. And yeah, they're corrupt, as is the Olympic hierarchy. But that's the way things are. You either play their game and abide by their rules, or you don't get your record."

Danny nodded. "Politics stink. I still haven't clearly defined mine, and I'd hate to be labeled. I'm liberal in some areas, conservative in others. But I'm clear on rights issues. And I feel my greatest right as an American citizen is the right to be left alone. As far as I'm concerned, track and field organizations, governments, big business, and religions have a lot in common. They're all control freaks preying on the little guy without a voice."

"I guess you could say that," Gabe said.

He stroked his chin, aghast at the teenager's spin on the world, Murray verbalizing many of the same firebrand philosophies that he kept bottled up inside him but never spoke. Murray was a rebel at heart, a kindred spirit to the founding fathers that led the colonies into revolution against Great Britain.

"Okay. I'll join their damn organization," Murray said. "I know I have to, to play their game. Otherwise I'm biting off my nose to spite my face."

Gabe just nodded.

"Where can I get a form?" Danny asked. "I need to join before the next all-comers meet in Eugene. I'm going to take the 5,000-meter record that night. I'll send out the word. Hopefully, a few folks will show up to watch me run."

Gabe's eyes widened. "I just sent in my membership. And I happen to have an extra form in my truck. Let's go get it."

"Okay."

As the two walked to Seward's truck, Danny gave him a detailed version of how he would run his upcoming race. Gabe just listened as Danny's flawless memory detailed the contest, right down to each 200-meter split. Seward reassured him that his time would be official since the Eugene meets were certified and had electronic timing.

As Gabe handed Danny the form, Danny said, "Thanks. This is for your ears only. I'm going to break the record, but only by a second or two. That way I can continue setting records for a long time in the future. Twelve minutes and thirty-nine seconds is soft. I can obliterate that. But there's no sense in doing it all at once. I'll take my time and milk every big meet here and in Europe and Asia that I can, chipping off a second or two at each one, each time getting a new record. With endorsements, I'll be a multimillionaire by the end of the season. And Cindy will never have to live in a rat hole again. I'll give her everything she's never had and more. She'll never have to want for anything."

Gabe said softly, "You really love your little sister, don't you?"

Danny said in a hushed tone, "She's the only thing in my life that gives it meaning. She's never had a chance."

Seward said, "Now she will."

As Danny Murray jogged away, Gabe Seward watched him move. He wasn't a 17-year-old kid, Seward thought. He had an adolescent's face and body, the structure belying the incredible strength housed within, and an adult mind that was dazzling.

He was the greatest raw running talent that Seward had ever witnessed in his life. The teen's bravado, that he would shatter world records, was not implausible. If Murray possessed any vulnerability, it was perhaps his affection for his little sister Cindy. It was apparent to Gabe Seward that she was more important to Danny than anything in his life, his running included.

CHAPTER 13

EUGENE, OREGON—THE FOLLOWING FRIDAY
MURRAY'S RECORD ATTEMPT AT 5,000 METERS

"Final call, men's 5,000 meters."

Gabe Seward eyed Danny Murray from the packed Hayward Field stands on the University of Oregon campus. The redhead was stretching on the infield, but this time not without notice. Almost every track and field fan in the stands had come to the all-comers meet just to watch him, the buzz in Eugene that Danny Murray, the mystery runner that listed his age as 17, was guaranteeing to obliterate the teenage marks of Steve Prefontaine and Jerry Lindgren, and the American open record held by Bob Kennedy.

Depending on the size and enthusiasm of the crowd, he had also said he might take the world record of 12:39 held by the Ethiopian Haile Gebrselassie. An American record would be almost a minute faster than his "fated shoe" run, where he had come back to catch the field after appearing finished; a world record run required another nineteen seconds quicker.

His predictions were of a boldness that bordered on delusional grandeur, a megalomaniac madness that was uncommon to a sport characterized by reflective thinkers. It was the type of braggadocio reminiscent of the young Cassius Clay, a man who would back his claims and more under the adopted name of Muhammad Ali. But a single all-comers meet did not make a Muhammad Ali, and Danny Murray was still an unproven product. Murray's initial run in Eugene had triggered a series of doubts and what-ifs among the track and field addicts drawn to Hayward Field—knowledgeable men and women who understood the remoteness of records coming from unknowns—unlike any in years past. Many could not believe what had happened.

In Murray's maiden race in Eugene, he had stunned track and field fans by running one of the most improbable races anyone had ever seen. Listing his age on his entry form as 17, he had run 5,000 meters, or 3.1 miles, in the time of 13:55. It was just a few seconds shy of what the immortal Steve Prefontaine had run as a teenager, and eight seconds short of Jerry Lindgren's U.S. teenage record of 13:47. But it was the fashion in which Murray had shaped his run that set track and field fans ablaze.

At a critical juncture of his run, leading the race by a wide margin, he had stepped out wide on the track, sat down on the sixth lane, and worked patiently to unknot an insidious shoelace. As he sat, the whole field passed him. And when he got up to start running again, barefoot and clutching a spiked track shoe in each hand, the pack of runners that he had led by such a hefty margin were a good 150 meters ahead of him.

It was a margin that anybody who knew anything about track and field would have understood as insurmountable. But the skinny redhead, with a look that never wavered, picked up where he had left off and went after the field. By two and a half miles he had caught them and recaptured the lead, redefining "insurmountable" as a barrier that only lesser minds erected. By the race's conclusion, the conjecture of what he might have done in an unencumbered contest was boundless. How much time had he lost as he sat and picked at his shoelace? How much extra energy had he exerted to bring back the field and go on to win? What finishing time would he have run if the incident had never happened?

Some said that Murray had conservatively lost a minute, while others said as much as a minute and a half. The first would have given him an American record, the second a world record. And then following the race's completion, Murray had hightailed out of Hayward Field, answering no questions and casting an even larger shadow of doubt on a run that was already so improbable.

He had listed his age as 17, which seemed wrong. He had left his address as a post office box, which seemed wrong. He had no affiliation with the United States Track and Field Federation or any track club, which seemed wrong. And no one had ever heard of him, which was worse than wrong.

His run set off flurries of speculation that he was the product of some wealthy and secretive cabal, a kid monitored by physicians and chemists on designer drugs, too sophisticated to show up by the current standard testing. Following Murray's run he had not been tested, further darkening the shadow of doubt cast by his performance.

If things went right, Murray would dispel those rumors this evening, Seward thought. He had taken all the right steps to insure his run would be entered into the record books without an asterisk. Gabe had been with Murray when he filled out his entry form and paid his money to the United States Track and Field Federation. And the kid had given him his word that he would stay around after his race and take both urine and blood tests, both of which Gabe had requested for lifting any shadows of doubt on Danny's record attempt.

The whole idea of Danny Murray being a pawn of some clandestine group attempting to chemically engineer a record-holding distance runner was so ridiculous to Gabe Seward that he hardly thought it worth addressing. This was a kid who was living in a dilapidated trailer with his little sister, a youngster surviving at a subsistence level on pasta and day-old bread, with barely the funds to pay for electricity and water.

But rumormongers sparked malicious attacks, and none were worse than those, Seward was certain, that were coming from Barry Swill's camp. He and his team of hack writers for his track and field magazine had been vicious in promoting a buzz among the sport's powerbrokers. Their telephone conversations and face-to-face meetings labeled Murray a fraud, a chemically engineered pawn of some secret and powerful group yet to be identified.

As Danny stretched, several competitors acknowledged him by eye contact and nods. It was the kind of recognition that athletes receive from each other only when there is respect involved, approval that can only be gained through past performance. As the competitors watched him, what became clear to them was the serene look of confidence and positive body language that Murray exhibited. He showed no signs of stress, a kid that looked like he may have been going out for a jog around the block. He had a sense of calm about him that spoke of being in another state, focused but not overly concerned. It was a look that an unknowledgeable observer may have mistaken as lacking conviction but Gabe Seward knew as other. He realized that Danny Murray's focus and calm were so complete that he had literally removed himself from his surroundings and was existent on a different level.

His higher plane was one that differed little from Tiger Woods threading a needle with a brilliant iron shot or Michael Jordan hitting an impossible game-winning fadeaway jumper at the buzzer. It was a zone that spoke of otherworldliness, perhaps Zen in nature, or whatever higher-level term aptly applied. It was a state that only a handful of athletes ever achieved, the elite few who were clearly superior to their competitors, a rarity in a world so full of talent.

Murray peeled off his gray cotton sweats and shoved them in his athletic bag. Then he knelt forward and rechecked his shoes. He had rethreaded his racing spikes with fresh laces and inserted new steel spikes. The clean whiteness of the lace, and shiny silver of the spikes were in stark contrast to his aged mottled gray shoes.

He stood up, leaned forward, and touched his palms to the track. Then he ran in place on his toes, his spikes making a light pitter-patter sound as they gently kissed the tartan-surfaced oval.

Then he jogged toward the start line where the competitors were lining up. The race was starting on the 200-meter curve, an equidistant 200 meters from the finish line. It would be a total of twelve and one half revolutions of the 400-meter oval, a distance of

3.1 miles. Danny lined up in the middle of the semioval line that extended out from lanes one to eight.

Unlike horse racing, where an outer post has a clear disadvantage because of the additional distance from the inside rail, in track running each competitor covers the same distance. The start line for the outer lanes is positioned further up the track; another designated area further down the oval, a spot where runners can break to the inside rail.

In a race as long as 5,000 meters, the start position is generally of little consequence, runners traditionally in no great hurry to rush to the inside rail to assume a lead. It is a race of patience and tactics, a contest where a rushed start is almost always fatal. To go out too quickly results in oxygen debt, a state that spells doom. In simple terms, it is like letting all the air out of a balloon at once. The runner's body then goes into an anaerobic state, or running without oxygen. Like a diver in the ocean, once the oxygen supply has been depleted, the results are disastrous.

The optimal way of running 5,000 meters is for the athlete to remain as close to his oxygen threshold as possible without exceeding it. For Danny Murray speculators, that was an unknown quantity. But Murray didn't have those kinds of doubts. He didn't need exercise physiologists or coaches to quantify his running and tell him what he was capable of doing. His strategy was based on what he had accomplished in practice and on his intuition. All the rest meant nothing to him, just strictures that those of lesser vision might tie him to.

As Murray and the men surrounding him leaned forward in anticipation of the starter gun, his resting heart rate of 36 rose. But as the gun cracked and he sprinted down the track, it rose quickly.

Murray went out like a flash, and at the break line for the inside lane he drove to the rail. He was already clearly ahead, and Gabe Seward checked his chronograph as Danny crossed 200 meters far ahead of the field. His time was 25.8 seconds, absolute insanity. "Holy moly," Gabe said to himself softly. It was a frightening start, even in light of what he had witnessed in Murray's astounding prerace workout. If he continued that way, he would certainly crash and burn.

Seward was sitting surrounded by strangers in this contest, Barry Swill and the rest of the press that had come to view the race assigned to a designated area for reporters in the far stands. It was just as well that they were not near him, Seward thought. Their acerbic quips would make it difficult for him to concentrate on Danny's performance, and he would derive no joy from needling them if Murray indeed ran the kind of race he had predicted.

Murray went through the first 400 meters in 52.5, and as he spotted Seward in the stands gave him a thumbs-up. He appeared to be about a hundred meters ahead of the pack behind him. Then he noticeably decelerated. His next 200 meters was a pedestrian 35 seconds, and his 800-meter split just under 2:02.8. As Murray passed by Seward, he had a grin on his face. Seward understood.

In the far stands Barry Swill checked his watch. "Slowed down to a 70," Swill said. "He's screwed."

"Yeah," a cowriter for his magazine said. "The cocky little s.o.b.'s in oxygen debt. He won't be able to come back in this one."

Danny Murray then settled into his intended pace, having built a large lead on the field. It was his strategy, going out quick and then relaxing, not wanting to chance being impeded by other runners. The last thing he needed to deal with would be a bump or a trip on a record-intending run.

Like clockwork Danny began to reel off 61-second quarters, his first mile time just under 4:04. His two-mile split was 8:08, and on the tenth lap he began lapping the slower runners in the field. With a lap and a half to go, he had lapped everyone; and with 200 meters to go, Seward checked his watch. His time was 12:07, meaning a 32-second final 200 would tie a world record. The roar in the stands was deafening as he headed for home. It was so loud that even Murray was jolted from his trance. It was difficult for him to refocus as he made his way for the finish line. Not wanting to chance losing the possibility of a record, he picked up the pace a bit more than he had intended. His final 200 meters was 29 seconds, and he crossed the finish line with a new world record of 12:36.

Everyone in the stands was on their feet screaming and yelling, the loudest and most vociferous crowd that had packed Hayward Field's fabled stands in years. Murray grinned sheepishly as he finished, continuing to jog on an outside lane as he acknowledged the crowd with a wave. The remaining runners in the race continued to come around, the second-place runner more than a minute and a half behind him.

Murray spotted Seward who was on his feet clapping and cheering. He gave Gabe a double thumbs-up and Seward responded the same. As Seward studied Murray, it appeared that the redhead was not even breathing hard. He looked as if he could continue running at the same pace for another 5,000 meters.

It was scary what this kid was capable of, Seward thought. He might have another twenty to thirty seconds in him in a 5,000, and to predict what he might be able to do in a 10,000 or the marathon was too mind-numbing to even contemplate. Most certainly he would destroy every distance record on the books.

But more importantly, Gabe knew that Danny's run this evening would be the beginning of a new life for him and his sister. The children of poverty and desperation would soon be living a life of privilege, a well-deserved change for two who had beaten unbeatable odds.

CHAPTER 14

POST-RACE INTERROGATION

Following the post-race drug test, reporters swarmed Danny Murray. A sports writer from the Portland paper began the questioning.

"Danny, you've just demolished a world record that few of us thought could be touched for a long time. And none of us have ever heard of you. Could you fill us in on your background?"

"What do you want to know?"

"Where were you born? Where did you live?"

"I was born in Kansas. But I've lived in a lot of places. Right now I'm based in Oregon."

"Where are you living right now?"

"Oregon."

"Where in Oregon?"

"I'm not going there with you."

"Why not?"

"Leave it at that," Danny snapped.

"That was one hell of a performance you ran today," a writer for the Eugene paper said. "Many of us would term it as shocking."

"Maybe to you. Not to me."

"You don't consider a world record by an unknown shocking?"

"Nope. I ran what I intended to. Almost right to the second. I got a little carried away the last 200. Actually, I was planning on a 12:38."

"Doesn't sound like you have too much doubt concerning your abilities," the reporter said. His words elicited laughter from the group.

"When it comes to my running, none," Danny fired back without missing a beat.

"Where does all that confidence come from?"

"It's not that hard. I know what I've done in workouts. I know my capabilities. Having an idea of what kind of times I can run is based on that. It's not exactly rocket science."

"Who's coaching you?"

"Nobody. I coach myself."

"Why is that?"

"Why would I need a coach?"

"All the obvious reasons. Especially planning workouts."

"I design my own workouts. I'm literate, and there's a lot of source material out there. Why would I want to get involved with some coach to control me and take credit for what I've done and what I'm planning on doing?"

"You think you can better the record you ran tonight?"

"You bet. I'll airmail it when I'm ready. What you saw tonight was just scratching the surface. There'll be records to come for a long time."

"When is the next?"

"That depends on what type of money is on the line."

"Do you have any endorsements?"

"No. But you can bet they'll be coming."

His words brought more laughter.

"What do you think of performance enhancement drugs?" Barry Swill asked.

Murray's eyes narrowed as he focused on Swill. "Unlike you, I despise them. I've read the crap you've put up on Internet chat groups. You enable cheaters. I think they should be thrown out of the sport for life."

"Your run today is going to raise a lot of suspicion, partner," Swill said in a condescending tone.

"As should every record performance that's run, regardless of the competitor. But I've just taken a urine and blood test. And understanding your affinity for tangible evidence, I'd be more than willing to send you a stool sample, Barry."

Danny's quip sparked more laughter.

"Cocky little guy, aren't you, kid?" Swill said.

"Nope. I'm a pragmatist. I know what I'm capable of doing. When you know you can do something, state it, and then do it. That's not cockiness, that's fact."

Swill mummed up. The rapidity, maturity, and clarity of Danny's speech were unsuspected. He spoke like a well-educated adult, nothing like Swill had suspected.

"You said you're just scratching the surface," a reporter from the Eugene paper said. "What kind of times can we be expecting?"

"Stay tuned," Danny said. "The fun is just starting."

"Danny, can you..."

"Sorry guys. That's it for this evening. See you all soon."

Danny turned and ran off, clutching his spikes as he made his way out of the Hayward Field track stadium. The stands broke out into applause as he moved. He waved to them and smiled, acknowledging their appreciation. And then he took off running across the campus, his ancient pickup parked far away from the circus.

A group of frustrated reporters were stranded behind down on the field, clutching palm-sized tape recorders and notepads. Gabe Seward had also sidled up to the group quietly, standing just outside the circle.

"He's hiding something," Barry Swill, the publisher of Track and Field Universe pronounced in an authoritarian tone. He was a short, middle-aged man; a pudgy little character who Seward knew was never an athlete. "Nobody runs a damn world record coming out of the woodwork. I've been covering track and field for a lifetime, and I've never witnessed anything like this. This has a bad smell to it. This guy's hiding something."

"I agree, Barry," a reporter for the Eugene paper said. "I've done some digging on this kid, and I came up empty. Just that he lists himself as Danny Murray, a 17-year-old, with a post office box that doesn't exist."

"What do you think he's hiding?" a reporter from a local Eugene television station asked.

"I don't know," Swill said. "But if I had to bet, I'd say he's probably, number one, lying about his age; and number two, he's on some new designer drug that doesn't have a test for it."

"How about that maybe he's just the greatest distance runner who's ever laced up a pair of spikes, and he's wary of adults?" Gabe Seward posed the question. The sports writer from the Eugene newspaper recognized him as the slender spectator with the thinning hair and owlish glasses who had been sitting in the stands behind him and Barry Swill in both of Danny's all-comer meets.

"And how about he's the second coming of Christ?" Swill hissed. Sardonic laughter followed his caustic quip. It was obvious to Seward that Swill possessed a degree of standing among the reporters who had formed a circle.

"Could be," Seward countered. "But my money's on his being the most phenomenal distance runner that has made the scene to date."

"Who the hell are you?" Swill hissed. "And what the hell do you know about track and field?"

"I'm Gabe Seward," he answered in a calm tone. "And I've done a bit of running myself."

"Seward?" Swill asked. His beady eyes narrowed as he summed up Gabe. "Yeah, I remember you. You bombed out in the '72 and '76 trials, right here in Eugene."

"Good memory," Gabe said, his voice still calm and without emotion. "You are correct."

"How's your buddy Len Hilton doing? He could never win the big one either. Choke artist supreme."

"Len is doing quite well. Though you need to brush up a bit on your history. National titles in the 1,500 and the mile aren't exactly small ones. And making an Olympic team isn't bad either."

116

Swill cackled, the chubby flesh on his flaccid frame seeming to shake like Jell-O. "You got some vested interest in this Danny Murray kid?"

"No," Gabe said. "Other than I hope we get to see him run again. He is 17 years old and has run the greatest 5,000 in history. I would say his bounds are limitless as to what he can do in the future."

"You know, Seward, now that you're talking, I remember you better from the trials in '72 and '76. You struck me back then as being the dumbest turkey of the whole group. A damn Pollyanna who thought everybody and everything was peachy-keen."

"Not everybody," Gabe said in the same measured tone. "Perhaps all the competitors at the trials, but unfortunately not all the press."

Seward's response brought some nervous laughter from the reporters surrounding the two men.

"I'll tell you what, Seward," Swill said, "I'd be willing to bet you ten thousand bucks that this kid's record won't stand. They're going to find something's wrong, big-time stuff. My guess is that, first, he's on some kind of designer juice that they don't have a test for yet. And second, that he's not 17, 27 more likely."

"Right, Barry. And a Kenyan to boot, with skin and hair color dyed to make the ruse even more plausible."

More nervous laughter followed Seward's response.

"You think he's 17?" a reporter from the Eugene paper asked Seward.

"Most certainly," Gabe said. "You gentlemen saw him up close. He's obviously a youngster. Seventeen is not a stretch at all."

"Bullshit", Swill hissed. Who are you to judge age?

"And who are you?" Gabe asked calmly.

"I've spent a lifetime around track and field," Swill said.

"So have I," Gabe said. "But I've also spent a lifetime around youngsters. And I would bet my life that this is a young man who is most certainly the 17 that he says he is."

Swill wiped a bead of sweat off his forehead that was shiny. He said "They have his urine and blood samples, Seward. And he's going to test positive right now, or some time down the road, for some kind of designer drug that's not out there yet. I'd bet my life on that."

"Don't rate your life so cheaply, because he will test clean now and forever."

"You're a fool, Seward," Swill said.

Gabe grinned. "I've been called much worse."

"Why didn't he stick around and answer more questions?" Swill spit.

"I couldn't tell you the answer to that one. I could only guess."

"Then guess, Einstein. We're all waiting with bated breath for more of your brilliance."

"Nothing too profound. Probably that he's just painfully shy and mistrustful of adults."

"How would you know that?" the reporter from the track and field journal said. "Drawing from your personal experience?"

"Precisely," Gabe said. "And the many youngsters that I've had the pleasure of working with."

"What kind of work do you do?" Swill hissed.

"Youth counselor," Gabe said.

"A damn social worker."

"I'll accept that label. But my job title is youth counselor."

"Seward, if you had another two I.Q. points, you could be a card-carrying grape," Swill said.

"Which would make me ineligible to write for your magazine where your high-end hiring number is considerably lower."

Laughter followed. Swill's neck reddened. His eyes panned the circle of reporters. "You guys have all been around the block. And I know you can smell the bullshit in this one. Let's find out who this Danny Murray character is, expose him and the group that's engineering this goddamn fraud."

A few heads nodded, but nobody answered. Swill turned to Seward. "I don't know what kind of connection you have to this Murray character, Seward, but there's something. I'm going to find that out and expose you too."

Seward smiled. "Barry, you bring back fond memories of my youth. Though I must admit that neither J. Edgar Hoover nor Richard Nixon were heroes of mine. Good luck on your investigation."

Seward turned and walked away, wondering when he'd see Danny Murray again.

CHAPTER 15

PORTLAND, OREGON
THE NIGHT AFTER MURRAY'S RECORD-SETTING RUN

"You can have whichever one you want."

Cindy's big eyes glimmered like blue diamonds as she stared at the rows of stuffed animals in the Portland toy store.

She made her way up and down the rows slowly, stopping and gently stroking the stuffed pets like they were sacred. "If you see one you like, go ahead and pick it up," Danny said.

Cindy stared at her brother, the wonderment in her eyes lifting his spirits to a level it had seldom reached in his 17 years. It was a joy he'd yearned for since early childhood, knowing that his little sister would finally be well taken care of and having what she desired.

Endorsements from athletic companies would be coming soon, followed by the rich purses from the track races that would take him around the world. Having read what the top names in the sport made through their racing and endorsements, he knew that he'd be a millionaire within a relatively short period of time. And with that money he'd earn, Cindy would have all the things she'd been deprived of growing up.

Most important of all she'd have a decent home to live in, in a good neighborhood. It would be a place where Danny would no longer have to worry about her safety, a house surrounded by upscale neighbors where crime would be almost unheard of. It would be a refuge where the fears that he dealt with in his daily existence in a low-rent trailer court would no longer be present.

Cindy would get the best education and have the best clothes and anything else that she desired that he never had. It would be a new life, one where the fantasies of his childhood were on the cusp of becoming reality.

Today in Portland was the start of that new life, and in celebration of the moment, he'd given Cindy a day unlike any she'd ever had. In the morning they had gone to the Portland Zoo, dined at a pizza parlor for lunch, and then to the movies. The toy store would be their final destination before heading back toward Eugene and stopping some place along the way for dinner.

He still had some yards to cut in the morning, a job he'd continue right up until the time his endorsements and track winnings began to come in. It was the product of hard times that made him that way, wary of the fickleness of success. He was mistrustful of future monetary promise, money that he had in hand his only reality.

Cindy took her time as she eyed the furry pets in the toy store, and Danny was patient not to rush her. He would let her enjoy the moment, one that would be the first of many in a future where he'd spoil her rotten with the things she desired.

His lust for things had never been intense, his craving for fame and wealth more a need to prove to the world his worth. It was a hunger accompanied by way of a will of iron, the unflinching mindset of a youngster who didn't know the meaning of "quit." He had overcome insurmountable odds in achieving what others could never dream of, and any outward trappings that he'd now accumulate would merely be validations of that triumph.

Murray imagined himself someday retiring from his running with the luxury of returning to school and formalizing the education that he'd never had. Again, he felt more learned than most adults he had met, those with college and advanced degrees, all by way of voracious reading and study. But a college degree would be formal validation of his knowledge, a missing element that he needed more than the tutoring. His life experience and extensive reading had shaped a mindset that had very definite ideas. He'd come to learn that critical thinking was rare in a culture that lavished praise on sameness, and that independent thinkers were frequently buried and forgotten in a society where original thought was ridiculed.

CHAPTER 16

THE NEXT NIGHT—CONSEQUENCES BE DAMNED

The following night Danny Murray was out running late at night, contemplating his next course of action. Both the Portland and local papers had given extensive coverage to his record run, and a visit to an Internet café in Portland had confirmed his thoughts. News of his run had streaked around the globe, igniting an interest in him that was at fever pitch.

He realized that his prediction of becoming an overnight valuable commodity had materialized, and now it was just a question of deciding on a proper course of action to take advantage of that window. His inclination was to contact an agency that dealt with name athletes, a place where contracts, marketing, and scheduling could all be handled in one place. It was an action that he would likely take the next day, contacting agencies on the east and west coasts to measure their level of enthusiasm and listen to their proposals.

He ran deep into the night and, as he jogged into his trailer court, realized that the trailer of the stripper who worked in Eugene was gone. Then he saw a sight that chilled his blood. The Hispanic looking man with the black mustache and scarred lips that he'd seen with the stripper was moving quickly to his vehicle, the silver Porsche 911. In moments the Porsche's engine roared as it zoomed out of the parking lot, shell and dirt kicking up dust as it blew past Danny. For a brief moment the man behind the wheel of the Porsche made eye contact, and Murray sensed that something was horribly wrong. As the car sped off, he focused on the California plates and committed them to memory. Then he sprinted toward his trailer and knocked at the door having left Cindy with his key, an action that somehow gave her a sense of security. Nobody answered and he banged harder. "Cindy?" he yelled.

There was no answer.

With a shovel that he kept in a small garden area outside his trailer, Danny smashed in a window, lifted it, and crawled inside the trailer. The trailer was dark and he turned on the light. His whole body shook as he spotted Cindy. She was lying on her bed face down, her pajama bottoms pulled down. The bed was soaked in blood.

"No," he screamed, his eyes hot with tears. He gathered her in his arms and grabbed his keys and wallet as he bolted out the door. And then he drove to the local hospital, accelerator to the floor as tears gushed from his eyes. Cindy lay on the seat next to him, her chest faintly rising and falling as life left her tiny body.

...

Danny waited in the emergency room for less than thirty minutes before the resident in charge made his way out into the lobby to meet him.

He looked at Danny firmly in the eyes and said, "I'm sorry. Your sister's gone."

"No!" Danny cried. "No, no, no!"

Tears gushed from his eyes as he sobbed.

As he cried the physician said, "Your sister was raped and choked. You'll need to wait here until the police come."

The face of the Hispanic man he had spotted zooming out of the trailer court parking lot flashed in his mind. With the vision vivid on his screen, his mind kicked into gear as rage replaced sorrow. He bolted from the emergency room and then out the door to his pickup.

Minutes later he was back at the trailer he rented. He hastily loaded his belongings in his pickup truck and drove off. Everything spun out of control as he drove in the soft rain that had begun to fall. Cindy was dead, raped and murdered. He'd seen her killer, a fact he was sure of. The new focus of his life was clear: He would find him and kill him. It was what he had to do.

...

In Eureka, California, Danny read that he was wanted for the rape and murder of his sister. The story also mentioned that he had set a running record that was pending, but which track authorities would not validate until his name was cleared.

As Danny's thoughts slowly cleared, he recalled the man's silver Porsche 911 and the California license plates he'd memorized. He was certain that he was of Hispanic origin, a slim lead in a state heavily populated by immigrants from south of the border. He rationalized that the probability of his base being either Los Angeles or San Diego was great, both large metropolitan areas where a heavy drug trade flourished and there would be many Hispanics for him to prey upon.

From Eureka he headed south, and a check of a data bank of driver's licenses from a site he pulled up in a San Francisco Internet cafe confirmed his suspicions. The plates linked the car to LA and a man named Rafael Gonzales. More checking revealed that Gonzales had an arrest record as long as his arm, everything from the drug dealing he suspected to immigration smuggling and imprisonment, child pornography, rape and murder. He had beaten most of the charges but had done his share of jail time.

At a Wal-Mart Danny bought some cheap black dye and colored his hair. He purchased a pair of steel-framed glasses with non-magnified lenses, and pierced his right ear with a faux diamond. In a novelty shop he bought a series of wash-off tattoos. And outside of a diner in San Jose he stole a set of license plates and inspection stickers. It had been almost four days since he'd slept, and at a roadside between San Jose and Monterey, he dozed for almost ten hours.

A dream of Cindy awoke him in the heat of the night. As he gazed out onto the highway, soaked in sweat and grimy, he began to weep. His whole body shook as he cried, his sense of loss overpowering. His purpose for living was gone, the only thing that had been precious to him taken away. At that moment he realized he had no fear of losing his own life, only of dying before Cindy's killer was found. His record run in Eugene and the life of what might have been no longer held meaning for him. His new obsession was to find Cindy's killer and put him down. To hell with the legal system and gutless society that lacked the spine to justly punish violent criminals, he thought. He would mete out his own form of justice.

...

"Silver Porsche 911? Friend, you know how many silver Porsche 911s we come into at this lot in a year's time? This is LA, California, chief. Land of hot chicks, big dicks, and boss wheels. Porsches are a dime a dozen out here and we turn them quicker than a hiccup."

"I've got the license plates of the vehicle," Murray said.

The salesman--a middle-aged guy with a bad toupee, Hawaiian shirt unbuttoned to midchest, and fleshy neck bound by a gold-plated serpentine chain-- flipped back his aviator sunglasses onto his hairpiece. His yellow-brown eyes narrowed. "Do you now, stud nuts?"

Danny nodded.

The man reached into the breast pocket of his flowered shirt and pulled out a pack of Marlboros and a nickel-plated lighter. He lipped a cigarette from the pack, and the lighter hissed as he sucked in flame. He sucked hard and a cloud of smoke followed from his lungs and mouth. "Why do you want to find that car, chief?"

"I've got reasons," Danny said.

The man nodded and continued smoking. "I'll need something to refresh my memory," he said.

"How much?" Danny said.

"A couple of Franklins could make me real smart."

"I've got one," Danny said.

"Two's my number, chief."

"Then we don't have a deal," Danny said.

"Listen, chief," the man said. "I go into that computer bank and my ass is grass if the owner finds me."

Danny shrugged his shoulders. "Your choice."

126

The man continued smoking, and following a lengthy pause shook his head. "Nope. I'm making good dough here. I'm not going to risk my job for a measly hundred bucks."

Danny nodded. "No sweat."

Then Murray walked to his pickup truck and drove back to the dive he was holed-up in, in South LA. As he got on the on-ramp of the freeway, he reached into his pocket and extracted the set of keys he'd lifted from the car salesman's trousers. He fingered the keys as he drove, wondering which one got into the showroom.

...

At 2 a.m. Danny was inside the dealership showroom. Ten minutes later he'd picked the lock of the owner's office and was into the computer system that held the car dealership's records. Minutes later he had Rafael Gonzales' former address. After getting the address, he exited the Contacts program and went into Word. There he typed out a note: "Your system is insecure. And your salesman with the toupee is a troglodyte."

Murray printed out the note, laid it on the owner's glass-topped desk, and on top of the note placed the keys he'd lifted off the salesman. Then he left the car dealership and drove back to his place.

...

"Who are you?"

"I'm looking for Rafael Gonzales."

"Are you a cop?"

"No."

"Then get go fuck off."

"I can make it worth your while."

"I told you to go fuck off."

"Listen, all I want is an address. I'll pay you."

"Just a second."

The woman Danny was speaking to behind a cracked door held by a chain was a washed-out Caucasian brunette, mid-40s, in a see-through negligee.

Moments later the chain lifted and the door opened. Standing behind it was a muscular black man in a white tank top brandishing a shotgun. "You got business here, bitch fuck?"

"I'm trying to find the location of Rafael Gonzales. That's all. I'll pay."

The man walked forward and stuck the barrel of the gun in Danny's face. "Open your mouth, bitch."

"I just want..."

The man pumped the shotgun and said, "Open your mouth, bitch, or I paint the sidewalks with your brains."

Danny opened his mouth, and the man stuck the barrel of his gun inside. "Now you my nigger, home. How it feel?"

Danny didn't blink, and the man said, "Now you go to judgment day."

He pulled the trigger of the shotgun, and a click followed. The black man then burst out laughing, displaying pearl white teeth. Then he reached into his pocket and pulled out a shotgun shell that he loaded. He pumped the gun once more and said, "You leave now or I blow off your honky head."

Danny just nodded, turned, and left.

...

Later than night Danny drove back to the same neighborhood where he'd been threatened at gunpoint. From a 12-year-old trying to score drugs, a kid he met down the block from the home he'd been to earlier in the day, Murray got his answer. According to the kid, Gonzales was known to the neighborhood and was rumored to operate out of the Hispanic areas of major Texas cities, his home base Houston. It was ironic, Danny thought, the man he was chasing was possibly located in the same city where Gabe Seward lived. He wondered if it was safe to contact Seward when he reached Houston. It would be a huge gamble, revealing to anybody his whereabouts.

...

Danny left LA the next morning and drove east toward Phoenix, hoping he was on Gonzales' trail.

It was hot as hell in the desert as he drove toward Arizona, temperatures in the 100s. He made the city limits on a Saturday night, and at Denny's off the Interstate, he read of a 10,000-meter road race to be held the next morning in Scottsdale. There was prize money, $750 for the open male winner, and $500 for the female winner.

The next morning, equipped with a fake driver's license he'd purchased in LA and his disguise intact, he took a risk that he knew was large. He paid the $25 dollar entry fee to get in the race. He was down to his last hundred dollars and was desperate for money. If anybody spotted him in the race, he would have to chance it. His biggest fear was that a name runner may show up, a condition that would raise a red flag in the running community were he to win.

But Murray's luck was running well that Sunday morning. Nobody to speak of showed up, and he hung with a pack of runners for six miles, running a pedestrian pace until the last 200 meters of the race before he kicked in. His finishing time was just under thirty minutes, a decent time for most road racers, but a good three and a half minutes slower than what he was capable of running if pushed.

Danny collected the prize money, and took off quickly. He changed his plans, driving back northwest toward Las Vegas, a detour from his original schedule.

...

In Las Vegas Danny got a room at a cheap motel downtown, and that evening engorged himself in the first decent meal he'd had in days at a $5.95 buffet.

At Circus Circus he waited patiently at a Black Jack table, counting cards before the deck moved in his favor. Sensing that to get greedy would call attention to him by the many trained eyes that watched the every move of every gambler, employee, and bystander in the casino captured by hidden video cameras, he bet relatively small, quitting when his winnings hit $500. Then he went to the Mirage and repeated his system.

He continued his same style of betting and play all night long, never making any unusually large bets, never sticking around at any table or hotel too long. He moved from one gaming resort to another throughout the night, and by morning had pocketed over $15,000 in winnings.

He left the city as soon as he got back to his hotel room, not chancing the risk of being discovered and caught. Casino management, who had obvious stroke with local authorities, despised card counters. Danny realized he'd pulled off a minor sting, but Vegas was too smart a town to continue. He wouldn't press his luck. It was time to take his profits, leave, and not look back.

As Danny drove back toward El Paso, he felt he'd moved a step closer to honing in on Gonzales. Money was the major player when it came to getting information, or anything else that would aid in finding Gonzales. Fifteen grand could buy him some time in that quest. Life was a hustle, he'd learned at a tender age. And he wasn't beyond hustling or anything else when it came to hunting and putting down Cindy's killer.

CHAPTER 17

HOUSTON, TEXAS
EIGHT DAYS AFTER CINDY'S MURDER

Danny made the Houston city limits on a Tuesday night at a few minutes past 11 p.m. He came in on the Katy Freeway, his previous stop San Antonio where a hunch that he could glean more information concerning Gonzales proved wrong. He continued on I-10 East, and at 610 took the Woodway Memorial exit. He went east on Woodway and headed into Memorial Park, making a left at the first light. He drove into the park, the golf course, and 2.9-mile jogging trail that circled it to his right. He continued past the tennis center and parked his car near the softball fields. He was nervous about a police car that periodically drove by as he sat, but fatigue won out and he was soon sleeping deeply.

A nightmare replay of Cindy's murder followed, and he woke up soaked in sweat and shaking. The dream of his sister triggered an emotional outburst, and he wept uncontrollably until falling back into a troubled sleep. He awoke early the next morning, and spotted joggers circling the cinder trail that looped the park's golf course.

He went to the back of his pickup truck, got out a pair of jogging shorts and shoes, and changed inside his truck. Then he jogged across the road to the cinder trail. He ran four loops of the 2.9-mile oval, easing his normally quicker pace so as not to call attention to himself. As he finished his run at a stone marker fronting the tennis center parking lot, he saw joggers walking into the center with athletic bags and street clothes.

He followed them inside where he learned there was a public locker room and showers that were available for a nominal fee. He went back to his truck, packed his athletic bag with some clean clothes and a dop kit, and walked back to the tennis center. There he showered and changed into clean clothes, both a welcome relief after the lengthy travail of being on the run and living out of his truck.

His stomach was gnawing as he got back to his truck, and he drove out of the park in search of a restaurant. At Shepherd and Memorial he headed south, and just before Highway 59 spotted a restaurant named the 59 Diner. There he consumed a large breakfast of eggs, sausage, biscuits, and hash browns, washed down by endless cups of coffee that his waitress continued to fill. As he drank, he debated the merits of calling Gabe Seward. At a few minutes past 10:00, he made his decision, paid his bill, and walked to a pay telephone outside the men's washroom. He dialed Gabe's work number and waited.

"Wellsley House." It was a woman's voice.

"Gabe Seward, please."

"Just a moment."

Gabe picked up the phone on the second ring. "Hello?"

"Gabe? Danny Murray."

"Danny? My gosh! Where are you?"

"In Houston."

"I'm glad to hear from you."

"Can I see you?"

"Absolutely. You name where and when."

"What time do you get off work?"

"I'm usually out of here by 5:00, 5:30."

"How far are you from Memorial Park?"

"By the time I leave work and park, I can be there by 6:00."

"Can we meet at the tennis center?"

"You got it, big guy."

"You have any idea what's gone down with me?"

"Just what I've heard on the news."

"Do you believe I did anything to Cindy?"

"Hell, no."

"You have any problem with meeting with me?"

"Hell, no."

"You won't say anything to anybody about this, will you?"

"Hell, no."

Danny felt relieved, Gabe's tone convincing. "I'll see you then."

"I'll be there."

"Thanks."

...

Danny waited for Gabe on a wooden deck by the stretching area just outside the tennis center parking lot. He was amazed at the sea of cars and people that converged on the park, primarily men and women who had finished their day at work. Most of them would either walk or run the 2.9-mile loop that circled the park, a cinder trail that circled the golf course that for many years had hosted the Houston Open.

It was an area resplendent with rolling green sod and towering pines, an oasis in a city bereft of park space. A plethora of late-model, expensive vehicles driven by young urban professionals converged on the precious parking spaces. Many cruised the park in fancy sport utility vehicles, unlike what Danny had experienced in the Midwest, New Mexico, and Oregon. He wondered if Houston had a disproportionate number of wealthy young people, or if they were like the many Americans he read about that lived heavily in debt. He wondered what it was like being a child of privilege, a dream that he'd fantasized for his sister Cindy that would never be realized.

As the 9-to-5ers walked and ran on the cinder jogging trail, some with dogs on chains, others pushing baby joggers, it was apparent to him that Houston was a fashion-conscious city. Everyone seemed to have the latest running shoes and attire, few looking to Danny like competitive runners. It was glaringly clear to him that some of the women had undergone plastic surgery, breast augmentation the most noticeable. He wondered what kind of pressures would drive women to alter their bodies in that way, and if big cities exerted stresses that smaller towns didn't.

133

As he waited for Gabe and the trail swelled with walkers and joggers, he sensed the park was a scene, a rat-race gathering place that was far removed from the type of isolation that he relished on his runs. He knew that he looked out of place here, his attire sticking out awkwardly in a crowd of hip-looking urban exercisers. The feeling of looking wrong exacerbated his paranoia, the danger of calling attention to himself a fear that could have dire consequences. He would get the right clothes to conform, he thought, anything to blend into the sea of urban dwellers that made up the melting pot known as Houston.

He walked over to the tennis center at a few minutes before six, and at the entrance spotted Gabe Seward who was already dressed in running gear.

Gabe stuck out his hand that Danny took. "How are you, Danny?"

"As well as can be expected."

Seward nodded, having difficulty trying to imagine what Danny was experiencing following his sister's murder, and being wanted for her rape and murder.

"I'm going to weigh in," Gabe said. "I'll be out in a second."

"Okay."

Gabe went into the tennis center, and weighed himself on the medical scale that Danny had seen in the back when he'd showered earlier. When he came out he rubbed his hands together and said, "Let me stretch out this old body, and then we'll get going."

The two walked back to the stretching area where Gabe leaned and stretched for several minutes as Danny watched.

"Ready?" Gabe said.

"Yup," Danny said.

As they got going, Gabe eyed Danny. It was obvious to him that the youngster was uncomfortable with the vast sea of people that they ran through and around on the crowded cinder trail. Sensing that Murray would be reluctant to talk in such confining quarters, Gabe said, "Why don't we leave the park and run to town? That way we'll be on our own."

"Good," Danny said.

The two headed east on Memorial, running toward town. It was a run that would be about ten miles, about five miles from the tennis center where they left, to the Sabine Street Bridge just before downtown Houston.

As they left the park, Danny said, "A lot of stuff's gone down since the last time I saw you. And now I'm wanted for rape and murder."

"I know that."

"You don't believe any of that, do you?"

Danny eyed Gabe to get a visual confirmation of what Seward had told him on the telephone.

"Hell, no."

"Okay. I trust you. At this point I've got no one else in the world to trust. Let me tell you what's happened up until now."

After the first five-mile loop of the Parkway was completed, Danny was still deep into his story. Gabe listened intently as the duo headed back to town for an additional five-mile Parkway loop, the added-on distance extending their run to fifteen miles. At the end of the second loop Danny was still deep into his story, so the two headed back to town for another five miles. The additional distance would make their run twenty miles.

As Danny finished his story midway through the third loop of the Parkway, he said "I've got plenty of money, so I won't need any help in that area. But if you'd be willing to stick your neck on the line and rent me a place, I'd be grateful. I'll pay you in advance for as many months as a landlord requires. I just don't want to chance getting caught executing a lease."

"No problem," Gabe said. "I know someone who has some rental property that should be perfect for you and won't ask any questions."

Danny glanced at Seward. The thin man's expression had not changed.

"You know, Gabe, you could end up in some deep trouble in this deal if I get caught. You'd be aiding and abetting a criminal."

"Let me worry about that. If that sucker that killed your sister is here in Houston like you were told, then we need to find him. Once that's done, everything else will fall into place."

Danny nodded. "That's what I'm counting on."

"But, Danny, don't take the law into your own hands. Can I have your word on that?"

Danny shook his head. "No. I can't give you my word on that."

"What do you plan on doing if you find him?"

"I can't tell you that either."

Gabe was silent as he considered his options. Danny's sister had been brutally raped and murdered, and the kid had been wrongly charged with the crime. Of that, Gabe was certain. But if Murray were to take the law into his own hands and wantonly take a life, he would be facing double murder charges. And Gabe knew he would be risking his own neck also. As an accessory to harboring a murderer, he could be facing a lengthy jail sentence if caught.

Seward weighed his options before saying, "Where are you staying?"

"Last night I slept in my truck in the park."

"You can crash at my place tonight," Gabe said. "I've got a contact who will rent me a garage apartment with no questions asked. It's close to where I work and not far from the park. I'd guess we should be able to get you in there within the next few days."

"Good."

"Please don't take the law in your own hands."

"I can't promise that."

"Okay, Danny. I won't say anymore."

The two ran back to the tennis center in silence. They went back to Seward's apartment and showered, and ate a dinner of peanut butter and jelly sandwiches and pasta.

Danny crashed on some blankets on Gabe's living room floor. He fell into a deep sleep, but was wakened by the recurrent scene of Cindy's murder. He was shaking as he woke, a condition far removed from his normal nerves of steel. Weeping followed and he sobbed himself back asleep, the wound of his murdered little sister raw and exposed.

CHAPTER 18

HOUSTON, TEXAS
MAY, 2006

On a Friday night, half past ten, Danny took off running from his garage apartment on Houston's north side. It had been almost four years since Cindy's murder and Danny was no closer to finding Cindy's killer. But Rafael Gonzales' footprints were all over Houston, and he was determined to remain in the city to hunt him down.

At the Wellsley House he met Gabe Seward, and the two began a 20-mile run. It was a workout route that would wind through Memorial Park and River Oaks, tracing the Allen Parkway east and Buffalo Bayou on its way downtown; and then head back west, up Memorial Drive on the other side of the bayou, before cutting north across the Heights, and ending back on the North Side at the Wellsley House. It was a run that would take them through diverse areas of the city, from some of the poorest high-crime areas in the North Side and the Fourth Ward, to River Oaks, a neighborhood of palatial, colonial-style mansions.

As the two advanced to Memorial Drive, they ran flanked by towering trees, cocooned in the night shadows of Memorial Park. Houston was woefully lacking in park space, Memorial Park its emerald gem. It was an oasis in a city carved out of the tropics; a sprawling, overgrown village where countless acres of lush flora had been replaced by endless miles of tar and cement.

Seward had been surprised when he first moved to Houston, learning that the city had mushroomed with no zoning laws and woefully little public planning. The cowboy mentality had culminated in an urban apocalypse; a place where opulent homes could be seen sharing block space with junkyards and rotting warehouses; where towering monuments of glass and steel erupted from the prairie with no apparent rhyme or reason; where hard rains resulted in disastrous floods from overbuilding; and where traffic jams were as predictable as the six months of sweltering heat, the air-conditioned nightmare a town where its wealthy fled to the mountains to survive summer. On days when it was clear, the skyscrapers of downtown Houston reflected like sharply cut diamonds under the big Texas sky. But those were rare occurrences, anomalies in an industrial wasteland tainted by refineries to its east.

On the bad days--hot, humid, sticky affairs that lasted from mid-April until October--waste products mated with the fumes of the millions of automobiles that buzzed its freeways and arteries, the noxious haze like a gray soup. It seemed to feed the traffic jams that stifled the loop like a lethal poison, fuel for the road rage that sometimes escalated into violence and death.

But for all its shortcomings, the city had fascinated Seward. Conceived by two hustlers from New York known as the Allen brothers, he had chuckled when he'd read their story. They had purchased a fetid swamp in the middle of nowhere for a pittance. And then they'd had the moxie to advertise their quagmire in Eastern newspapers, touting it "an oasis, an Eden of luxuriant tropical flora, a city of the future where year-round temperate weather was cooled at night by gentle Gulf breezes from the east."

Little did the unsuspecting romantics who read the ads know what was confronting them. What they found was a festering swamp, a place where sweltering heat was coupled to unbearable humidity; a morass where swarms of palm-sized mosquitoes sucked blood and devoured flesh without impunity, spreading malaria and other tropical diseases as quickly as fresh graves could be dug. The breeding grounds for the mosquitoes were bayous, putrid waterways that snaked through the jungle-land like giant open sewers. Alligators and gar lurked in their oily waters, while the banks teemed with snakes, huge rats, and winged cockroaches that could blanket a baby's face.

The Allen brothers' village that budded along the banks of the Buffalo Bayou stayed a nonevent until the hurricane of 1900 reduced the port town of Galveston, 50 miles to the east, to a pile of rubble. Before the Great Storm, Galveston had been the state's largest metropolitan area, a gateway for European immigrants who would reshape a burgeoning nation. After the storm it was reduced to a decimated island, a hellhole strewn with piles of timber encasing rotting corpses. The rancid stench could be smelled miles away. But as the final morsels of putrid flesh were picked clean by hungry maggots, the seeds of opportunity sewn in the Allen brothers' swamp began to germinate.

The Bayou City grew steadily after the storm, but it was visionaries who imagined it a port linked to the gulf by a ship channel that made it a world power. Dreamers sold that idea to a gullible public, who bought it without question and made it reality. In an engineering feat that took the lives of countless workers, the Gulf of Mexico was mated to the Bayou City. Dredging through fever-teeming swamps and inhuman conditions, they sacrificed themselves for a city that was to become the nation's fourth largest, and second to none in total tonnage.

It was a town where its engines had originally been fueled by oil, a place where gamblers made fortunes and lost them just as quickly. It was a metropolis that Seward sometimes had trouble understanding, difficult for him to fathom the utter contempt of the haves for the have-nots, and the prevailing mentality that all those who did not make it were either lazy or stupid.

But Gabe understood that the problem was not just Houston. It was largely him, a '60s-style dreamer who had difficulty comprehending greed. It was a town that, in spite of all its faults, Gabe had still come to love, the place that housed his extended family of the rough North Side that he'd come to embrace.

As Danny and Gabe reached Shepherd, they looked both ways before scooting through a red light and continuing south, following a wall to their right.

At Inwood the wall opened, flanked by concrete pillars. There they turned right, running west on a boulevard rife with verdant acreage, towering oaks hovering overhead, shading plantation-style homes that housed some of the deepest-pocketed business titans in the world. It was the entrance to River Oaks, the once all lily-white enclave the history of which was deeply rooted in the prejudices of the Old South, a country club fiefdom that until just recently had been completely closed to minorities.

It was a neighborhood where oil and gas dealings had made its residents filthy rich, a highly restricted zone that now housed some of the most powerful and wealthy business magnates in the world, along with a host of flamboyant attorneys who reveled in their love of courtroom battles. They were unlike their eastern counterparts that were inclined to settle big cases, the gunslinger mentality of the Wild West still alive in the Bayou City. River Oaks embodied the stereotype of how the press played Houston to the rest of the world, a place where money was everything and nothing else a distant second.

The Enron scandal had exposed River Oaks worldwide, a guarded community that housed many of the company's most powerful executives and board members. It was a place where greed, thievery, deception, and lies, were hidden from a public they viewed as largely ignorant and stupid.

"They just don't get it," was a favorite aphorism of one of the company's former CEOs, a phrase in which the double entendre ironically came to include both understanding and assets. River Oaks residents lived largely in their own cloistered world, one that Gabe and Danny were largely ignorant of. They were untouchables in the eyes of the super-rich: a social worker who dealt with the city's have-nots, and a fugitive who'd been charged with murder.

141

They crisscrossed in and out of the guarded streets harboring palatial palaces, aware all along of the neighborhood squad cars manned by off-duty Houston police who kept tabs on the neighborhood, before continuing back toward Shepherd and the Allen Parkway. They crossed the Parkway running east, continuing on an asphalt hike and bike trail that paralleled the murky waters of Buffalo Bayou. They ran toward downtown, the skyline of Houston's lit skyscrapers--monuments forged through the fortunes of oil and gas-- shimmering in the dark.

It was a city of dreams for those who chased the American fantasy of power and wealth, a place of something else for those who lived on its streets, under its overpasses, or wherever a body could sleep without authorities hassling them. Along the Allen Parkway, Danny and Gabe spotted several of those displaced souls, their bodies and heads covered by sleeping bags or blankets, their shopping carts or backpacks beside them housing all their possessions.

It was a life that Danny had remained a hairsbreadth removed from, one that Gabe realized could also be his should fortunes change. Homelessness was a condition that Seward had come to rationalize as both complex and disturbing. Though he understood that there were no simple solutions, he was troubled by its presence in a society where there was such vast wealth. In just the distance of a few blocks, he and Danny had left a neighborhood of multimillionaires to be sharing the asphalt hike and bike trail of the Allen Parkway with the homeless.

It was a phenomenon that Gabe could never feel settled with; the fantasy of a kinder, gentler society, merely blather for the meanspirited reality that trapped the disenfranchised in their faceless lives of utter despair. Unlike himself, Seward knew that Danny was largely unconcerned for the plight of the underclass. He viewed the lack of compassion as an understandable reality for a young man who had battled for survival since early childhood.

As they ran past downtown and into the Fourth Ward, the contrast was sharp: gleaming high-rises of steel and glass towering above dilapidated homes and rotting shacks. It was a neighborhood that for years had been all black, dating back to the pre-Civil Rights era when the city was an apartheid society. The physical neighborhood had deteriorated further, and, like the North Side, was a haven for drug dealing and crime. But unlike the North Side, the Fourth Ward was experiencing pockets of gentrification. It lurked under the shadows of downtown skyscrapers, real estate that was far too valuable for hungry developers to let slide unnoticed.

They viewed it not as a place where people lived and had homes—some whose families had roots dating back to the city's founding in 1836—but as investment fodder, chattel that could be churned into profit, money that could separate them further from the poor they uprooted and displaced.

As large social issues swam through Gabe's mind, Danny focused on the inequity that had shattered his small world. His mind replayed the scene of finding his sister murdered, and the subsequent nightmares that haunted him. Most vivid was the image of the scar-faced man whose visage he would never forget. He recalled his flight from authorities, and his struggle for survival.

His gut had been correct in throwing his trust in Gabe Seward, the only person he knew that he might trust. Seward had proven far more than trustworthy, providing him with the means to exist, enabling him to work and live as a shadow-person while hanging on to the slender thread of hope that he would eventually find Cindy's killer.

Danny Murray had remained in top physical condition, but his dreams of running again on an elite level were gone. Cindy's death had done that, eradicating a dream that had been so near that he could once almost taste it. Now his nectar was revenge, punishing his sister's killer his obsession, clearing his own name his ancillary motive.

But Gabe Seward, the eternal optimist, did what he could to keep Danny's running dreams alive. He would gently remind him on a regular basis that he'd likely lost none of his youthful running skills; but more likely, as a fully mature man would just begin to reach his physical peak years as a runner which could extend well into his 30s. He would tell stories of the great distance runners of the past whom he had competed against or watched run, men who had set world records well into their 30s and beyond. He told Danny of Carlos Lopes, the great Portuguese runner who had won the Olympic gold medal in the 1984 marathon in Los Angeles at age 37, and come back at age 38 to set a world record at the event in Rotterdam. He told him of the great Ethiopian runner Miruts Yifter, the man who had won Olympic gold in Montreal at 10,000 meters. Yifter's age was never confirmed, but common knowledge in the running world held that the tiny African was either in his late 40s or early 50s at the time of his Olympic triumph.

It was narrative that Gabe never addressed directly to Danny as inspirational motivation, but words cleverly disguised as dispassionate fact, powerful suggestions that Seward hoped would keep Danny's running dreams alive.

Gabe's queries concerning Cindy's killer were hushed conversations that he only shared with trusted confidants whom he had nurtured since childhood. They were men who would literally take a bullet for him. The questioning yielded several positive responses, most notably of a man who fit the description Danny had given. Even more remarkable was the assertion that he had been spotted right in the same neighborhood where Gabe and Danny lived. It would be truly ironic if the man was living right under their noses, Gabe thought, a notion that seemed implausible but not impossible.

Seward, the half-full glass optimist, prayed for a miracle. Secretly, he hoped that if Cindy's killer were spotted that it would be he, not Danny, who would make the discovery. He knew that Murray had no fear of losing his own life in tracking down his sister's killer, a sense of fearlessness that could backfire and result in his demise.

Seward had yet to formulate a plan as to how he would proceed should he spot Cindy's killer or receive information leading to him. His inclination was to deal with police contacts that he trusted, men who had been the same youngsters he had dealt with as juvenile delinquents. He realized the irony of that possibility. He would be relying on former juvenile delinquents, who under his care had stretched him to the limits. Now as adults, they were the same legal authorities they had tortured as children. But Seward had a bond with them that was ironclad, and he never doubted their unqualified indebtedness.

It would be tragic if Danny circumvented the legal system to mete out his own justice, Gabe thought, especially as advances in technology—namely DNA testing—could now clear Murray and finger Cindy's killer. Cindy had been raped, and the crime lab in Oregon still had samples of the bodily fluids they had found within her.

Sometimes Gabe chastised himself, aware that fabricating what-if scenarios had no firm root in reality. Cindy's killer was on the loose; and if he was dealing drugs, enslaving illegal aliens, and the litany of other illegal dealings that Gabe's contacts had informed him he was involved in, chances were likely that he was already dead. His body was probably encased in a cement block somewhere, or had been ground up as feed for hogs, fodder that had been consumed on some Mexican farm where life and death were cheaper than the meal for fattening its swine.

As Murray and Seward approached the Wellsley House, Gabe turned to Danny. "How are you doing, big guy?"

"Tired," Danny said. "I've been working straight the last three days cleaning custom homes ready to close. They're punched out and I'm exhausted."

"Going home to get some sleep?"

"Yeah. I've got tomorrow off."

"Then I will see you at the park next Monday, about 10:00?"

Danny nodded.

"Gabe, any more leads?"

"No. Not a thing."

"Keep on it."

"I will. Don't lose faith."

Danny nodded and took off running to his house. He had run less than four blocks before he passed a convenience store and saw a sight that stopped him in his tracks. Blood rushed from his head. He felt as if he was about to fall. Coming out of the convenience store, and walking toward a black Lincoln Navigator with Texas plates parked next to a gas pump, was Cindy's killer.

Danny was paralyzed for what seemed to him like an eternity before he was able to instruct his body to move. He ducked behind a parked car on the street, and lay low as he watched the man open his gas tank and insert the pump. His pulse rate, which was normally in the 30s, went up sixfold. It was like he was running in an all-out race, his heart pumping furiously.

Cindy's killer stared in his direction for what seemed forever, before removing the gas nozzle from his tank, screwing on the lid. He tapped the unlock button on his key chain, a beep sound following as the Navigator's interior lights turned on. The man slid into the SUV, started its engine, and eased out of the parking lot as Danny memorized the license plate. He watched the black Navigator as it headed down the street before making a left turn two blocks down.

When it was out of sight, Danny got up and ran down the road, turning left two blocks later as he headed in the direction of the vehicle. Knowing it was a long shot, he combed the neighborhood for the Lincoln. He crossed and recrossed every street within a mile radius for the next two hours, and had given up pursuit and was jogging back to his apartment when he turned on a secluded back street he'd never been down. There he spotted the Navigator for a second time.

It was parked in the circular driveway of a large home set back on a lot framed by tall oak trees. A fifteen-foot-high chain-link fence topped by razor wire cordoned off the property. It was a recently built home that was totally out of character with the neighborhood. Murray spotted two large dogs padding back and forth inside the fence. Sensing that he was watching them, they hurled themselves against the fence and barked ferociously. They were two of the largest pit bulls he had ever seen. He took off down the street running at full speed, fearing that the barking dogs could urge Cindy's killer out into the yard.

By the time he reached his apartment and was safely inside, his pulse was still wildly elevated. Though he'd had little sleep the last three days, working overtime cleaning and making ready new custom built homes, the rush of finding Cindy's killer electrified him, like a high-voltage jolt standing every nerve on end.

The bastard was going down, Danny thought, and he would do it. It would take time formulating a plan, but time was on his side. As he lay in his bed that night, staring emptily up into the darkness, he replayed every detail of the killer's compound that he could recall. It was a space that would be hell getting into. But hell was where he was determined to send Cindy's killer. That was a reality that was clearer in his mind than the running vision he'd clung to as a youth. Failure was not an option. He was obsessed with taking down Cindy's killer at all costs, even if it meant losing his own life.

CHAPTER 19

AN ASSASINATION PLOT

For the next three months, a night never went by that Danny didn't run by the home of Rafael Gonzales. When he got home he recorded everything in a journal, detailing Gonzales' coming and going and the sea of characters that spun through his doors, all with precise times. If the hit he was planning were executed correctly, police would chalk it up as a drug deal gone sour or a gangland assassination. Authorities would accept either scenario with minimal scrutiny, he reasoned.

Murray knew that Gonzales had a long criminal record, and had learned from street sources that drug dealing and other criminal activities were going on in the ex-con's home. But Murray's dilemma of penetrating the compound undetected encompassed a host of problems.

He brought throwaway pocket cameras with him when he ran and photographed Gonzales' grounds from as many different angles as he could. With the prints he got back from a local drugstore pinned to a large corkboard hung on a Sheetrock wall and his copious notes spread out neatly on a work desk, he was methodically mapping a detailed blueprint that would be the foundation of his plan.

A predictable pattern of Gonzales' movements emerged as Murray's investigation advanced, and with that knowledge his course of action became clearer. His recurring vision had him breaking into Gonzales' compound and house late at night when the ex-con wasn't there. Once inside he would wait in hiding for his return before killing him.

The hard data that he collected grew, as did the plethora of options for a course of action. It became clear to him that hard choices had to be made and narrowing his focus was essential. To accomplish that, he began breaking down the operation in distinct parts.

First, he would have to choose a method of transportation to and from Gonzales' house the night of his attempted murder. Second, he needed to figure a way of getting either under, through, or over the fifteen-foot chain-link fence topped by razor wire that guarded the compound. Third, he had to come up with a plan of dealing with Gonzales' pit bulls once he was off the fence and into the yard. Fourth, he had to figure out a course of action in disabling Gonzales' security system, if there was one, before breaking into the house. Fifth, he had to devise a system of breaking into the house. And finally sixth, he had to decide on the type of weapon and form of execution he'd employ to take Gonzales out.

Addressing the first issue, he debated the merits of driving up to Gonzales' home in either a car or truck as opposed to on foot. The upside of a vehicle was the obvious quicker escape mechanism that it would afford him and also, the ease that it would provide him in transporting break-in materials and weapons to the compound. Murray still had his old truck from Oregon, and it was in good running order since Gabe Seward had hooked him up with a mechanic on the North Side. The man had asked no questions and put the vehicle in good running condition cheaply. But Danny feared that driving his own truck to Gonzales' home would be super risky.

He had purchased the vehicle for cash in Oregon years before, and had driven it with black market driver's license, plates, and inspection sticker. His truck had slipped under the radar screen of authorities so far, but he realized the odds of that continuing were slim. Just one call-in by a suspicious cop checking plates could come back to haunt him. Understanding the incumbent risks, he had rarely used the vehicle since coming to Houston. It was a city that swarmed with police, in stark comparison to Eugene, Oregon where there were few.

Murray kept his truck inside a locked garage under his apartment, regularly starting it up but rarely driving it. He also debated the merits of renting a vehicle, but realized it had few upsides. Car rentals required a credit card and a valid driver's license, neither of which he had. And even if he were able to somehow rent a vehicle, he realized it would necessitate dealing with car rental employees who, in a lineup, could identify and finger him in a heartbeat.

He also considered the option of stealing a vehicle and dumping it after its use. But that was risky too, for all the obvious reasons. Police were always on the lookout for stolen vehicles in Houston, especially on the North Side. A stolen car or truck could quickly be verified by any cop cruising the neighborhood, the computer systems equipped in their vehicles coupled to a deep database.

And then there was the issue of trace evidence. Fragments from an individual's body and clothing had uncanny ways of adhering to a vehicle's interior no matter how much care was taken. They were the bits and pieces that could indict and convict him of murder.

His second issue of dealing with the fifteen-foot chain-link fence topped by razor wire that guarded the compound also presented immense problems. The fence offered three opportunities of penetration: under, through, or over. Digging under the chain-link fence and sliding on his back to get inside was an option that seemed ridiculous on its face. It would take time and effort to dig under the fence, slide beneath it, and then cover up the hole made before continuing toward the house. It would also entail the use of awkward tools, devices that would likely necessitate the use of a vehicle for their transport. But he also realized that going under the fence provided a distinct advantage the other two did not. If done correctly, Gonzales, upon return to his compound, wouldn't realize that somebody had broken in. It would be time-consuming and awkward to go under, he reasoned. But he was thin and reasonably certain that he could accomplish the task relatively quickly. Underneath the chain-link fence was grass and dirt, both of which could be replaced once he was inside.

Cutting straight through the fence by the use of a wire cutter would be the easiest, quickest, and safest way of gaining entrance into the property. But the dilemma of a gaping hole that would be readily detectable to Gonzales upon his return to his house spoke for itself.

Murray's final option of going over the top, presented the obvious conundrum of the razor wire. He was uncertain how difficult it would be to cut and remove a section of razor wire without shredding himself. And once the wire was severed and removed, he wondered if Gonzales would spot it upon his return to the compound.

Once inside the fence, he would have to deal with the ferocious pit bulls that guarded the grounds. He knew they would excoriate and eviscerate him within a matter of moments if given the opportunity. An option that became clear to him was drugging the dogs. But to accomplish that presented a host of other problems. He went online and read about different drugging techniques employed by the CIA, KGB, Mossad, and other secret police organizations throughout the world. In his research, he found no method that was without great difficulty. The mechanics of hitting the animals with drug-tainted darts through a chain-link fence presented all types of logistical problems, as did shooting them with a stun gun or some other type of weapon. Both the purchase of knockout drugs and delivery weapons meant contact with more strangers, each new contact increasing his odds of future problems.

And then there was the security system issue. If Gonzales had one it would have to be disabled.

And finally, his most perplexing issue was the actual killing of Gonzales. He would have to decide on the most efficient method of taking him out while making it appear as a drug deal gone wrong or an assassination. There were infinitesimal choices to be made in carrying out his operation, each with its own set of high-risk components.

At night Danny rarely slept, the same scenario that plagued him during his waking hours still fresh in his mind: the obsessive reenactment of Gonzales' murder from beginning to end. The thought process sharpened when he ran, as he visualized every piece of his plan, from the time he would leave his home until arriving at Gonzales' house and fleeing. He would see himself clearly breaking in, waiting, carrying out the kill, and then slipping out unnoticed, before ridding himself of potential evidence that could be linked to him.

His final vision would be returning to his apartment and waiting to see how the police would rule the murder. The more he researched, plotted, and planned, the more apparent it became to him that simplicity was his best tactic; that attempting a killing that was too complex and sophisticated was not only risky but unprofessional.

He came to learn that professional hits were very rare, a fractional subset of premeditated killings that were also uncommon. The vast majority of murders were heat-of-the-moment reactions void of preplanning. In Murray's research, he further learned that most killings that went unsolved had two common components: the lack of witnesses and recovery of a murder weapon.

Ridding oneself of all trace evidence was also essential, especially gunpowder residues if a gun was the murder weapon of choice. Danny's inclination was the use of a handgun fit with a silencer, both items he could purchase on the black market with minimal difficulty. Stolen guns in tough Houston neighborhoods were as easy to buy as drugs. And though he'd never used a handgun and knew that he'd have to learn how to shoot, those were operations he was certain he would master in short time.

There was a long list of obstacles that had to be dealt with, he reasoned, but nothing that couldn't be overcome. He had lived by his wits since early childhood, and relying on his exceptional mind, gut instincts, and street smarts had been his salvation. It became increasingly clear to him that his current conundrum had a lot of moving parts, a situation that demanded total commitment and focus.

But it was those attributes, along with innate talent, that had placed him on the cusp of becoming the world's greatest distance runner as a 17-year-old youth. Now, with that dream shattered and no longer an issue, his sole purpose in life was to avenge his sister's rape and murder. It was the type of compulsion that only one who had experienced a like loss could truly comprehend.

...

On a Tuesday night at 11:15 p.m., a time frame when Danny knew Gonzales regularly left his home; he hid in a neighbor's hedge down the block. Almost right on cue, the Hispanic emerged from his house and moved to his Navigator. Moments later he pulled out of his driveway and headed down the block in the opposite direction from where Danny was hiding.

Equipped with a lightweight backpack, Danny made his way to Gonzales' property and stopped at the fence. Within moments the pit bulls were barking thunderously, pressing against the chain-link fence, the power of their thrusts pushing the metal links menacingly toward him. Murray didn't hesitate, removing from his backpack an aluminum pole that he opened, the device telescoping to about three feet. From the backpack he also produced a package wrapped in tin foil. He opened the package, displaying about a half-pound of raw hamburger.

As the dogs thundered and hurled themselves against the fence, Danny crammed a chunk of hamburger on the tip of his aluminum pole. He moved quickly and shoved it through an opening in the chain-link fence. The larger of the two dogs grabbed the meat and the pole with a ferocity that tore the tool from his hands. As the enraged pit bull clamped down on the end of the pole, Danny grabbed it with both hands and yanked back. The force of his pull ripped the pole from the dog's mouth, as Danny fell backward on the lawn. The action furthered the animals' frenzy, their jaws dripping with thick strands of white lather as their barks thundered through the neighborhood.

As Murray stood up and studied the end of the pole, he was shocked to see that the animal had severed the aluminum, likely swallowing both metal and ground beef in one gulp. He quickly repacked the pole and hamburger into his backpack and took off running, fearing that the dogs' uncontrolled barking would bring out neighbors.

When he got home that evening he assessed what had happened. Neutralizing the dogs would be no easy task. But it became clear to him that tranquilizing the dogs, as opposed to killing them, was out of the question. The animals would have to be put down. Attempting to measure the right amount of tranquilizer to put them to sleep without killing them was way too risky. The pit bulls, even in a drug-induced miasma could tear him to shreds in a matter of moments. He would have to kill them, even though the risk of Gonzales finding the dogs dead would be a strong signal that someone had broken into the compound.

Murray rationalized that Gonzales had many enemies, including neighbors terrorized by the dogs. He was banking that the Hispanic's paranoia would lead him to believe that one of them would be deemed culprit if he came home to find his dogs dead. Now it was just a question of determining the most effective way of dealing with the dogs at the appropriate time.

...

At a garage sale in the Heights, Danny picked up some wire cutters that were exactly the type he had been looking for. The woman who sold them to him had been recently widowed, her husband a lineman in Montana in his younger days. They were sheathed and in excellent condition, lightly oiled and free of rust. With an Arkansas whetstone Danny carefully sharpened them, and on a Tuesday night decided to give them a test. In an abandoned warehouse on the North Side, he severed a chain-link fence. It was difficult work, even with the sharp cutters, the heavy chain-link metal requiring two strong hands.

But the second test proved to be more difficult. He scaled the fence and began the process of cutting out a section of razor wire. As he finished a section of razor wire, he saw a vehicle down a dirt road approaching him. He scurried down the fence, but was not quick enough.

As he touched the ground a voice yelled, "Hold it there, or I'll blow your goddamn brains out." Danny didn't. Sprinting at full tilt, he ran as the repeated blasts of a twelve-gauge shotgun thundered, pellets of hot molten shot whizzing toward his head and body. Repeated charges boomed past him as he continued running at full speed through vacant lots and back alleys, fleeing the shooter.

When he got back to his apartment that evening, he undressed, and realized that his arms and hands were torn and bleeding. In his haste to get down from the chain-link fence, he'd sliced himself to ribbons on the razor wire that ringed the top. He bathed his wounds in alcohol and iodine before wrapping them in towels to staunch the flow of blood. As he worked, the pain of the cuts or the scars they would leave were not issues to him.

His focus was the razor wire that was thinner in gauge than the chain-link fence, and the knowledge that it could be severed relatively quickly. He was making progress, he thought. Like training for a distance race, what he was planning for Gonzales would take time.

At a Goodwill store off the Eastex Freeway, Murray purchased a jog bra and a blond woman's wig. And at a garage sale near Memorial Park, he bought a cheap woman's makeup set. Complimenting his natural red hair and milk skin was a very light beard. So with just a light sheen of subtle makeup applied to his cheeks, he had no visible hints of facial stubble. With practice he learned the art of applying makeup to his eyes, and with his blond wig fitted on mimicked a female visage that was stunningly realistic.

The jog bra, which was not padded, proved to be more challenging. But with patience and a firm hand, he fitted the cups with rubberized padding that gave them a shapely fullness. As he stood in front of a mirror he realized he presented a convincing female figure, an illusion that would be further fostered when he shaved his armpits and legs. It was a different realm he was entering, one far removed from anything he had ever envisioned.

...

At a gym in a rough section of downtown Houston owned by a former heavyweight boxer, Danny hardened his body by doing endless fingertip push-ups, pull-ups, and crunches, and scurrying up and down a thick-gauge hemp rope that dangled from the ceiling. A pegboard had also been constructed from chest-high height to ceiling, and the gym owner watched with wide eyes as Danny went up and down both devices quicker than anybody he'd ever seen. The kid was tough as nails, the ex-boxer thought. He could do more push-ups, pull-ups, and crunches than any fighter he'd ever trained, and go up and down the pegboard and rope quicker too.

His eyes shifted to Danny's legs, twin steel strands of lean, hard muscle. He wondered if the guy could take a punch. If he could, he'd be one hell of a fighter in the lighter weight divisions. The ex-boxer figured Murray to weigh between 120-125 pounds. He wondered what his background was, and what he was training for at his gym. Whatever it was, he'd be ready, the boxer thought. That was apparent in the guy's eyes, orbs that had total focus. They were the kind that he looked for in kids who wanted to box, killer eyes that would fight until death.

CHAPTER 20

SHOW TIME

Danny Murray sat huddled in Rafael Gonzales' bedroom closet, attempting to settle his runaway mind. As he sat, scenes of his past continued to play on his screen, the telephone book of horrors that had consumed him since childhood. He saw his father and heard the sharp crack of his knuckles as they struck his mother's once-innocent face, and her sobs that followed. The scene elicited his feeling of helplessness, his being too small to defend her as she was battered. It was a predictable occurrence prompted by alcohol-induced rage, times that happened with shocking regularity.

As he replayed the dark scenes, he recalled the blackest of all, a fateful evening when he finally took action. He was a nine-year-old at the time, a boy-man equipped only with a shotgun almost as large as him and an ironclad will. He had halted the horror by shooting his father, an action with long-term ramifications that he came to realize, solved nothing. The deed had not saved his mother from future misery as he intended. It had perhaps even backfired, as the chain of events that followed triggered a response that led her to take her own life. It was a loss that had torn him up inside, turning a child into an embittered man at the age of nine.

As his thoughts sped forward following his mother's death, he played back the dreadfulness of the foster homes that he and his sister had endured. Most were places where he and Cindy were abused and mistreated, hellholes for two children who had never experienced real love. Following a near rape at the last foster home they would ever step foot in, he and Cindy had hopscotched the country on a mission of survival. They existed in wretched conditions, dealing with hunger and sickness, anything better than the imprisonment of the abusive households they'd fled. But most vivid in the sea of hideous scenes that plagued him was the one of finding Cindy raped and murdered. It was a vision that would never be erased, not as long as there was a breath of air in his lungs to sustain him.

As he sat, he played back the sequence of events leading to the breaking in of Gonzales' home. It had gone easier for him than he ever could have fantasized. The consummate planner, he realized that he had over-prepared, his backpack that he ran with stuffed with materials and tools that were unneeded.

The pit bulls had engorged the poisoned hamburger meat that he chunked over the top of the fence in paper bags. They had died quickly and painlessly, and he'd followed their demise by climbing the chain-link fence. He had quickly cut a section of the razor wire at the far end of the fence, a portion that Gonzales would be unlikely to notice at night. And getting into the house had proven much simpler than he had anticipated also.

He was amazed that Gonzales' breaker box was on the outside of the house, making it easy for him to cut off the power. But taking that step was just extra energy, as upon breaking into the house he found that the Mexican had no security system. After scaling to the second floor with suction cups, he was able to open a window and hoist himself inside. The window was carelessly unlocked, meaning that he didn't need to use the glasscutter that he'd brought along. It had all gone too easily, he thought. He wondered if the ease of entry would be a harbinger of darker moments to come.

As he sat, fingering the cold metal of the silenced revolver that rested in his lap, the vision of Gonzales' face flashed menacingly on his screen. It was a recurrent vision as he waited in the dark closet, periodically punching the display light on his running watch.

The process continued until 2:13 a.m. when he heard vehicles entering the compound. The slamming of car doors followed the cutting off of engines, succeeded by the loud curses of an angry man's booming voice alternating between Spanish and English. The bellicose blasphemes were followed by the voices of other males as Murray heard the front door open.

At that point, all the thoughts of Danny's past vanished as he focused on the task at hand. Like the young runner who had once set a world record, the athlete in Danny Murray returned. He blotted out everything in his mind, his concentration total. His heart rate rose gradually as he sat, but well under control as he prepared for action. A dominant male voice boomed like thunder as Danny heard a group of men enter the living room downstairs. It was a voice that Murray was certain belonged to Rafael Gonzales.

Smashing glass was followed by Gonzales' thunderous deep voice. "I get my hands on that puta, and I'll cut off his dick and balls. I will make him eat them and the puke that comes from his gut as he vomits them up. He kills my dogs and he kills a part of me. I will take a razor and cut that puta from his shit chute to his navel, and bleed him like a fish. Then I will make him eat his own shit and cut his eyes out before I piss on his brains. The goddamn fucking puta. I will teach him what it means to fuck with Juan Gonzales."

Danny then heard Gonzales hawk up a wad of phlegm before spitting.

"Who do you think killed your dogs, Rafael?" another Hispanic male asked.

"I think it is the bastard that lives down the block. He has called the police before about the dogs. He says they are a threat to his children. I will teach him about threats. I will buy new pit bulls and feed his children to them as he watches. And then I will feed him to them, one body piece at a time as I cut him up like menudo. The stinking puta."

Danny heard Gonzales spit again.

"Enough of that bullshit.," another Hispanic male voice said. "I did not come here to hear you complain about your fucking dogs and your fucking cunt fantasies. You bring me cocaine to sample so I can make a decision. I have no time to hear your cunt sob stories."

"You have no feeling, Juan," another voice said. "The man has lost his dogs."

"Fuck his dogs," Juan said. "I am here to sample his cocaine. If it is what he promised, I will buy. If not, I leave. I have no time for his cunt bullshit.."

"I will bring you your cocaine, Juan." Gonzales said. "You wait here and I come back."

As Gonzales climbed the stairs and entered his bedroom, Danny held his gun with both hands. As he heard Rafael Gonzales rummaging around, he sat in the closet prepared to shoot, but knew that was a last option. He steadied his heartbeat, mapping out a course of action.

Killing Gonzales would mean dealing with the other men in the living room, a gun battle almost certain to follow where he would likely be cut to ribbons. If Gonzales entered the closet, he would have to shoot him and then bolt for the window. It would be risky to jump from the second story, but that would be his only option. Getting into a gun battle with the men downstairs would be certain death. He quieted his breathing to a whisper, undetectable to Gonzales who rummaged in his room before stopping. Danny listened in silence as Gonzales made his way out of the room and back down the stairs.

Gonzales' voice followed from downstairs in his living room. "Here is your coke. You sample. And if you don't like it, I will suck a donkey's dick."

"How we know you don't like a donkey's dick?" another man asked.

That brought nervous laughter followed by silence. Danny could hear each man taking turns as they snorted lines of cocaine on a glass tabletop from the bag of coke that Gonzales had brought them.

"Is this righteous shit or what, vatos? Would I fuck you over?" Gonzales asked.

"It's good shit," the voice he recognized as Juan responding.

"How much you have?"

"Two keys."

"Two keys? You bust my ass to come here for two fucking keys? Who you think you're dealing with, Chihuahua cock?"

"It's good stuff, Juan. Let's give him some time."

"Time? I ain't got no time to be playing games with no fucking amateurs. Fuck that time shit. He said he had the shit right now. He don't have the shit. Fuck him. I don't do business with no fucking amateurs."

"You're a stupid cunt," Gonzales thundered. "You ain't gonna get no better shit than this. You give me time and I get you more. You not the only fish in the sea, vato."

"Fuck you, puta," Juan said.

The booms of large caliber guns followed his words. More gunshots were followed by screams, and the house vibrated with the sound of gunfire and wails before everything came to a halt. An eerie quiet entombed the house, the smell of gunpowder choking the air as Danny clutched his revolver. His heartbeat had quickened, but was still in control as he visualized what had gone down in the living room.

He waited for a lengthy period of time, what seemed an eternity before he fitted on his backpack and made his way out of the closet. Silence entombed the house as he walked down the stairs to the living room, clutching his revolver in both hands, walking as lightly as he was capable.

As he reached the bottom of the stairs, he was unprepared for the sight that confronted him. Four men lay scattered on the floor, bleeding and without movement. But sitting on the couch was Rafael Gonzales, his legs riddled with bullet wounds, his left shoulder drenched in blood. His eyes looked glassy, and as he sized up Murray said, "You take me to the emergency room, white girl, and I give you more money and dope than you know what to do with."

It was apparent that Gonzales was in too bad a shape to even move from his perch on the couch, to reach his cell phone that was on a lamp table to Danny's right.

As Murray held his revolver pointed at Gonzales, he said, "You don't know who I am, do you?"

"I don't care who you is, white girl. You help me and I make you rich beyond your dreams."

"Let me introduce myself," Murray said. He pulled off the blonde wig with his left hand and laid it on the lamp table, still clutching the pistol in his right. The action revealed his dyed short black hair. "I am Danny Murray. Does that name mean anything to you?"

"No, man. It don't mean shit to me."

"How about the name Cindy Murray?"

"No, man. I don't know no Cindy Murray."

"How about Eugene, Oregon? That refresh your memory?"

Gonzales' eyes darted back and forth in his head. Following a lengthy silence he said, "Look vato, I don't know who the hell you is, or who the hell no Cindy Murray is. But you get me to the emergency room, and I put your white ass on easy street the rest of your life."

"No. Money wouldn't scratch my itch. I don't care about money. All I care about is making you pay for what you did. No amount of money can make any difference. I want you to die."

"I don't know what you're talking about, white boy, 'cause I don't have nuthin against you."

Following a lengthy silence Murray said, "Cindy Murray was the little girl you raped and killed in my trailer in Eugene, Oregon. She was my sister, all I had. Do you know what it's like to lose the only thing that has any meaning to you in life?"

"I don't know what you're talking about, vato. But you get me to the hospital and you a rich motherfucker for the rest of your life."

"You know, I've fantasized this moment for years," Murray said. "But it's not like I thought it would play out. I wanted to take you out whole. Not as a pathetic piece of crap that is already bleeding to death."

As Murray studied Gonzales, he realized that getting the type of revenge he had envisioned was a lost opportunity. It was apparent that Gonzales would bleed to death if left alone, the man unable to move himself from the couch where he had been riddled with bullet wounds. Killing Gonzales at this point would be worth little, Danny thought, like taking out a defenseless wounded animal. He realized that to do so could never satisfy his need, retribution that would always have a hollow ring.

As he pondered his course of action, he realized he had one of two options. He could remain with the drop on Gonzales until he bled to death, or he could call authorities and alert them before leaving. As he debated his choices, he calmed himself, clearing his mind as if he was running in a race. It was an act that squelched emotion, a time for rational thought to overpower animal instincts.

As he quieted his thoughts, he realized that he was not a cold-blooded killer. And that to take out Gonzales in his current condition would be lowering himself to the same mentality of the man who had raped and murdered his sister. It was a truth that was far removed from what he had fantasized. He had replayed the scenario of meeting face-to-face with Cindy's rapist and killer, before murdering him with the same cold-blooded callousness that Gonzales had employed in snuffing out the life of a defenseless child. But now that he was facing reality, he realized that the hard truth was unlike what he had imagined.

As he stared down at Rafael Gonzales, conflict addled his brain. Was he doing his sister an injustice, or was he just too cowardly to perform an act that he knew was rooted in a higher justice that no court would condone? As he pondered his dilemma, he realized that if Gonzales survived and was picked up by authorities, he would be put away for a long time, maybe even face the electric chair if a sympathetic jury was enraged greatly enough over the killing of an innocent child.

DNA evidence would surely link Gonzales to Cindy's killing, Murray thought. And at that time he could come forward, his exoneration almost certainly following. Danny sat down facing Gonzales, recalling the fateful chain of events that had led to him shooting his father. The action had halted his father's aggression, but Danny had been unprepared for its eventual consequence. It was an act that he later agonized over as having prompted his mother's suicide.

As Murray pondered his choices, he knew what he had to do. Dispirited, he picked up Gonzales' cell phone that was next to him and touched the power button. He would call authorities, give them Gonzales' address, and leave the crime scene before they arrived. And then he would contact an attorney to find his best course of action. Killing Gonzales was not the answer, he realized. As badly as he had sought retribution, staring face-to-face with a potential crime that would put him in the same category as his sister's killer revealed a greater truth. He was not the cold-blooded killer that he had envisioned himself as being.

As Danny sat, he punched the "on" button of the cell phone, his gun held in his right hand still pointed at Gonzales. The bullet-riddled man made a deep moaning sound and pitched forward, a rattling noise coming from his lungs. Murray wasn't prepared for what followed.

Before he could react Gonzales sat upright, clutching a Colt.45. in his right hand. The gun had come from the cushion behind him, stunning Danny. Murray realized that he had made a fatal mistake, but it was too late. Gonzales fired off a shot, and it boomed like an explosion in the quiet house as the bullet whizzed toward Danny. He could feel the heat of the charge as it sped toward him, a second blast following in rapid succession. Danny calmed himself, unaware if he had been hit, as he leveled his revolver and pulled the trigger. Everything froze in time as the two men sat, and Danny's life spun before his eyes.

He recalled his early childhood, from his time with his biological parents, to the succession of foster homes that he and Cindy were shuffled in and out of. He remembered his world-record-setting race in Eugene, and the brief moments of euphoria that he'd experienced before his ultimate tragedy. And then he recalled the scene of Cindy bleeding on her bed in their small trailer, and the horror of the surgeon's words who came out of the emergency room in Eugene to tell him of her fate.

But his last vision was of his sister's glowing face in a toy store in Portland, the promise of a new life beginning as she hugged a furry bear. She squeezed it with the kind of intensity and loving kindness that only a child is capable of. The vision of Cindy hugging her bear was his last before the reality of the gunfire battle that had just occurred hit home.

Danny never blinked as blood poured from Gonzales' forehead, the dark hole that had been opened by a small caliber bullet leaking matter and gore. The mustached man slumped forward, the Colt still clutched in his hand.

Danny remained motionless, assessing what had happened. His eyes checked over his body and he touched his face. Then he checked his hands. Both his body and hands were without bloodstains. He breathed deeply. Gonzales' two shots had both just barely missed his head, he realized, almost grazing his ear and cheek as they slammed into the Sheetrock wall behind him.

Gonzales had made his decision for him, Murray thought, forcing him into the act he had long plotted. Any sense of conflict that surfaced just before his action was now resolved. He had killed Gonzales in self-defense, his original notion of execution having been laid to rest.

Murray got up and moved toward Gonzales. As he reached the motionless body he reached into his pocket and produced a glove. With the gloved hand he grabbed Gonzales' hair, pulled up his head, and studied his blood soaked face. His cleaved lips looked like purplish slabs of meat.

The bullet had found its mark in the center of the Hispanic's forehead, a dead perfect shot. As Danny stared into Gonzales' lifeless dark eyes, he knew it would be the last and only act of violence he would ever commit. He picked up his wig from the lamp table and refitted it. As he ran away from the compound, he realized that justice had been served.

The run home was the freest one he'd taken since Cindy was alive. With her death avenged, and the knowledge that Gonzales would never prey upon a helpless child again, he felt a sense of relief. The fear of being caught was at that moment a nonissue to him, the knowledge that a predator of the worst type had been eliminated from society. At a trash bin in the back of a convenience store, he stuffed his gun in a black heavy-duty trash bag and retied the strings.

As he continued through Houston's North Side running toward his house, he sensed that he was on the cusp of a new life. The chances of authorities linking him to Gonzales' death were remote, he reasoned, especially when they found the dead bodies in his living room, the drugs and cash. Much of his preparation had been for naught. It seemd the winds of fate had shifted, his luck finally having changed. A new life lay ahead for him, he thought. Other than his record run in Eugene, it was the most hopeful day of his life.

CHAPTER 21

INVESTIGATION

The Houston Homicide Department is made up of men and women of diverse ethnicities and skin colors. And for obvious reasons, detectives are frequently assigned to areas of town matching their own racial and ethnic profiles. So it stood to reason that Hector Morales was heading the investigation into the death of Rafael Gonzales, a known drug dealer operating out of Houston's North Side, a predominantly Hispanic, hardscrabble neighborhood.

Gonzales had a rap sheet as long as an NBA center's arm, everything from drug dealing, armed robbery, pimping, and arson, to smuggling young Mexican women into the United States and imprisoning them as sex slaves. Few of the charges had stuck against him before his murder, as he put up large sums of cash, taking advantage of a legal system that was both corrupt and overburdened with an out-of-control caseload. Morales knew that, and it had done more than flavor his investigation, his contempt for predators like Gonzales a contained rage that continually roiled his gut.

Morales and Seward had a strong bond, the Hispanic youth having survived a rocky childhood of his own. A product of a broken home on Houston's North Side, living in a dilapidated house just a few blocks from the community center where Gabe was employed as a counselor, Morales had more than his share of run-ins with the law when Seward took him under his wing. The Hispanic youth had just turned 12, a big burly kid whose face had been scarred by knuckles, arms and torso opened by knife wounds. His background played like the same warped record that was standard press for almost every kid involved in the juvenile crime system: one-parent family with the mother as sole support; kids left to fend for themselves; mother stuck in a low-paying, dead-end job or on welfare; a deadbeat father, either in jail, or having disappeared, never making child support payments.

Sylvia Morales cleaned homes in affluent Houston neighborhoods. She commuted to her cleaning jobs by bus, leaving early in the morning and getting home late in the evening, frequently taking two cleaning jobs a day when they were available.

Naturally, the mother's absence left little time for Hector. Her young son was constantly in and out of juvenile court for a variety of offenses, including fighting, truancy, burglary, and assault. Hector's first outing with Gabe was one that Morales would never forget. Gabe loaded him in one of the vans provided by the community center, along with four other Hispanic kids, and drove him to Memorial Park. After sending the first four youngsters out on the three-mile jogging trail that circled the park--a drill they were all familiar with--Gabe said quietly to Hector, "I don't know how much of a man you are, Hector, but those three girls and that young fellow are all going to finish this three-mile loop. Apparently, they're not sure you can."

Hector's ears reddened. "No girls or punk kid going to beat me."

Gabe nodded and extended his hand. "I will see you here at the stretching area when you finish. Let's see what you have in you." Hector didn't take the extended hand as he sprinted out at a pace that Gabe knew was unsustainable.

Gabe had already run six miles, and was waiting at the stretching area adjoining the tennis center parking lot, as the kids straggled in one at a time. Hector finished a distant last. Gabe said nothing to the youngster, praising the group collectively for finishing, before loading them in the van and driving them back to the community center. Conversation in the van was sparing among the fatigued youngsters. As they got out of the vehicle at the community center, Gabe said, "Hector, I'd like to see you."

Hector shuffled reluctantly to him, looking both beaten and humiliated. "I'm proud of you, Hector," Gabe said. He put his hand on the stout boy's shoulder. "That was one hell of an effort you did today. Just between you and me, you're the only one of that group that was able to finish three miles the first time out. All the others were only able to do a mile or two. That shows me you have character. I think you and I are going to get along really well."

Hector grinned, the first time Seward had seen the youngster smile since he met him. "Come with me, Hector."

Gabe led the kid to his black Ford pickup truck, and drove him to a blue-collar buffet off the I-10 loop that Gabe frequented. There the two consumed prodigious sums of food, Gabe having to stop his meal frequently, shaking the hands and swapping stories with the steady stream of Latinos who came to his table to greet him.

Hector's eyes widened as Gabe queried his visitors about their family members and friends. It was obvious to the youth that Seward was intimately involved with them. Gabe seemed to know just about everybody who'd ever lived on the North Side, the product of a lifetime of working and living in the community.

After the meal, Gabe drove Morales back to his house, his mother not yet having returned from work. "We're having softball practice tomorrow at 3:30," Gabe said to the youth. "I suspect a fellow with shoulders like yours could probably hit a ball a pretty long ways. That is, if he was willing to learn."

Hector showed up the next day, and would follow Gabe around like a shadow as he developed. He graduated high in his class at Davis High School, before doing a tour of duty in the Marine Corps, and ultimately received a degree in criminal psychology from the University of Houston. He worked his way up to Captain on the Houston police force, and was now the key investigator for the North Side. It was a road that wasn't without bumps, the politics and backstabbing in the Houston Police Department no different from that of big city departments throughout the country. But Hector was a survivor who rose through the ranks, and never forsook his roots. He stayed in close contact with Gabe, whom he knew kept a firm pulsebeat on the tough Hispanic neighborhood.

Hector pulled his brown Plymouth into the Wellsley House parking lot and reached for a tan sport coat on the passenger seat next to him. He got into the coat, the garment shrouding the shoulder holster and Smith and Wesson that he'd rarely employed in his years as an investigator.

He glanced in the rearview mirror and smoothed his mustache. He was a no-nonsense-looking man with razor cut black hair, firm black eyes, and weathered brown skin. It was the face of a man who had seen the worst side of life in his profession, not far removed from what he experienced growing up. The neighborhood was still much the same, as were many of the cast of characters, the ones who hadn't made it out, along with their offspring and grandchildren who were likely to repeat the same cycle. It was a place where children gave birth to children, the father of the unwed mother's child often her own.

Morales got out of his Plymouth, locked the door, and hitched up his trousers before making his way toward the Wellsley House. His walk hadn't changed much from the way he moved as a youngster, a deliberate lumbering gait, the kind typified by a good-sized man who, by nature and training, never seemed rushed.

He made his way through the institutional white-walled structure and up a flight of stairs toward Gabe Seward's office. Scenes of his stormy youth and trips to the office came back to him as he climbed. He was breathing heavily as he got to the top of the stairs, out of shape, the years of police work, raising a family, and physical inactivity having taken their toll on his body. He knocked at Gabe's door that was half open. Seward grinned widely as he spotted Morales, popping up at his desk like a jack-in-the-box as he beckoned Hector in. Seward's extended hand was swallowed by Morale's beefy mitt, the homicide cop's grip as firm as iron.

"How are you, amigo?" Gabe said as the two men sat.

Morales leaned back in his chair and tapped his tummy. "Fat," he said.

"Well maybe a few pounds over fighting weight, but certainly not fat."

A thin grin curled Hector's lips. He studied Seward. "Gabe, you look like a damn piece of gnarly wire. How much do you weigh?"

Gabe stroked his chin, the bony protrusion sprouting white stubble. "About 140."

"One-forty," Hector repeated. He shook his head in disbelief. "Damn. Five feet ten inches, a hundred and forty pounds, fifty-seven years old, and probably still running like a fool."

"Eighty miles last week," Gabe said grinning widely.

"Eighty miles! Damn! That's crazy. You really are crazy. Gabe, why are you doing all that running? You think you're going to live forever?"

A Cheshire grin opened Gabe's angular face. "I plan on making it to at least 115. Which means that I still have several years left until I reach middle age."

"Why would you want that?"

"Because when I hit a hundred, I plan on marrying a young senorita in the 20-25 range. I want to be absolutely sure that I can keep up with her. It's the time of life when I'll seriously be thinking of starting a family of my own."

"You're still nuts, Gabe." Morales glanced at a sleeping bag that was rolled up on the concrete floor of the cramped cinder block cubicle. It was painful for him staring at the bag, understanding that Seward often employed it to sleep on the concrete floor without a cushion. That was Gabe, Morales thought. The few bucks that he could spend to purchase a cushion would instead go to his clients, kids that he'd take for dinner or whatever came up.

"And you're still crashing here on the floor when you pull a late-nighter, Seward?"

"On occasion."

Morales knew that Gabe would never say no when one of his clients--that included a vast number of young people and adults in the surrounding neighborhood--was in dire straits. He would stay late at night for them at the center, go to their homes when there was a domestic disturbance, or downtown to the city jail or juvenile detention holding center when called for. He'd risked his life in the Moody Park riots, trying to calm things down, a fact that was well known in the community.

The incident had been triggered when a Hispanic man was found dead, facedown in a bayou, his hands cuffed behind him. Everyone knew it was the Houston police force that had done the killing, and the truth came out, but not before angry rioters had set the park aflame. Gabe had tried in vain to halt the rioting, appealing to each adult and youngster he knew at the scene to retain their cool.

Morales realized that Gabe's work was his life. When he got back to the center it was often too late at night for him to return to his small apartment and get back in time in the morning, so he'd just sleep on the floor until clients began coming in to see him the following day. His clients became his extended family, Morales now rationalized, understanding as an adult what he could not have cared less about as a youngster.

Seward's work was all-consuming, filling a void in a life that was bereft of traditional family. He was too busy and too involved with his clients--who often later became his friends--to experience the type of loneliness that plagued many single people, Hector thought. But Morales had also come to rationalize that Gabe may not have been cut out for a traditional family life, the concept of boxing him in with a demanding mate and children, likely too stultifying for his carefree, hobolike existence. Gabe was a complex individual, Morales thought, a '60s carry-over who walked the walk of rejecting materialism in his quest for reaching a higher plane.

Morales rocked back in his chair. "Rafael Gonzales," Morales said slowly. Morales studied Seward's face and saw no change. "He was one bad ass."

Gabe nodded.

"You know I've been assigned to his case?"

Gabe nodded.

"Strange case, Gabe."

"Why's that, Hector?"

"You know, when a big-time drug dealer like Gonzales gets taken out, the first thing that comes to mind is business, that somebody else, in this case almost certainly a rival drug faction, put him down. Especially when the evidence is staring you right in the face. You walk into Gonzales' home, and there he is, slumped over dead, full of bullet holes, and four other guys are their looking just like him, dead on the floor. And their car is parked in his driveway, and their records reveal them all as well-known drug dealers. Slam dunk, right, Gabe? That's what my detectives thought."

Gabe nodded. "That sounds plausible to me."

"Yup. That's the consensus in the homicide. That those guys with him in his living room took him out. And you can imagine the sentiment downtown with the rest of the department."

"I think I can."

"Yeah. They're all as pleased as punch. And you know what? So far I've left it at that."

Gabe nodded.

Hector stroked his chin and leaned back in his chair. "Gabe, let's get real here. There's some stuff I want to discuss with you off the record. I need your word that nothing we talk about today leaves this room."

"You've got it."

"That's good enough for me. I've known you since I was a kid. And your word's always you're your bond."

"Same with you, Hector."

"Gabe, the guys downtown are glad as hell Gonzales is dead. Their thinking is that if there's a drug gang war going on, what could be better for the community? They don't give a damn who killed him. You share that notion?"

"To be honest with you, I do."

Morales nodded his head. "Way down deep inside, I feel that way too. You know how I feel about drug dealers. But you know what? My job is homicide, and I've got a problem in just letting things go conveniently like that."

"I can understand that."

"Gabe, you have any information as to who killed Rafael Gonzales?"

"I couldn't help you with that."

Morales leaned back in his chair. He cracked his knuckles. He smoothed his mustache. He studied Gabe's face that showed no signs of change. "Gabe, how come I think you know something that you're not telling me?"

"Hector, that's a tough one. I couldn't tell you what's going on in your head."

Morales grinned and chuckled. "I know you know something, Gabe. As well plugged-in to this community as you are."

Gabe just sat, his expression not having changed.

"You're just damn lucky that I owe you my damn life, Gabe. Because if I didn't, I'd have you subpoenaed by a grand jury in a New York minute to find out what the hell you know."

"And Hector, I can assure you my answers to them would be no different from what I would tell you today. That I know nothing in this case, other than the fact that a blight to our community has been removed. My hope would be that others like Rafael Gonzales may suffer similar fates if they are engaged in drug dealing."

Morales rubbed the back of his hand with his fingertips. He leaned forward and stared into Gabe's eyes. "I'm going to tell you what

I think happened to Rafael Gonzales. I don't think his murder had anything to do with drugs."

"Why is that, Hector?"

"Oh, multiple reasons. I checked that crime scene out with a fine-toothed comb. And I've checked with multiple street sources. None of that would lead me to believe that the guys in his home were there to kill him. This wasn't a turf war. Gonzales was taken out in his own living room, for Crissake, by a Saturday-night special. Does that sound like a professional hit to you?"

"I don't know. Crime reconstruction is not my area of expertise."

"You know what I think happened?"

"No."

"I think that somebody with balls the size of an elephant, a rank amateur, was hiding in Rafael's home when he came home with some guys he was going to do a drug deal with. I think they got in an argument, shooting started, and Rafie killed four of them. In the process he was wounded. But somebody who wasn't involved with the drug dealing finished him off. I think that the son of a gun got off a hell of a shot and popped damn Rafie right between the eyes.

"Rafie, apparently, got off a couple of rounds before he was shot. But from what I could put together, got nothing but Sheetrock. This wasn't a drugland hit, Gabe. Those guys that were in his home weren't professional killers. They were drug dealers there in the middle of a deal. Pros don't do things that way if there's a hit. If they'd wanted to kill Rafael, they'd have blown up his car or put him down with some heavy artillery. The kill shot that put down Gonzales was done by an amateur with big balls and a Saturday-night special. He got off a hell of a shot from halfway across a room. Hit that sucker right between the eyes. It was an amazing shot, the only one the shooter fired. Rafie got off a couple of shots before he was hit. Which makes me tend to believe that the shooter may not have originally intended to kill him. Or maybe he had, and then for some reason had second thoughts. I think the shooter popped Rafie in self-defense.

"No, Gabe, whoever pulled the trigger for the forehead shot that took down Rafie wasn't a pro. Though he did a damn good job of making it appear that way. Drugs started the shooting, but they had nothing to do with the kill shot."

"Interesting, Hector. Did you find drugs on the scene?"

"Yup. Rafie had stuff all around the house that wasn't touched. And cash too. Which lends more credence to my thoughts that this wasn't an assassination. Shoot, I was surprised when I checked the house out that Gonzales was so sloppy. I guess he wasn't too worried about being busted."

"I take your word for that."

"Yeah. That's why I'm betting that some amateur had gotten into his house, and was there with the intent of killing him. I'm clueless as to motive. But my bet is it was somebody who wanted to make it look like a robbery, or a gangland hit. And then lucked into a deal gone bad. I think the shooter finished a job that the boys we found murdered in the house had started."

"How did the shooter come in?"

"I'm not sure. But again, if I'd had to bet, I think that after he did get in, he was hiding in Rafie's house waiting for him. My guess is that he somehow got in the second story. Rafie may have gotten a little sloppy, and left his window upstairs unlocked."

"And how did he get up there?"

"Search me. Must have been a pretty agile guy. And I think that he was hiding upstairs when Rafie came in with his clients, their deal went bad, and the shooting started. I think the guy in hiding finished off Rafie after the gun battle. I'm guessing he went downstairs, found four dead bodies on the floor, and Rafie shot and bleeding. At that point, it's unclear what happened. But my guess is the shooter may have had second thoughts about killing him. And that as Rafie fired off a couple of shots, the shooter responded and took him out."

"Quite a scenario, Hector."

"You think I'm blowing smoke, Gabe?"

"I have no reason to doubt you. You know your craft."

"Yeah. Too many things that don't add up. The guys that we found dead in Gonzales' home had their car parked out front, right behind Gonzales' vehicle. They didn't break into the compound. They followed him in. They were sampling drugs, negotiating over a buy I'd guess. Then something went wrong, which happens a lot in those kinds of deals, and an argument ensued. And then the shooting started. Gonzales' gun was major firepower, as were the ones found on the guys dead in his house. All the casings were from major firepower, as were the bullets found in the bodies. Gonzales' legs and shoulder were hit by large caliber charges. But the coroner pulled a .38 slug out of Rafie's forehead. It was the only .38 piece of lead recovered from the scene. My guess is that somebody else pulled off that .38 shot that ended his life. And that somebody was an amateur with nerves of steel. It was an amateur that poisoned his pit bulls. And it was an amateur that hopped his fence and cut the razor wire. And an amateur that scaled the wall on the back of his house, and got through in a window. And it was an amateur that hid in that house waiting for Gonzales, and stayed in hiding as the fireworks started in the living room."

"Very interesting," Seward said.

"What that amateur did took balls, Gabe. To poison Gonzales' pit bulls in his yard, hop a damn chain-link fence with razor wire on the top, flip the switches on his breaker box, slither up his wall like a lizard, and break into his home like a damn cat burglar, took balls. And then to come face-to-face with him, nail him with a shot right between the eyes with a small caliber pistol as Rafie's pointing a .45 at him, and popping off two rounds before he goes down takes big balls. To get a shot off like that under pressure and put a guy down like Gonzales, takes major cojones. Elephant cojones."

Hector sat frozen, his expression not changing as he studied Seward's poker face. "You know what's a no-brainer with Rafie's shooter, Gabe?"

"No."

"That he was one hell of an athlete. He scaled a damn hairy fence lined with razor wire to get in the yard. He snaked his way up a vertical wall and hopped into a window. And he got off a hell of a shot with a .45 firing at him. And he left without leaving a trace of anything behind. That indicates to me a lithe body with ice water in his veins. Someone in damn good shape that doesn't choke with the pressure on. That's an elite athlete's profile. That, and one more thing."

"What's that?"

"An old lady that lives in the neighborhood across the street from Rafael, had taken her dog out in the middle of the night. She saw a figure running down the street not long after the time we determined Rafie was popped. She didn't get a look at the runner's face, but she said it was a woman, and she was flying. The only physical description that she gave of her was that she was thin, had blond hair, and ran like the wind. A very high knee lift and lengthy strides. Sounds to me like that could have been the woman who put down Rafael. But you know what? I'd bet my career on the fact that wasn't a woman. That was a guy disguised as a woman. Hey, I'd get fried by the ladies in my department for offering a theory like that. They'd call me a male chauvinist. But I'd still make that bet. Screw political correctness. That wasn't a female."

"I would take your word for that."

Morales shook his head. "You're not going to tell me anything, are you, Gabe?"

"I truly wish there was something I could tell you."

"Gabe, you're playing semantic games with me. I'm not the uneducated Mexican that you brought up as a kid. I know the difference between could and will."

Seward smiled widely. "Hector, you have come a long way. And I'm sure your language skills exceed mine."

Morales tapped his thigh. He leaned forward. "Seward, I'm not going to b.s. you anymore, because I know you know more than you're telling me. And you know that what I was telling you before about finding his killer is b.s. To hell with Rafael Gonzales. And all the other major drug dealers in this neighborhood. Let them all kill each other, as far as I'm concerned. And if you know who's behind this, that's your deal. But, Gabe, you know that if you're harboring this shooter, and push comes to shove, somebody else in the department could come down pretty hard on you if you're connected."

Gabe didn't respond.

Hector leaned back in his chair. He cracked his knuckles. He smoothed his mustache. He grinned. "Of course that's unlikely. Since I call the shots on what cases down here have continuing investigations, and which ones we let slide. And I'm closing this case. This one's going down as a turf war shooting. Done deal."

Gabe sat without moving.

"You're a tough old bird, Gabe. And a pretty convincing liar."

The smile left Gabe's lips.

Hector twiddled his thumbs. He leaned back in his chair. Then he came forward, his eyes penetrating Seward's.

"You owe me dinner," Hector said.

Gabe smiled broadly. "Name your time and place."

Morales shook his head. "No, I take that back. You don't owe me a thing. I owe you. Why don't you come over this Sunday to the house? I'm going to throw some steaks on the grill and my wife makes a pretty mean salad."

Gabe rubbed his hands, and stuck out his right one that Morales took.

Hector Morales left the Wellsley House knowing that he was betraying the ethics of his profession. But he didn't give a damn. He'd learned in his long career as a homicide cop that there were gray areas in law and ethics, and that doing everything by the book was a notion that didn't hold water in the real world. If Gabe Seward was hiding something, so be it. A drug dealer that had brought untold misery to his neighborhood--to the youngsters and their families who lived there--

179

was dead. It was true justice, far exceeding the reach of the legal system that employed him.

CHAPTER 22

LEGAL ACTION

Gabe took Danny to a Starbucks off West Gray on a Monday morning at 7:30.

There the two ordered coffee and took a table outside. As they sat, they observed the steady stream of cars that came into the parking lot and the people who got out. The vehicles were largely BMWs, Mercedes, Porsches, Lexuses, Infinitis, and Jaguars, along with a wide range of expensive SUVs. And most of the patrons who got out of them were nattily clad men and women, professional people clutching cell phones. Their stress levels appeared high to Danny as they queued up in line for their designer drinks, caffeine fixes that would take them through their hectic mornings. They were exotic-looking whipped cream-topped concoctions that Danny saw cost more than most of the meals he fixed in his apartment.

It was a world that Murray was far removed from; one that Gabe knew existed but had never desired to enter. Danny and Gabe sipped their coffee out of covered paper cups for about ten minutes, when a silver Jeep Grand Cherokee eased into the parking lot, taking a space facing them. An athletic-looking middle-aged man with silvering red hair, clad in charcoal slacks and a crisply starched white dress shirt with a red club tie, got out and walked toward them. He extended his hand to Gabe, who was on his feet and took it.

"Good to see you, Gabe."

"Same to you, Jerry. Jerry, I'd like you to meet the young man I told you about. This is Danny Murray."

Danny got up and took Jerry Martin's hand. Martin's handshake was firm and he had a pleasant smile and clear eyes.

"Let me go grab some coffee, guys. I'll be out in a second. Can I get you anything?"

Gabe looked at Danny who shook his head, no. "No, we're fine, Jerry."

"Be just a second," Jerry said.

He then walked to the door and into the shop, queuing up in the line that was starting to grow.

"Why don't we move to the table down there?" Gabe said to Danny.

He pointed to a vacant table that was furthest removed from the store, closest to West Gray that was now teeming with rush-hour traffic.

The two took the table, and Danny sat facing River Oaks, the neighborhood of palatial colonial-style mansions owned by millionaires that he and Gabe had run through so frequently. Seward sat facing the coffee shop.

Several minutes later Jerry emerged from the coffee shop. Gabe stood and waved as Jerry spotted him by the far table fronting West Gray.

As Jerry approached the table and sat, Gabe said, "I thought this would give us a little privacy."

"Good idea," Jerry said. He took a sip of his coffee, the same unfettered drink that Danny and Gabe had ordered. Then he put down the cup, pulled a pair of tortoise-colored sunglasses out of his shirt breast pocket and fitted them on. The sun had come out, the beginning of a warm day that by afternoon would be hot.

"How's everything with you, Gabe?"

"Good, Jerry. Everything's fine. Now, if we can just get this matter cleared up with this fine young man, everything will be even better."

Jerry turned to Danny. "Gabe told me a bit about what's gone on with you. If you feel comfortable, why don't you tell me in your words what happened."

"Where do you want me to start?"

"That's up to you. Whatever you consider the beginning would be fine."

Gabe said, "Would you like me to leave?"

"If you don't mind, that would probably be a good idea until we finish."

"No problem. I'll go inside the shop and have another cup of coffee and read the paper. And perhaps view some lovely ladies too."

Martin grinned. "There's some great eye-candy here."

As Gabe walked back to the shop, Danny sensed the attorney seemed relaxed. Intuitively, he sensed that Gabe had picked a good man.

"Whenever you're ready, Danny, go ahead."

Murray began his narrative, and detailed his life from his early childhood until the present. He gave a thorough accounting of what had gone on with Gonzales, and hid nothing as he told his story in full.

When he finished, Jerry nodded and said, "That's quite a story."

"You believe me?"

"I have no reason not to. Especially with what Gabe said. Gabe has spent a lifetime working with kids who have had problems. He tells the truth."

"Gabe has been my lifeline."

Jerry sipped coffee and readjusted his sunglasses.

"Danny, as far as the Houston Police Department is concerned, Rafael Gonzales was killed in a shootout involved with drugs. I'd say from your point of view, it's a good idea to keep them with that impression. Other than Gabe, did you tell anybody else about Rafael Gonzales?"

"No."

"Nobody?"

"No one."

Jerry nodded. "I'd urge you to keep it that way. Forever."

"No problem," Danny said.

"From that angle I think we'll be okay," Martin said. "But we've still got a few bridges to cross. The Oregon District Attorney still has a warrant out for your arrest. As far as they're concerned you're still wanted for your sister's murder. I'm going to arrange to have a DNA sample of Gonzales taken and flown out to Oregon. If that comes back matching Gonzales, that should be indisputable proof that he raped and murdered your sister. But there's still the issue of your warrant. My suggestion is that once the DNA has been cleared, we make arrangements to surrender you to Oregon authorities. We'll fly out there and you'll be arrested, and possibly be held for a day or two. I doubt under the circumstances that bail will be required. But if it is, I'll handle it. At that point the District Attorney will likely review Gonzales' DNA records, and drop charges against you."

Danny nodded. "What's a worst-case scenario?" he asked.

"You mean if the DNA doesn't match up?"

"No. I mean if they decide to go after me for fleeing following Cindy's murder."

Jerry shook his head. "That's not likely. If the DNA proves to be Gonzales', this thing should be a slam-dunk. I'm not anticipating anything after that."

"I've gone through a lot," Danny said.

"And I understand that. But I've been doing criminal law a long time. Once the DNA tests are confirmed, you should be home free. At worst you may have to spend 48 hours in a holding cell. Besides..." Martin paused and grinned, "I know the DA out there and we're good buddies. We were both prosecutors right here before he moved out there. I know how he operates. He won't screw us over. And it doesn't hurt that he eats, drinks, and sleeps running."

Danny just nodded. "Okay. Let's go for it."

"You have a phone where I can reach you?" Jerry said.

"No."

"No problem. But I want you to check in with me every day starting tomorrow."

"I'll do that."

"One more thing," Martin said. "Just a reminder to keep your lips concealed concerning Gonzales."

Danny nodded. "I don't have any problem with that. Gabe is the only person alive that knows anything about my life. I don't have any problem keeping my mouth shut."

Jerry nodded. Then he reached into his back pocket and pulled out a wallet. From the wallet he took out a business card that he jotted another number on and handed to Danny. "Call me tomorrow on my cell. I've written it on the back of my card."

"I will."

He got up and shook hands with Danny and said, "Hopefully we'll have this whole deal wrapped up within the next month."

"That would be great."

The two shook hands and Jerry returned to his car. Murray walked back into the Starbucks to get Seward with the first relaxed smile on his face that Gabe had ever seen.

...

Danny and Jerry flew out to Oregon four weeks later and surrendered to authorities after the DNA tests were confirmed. As Jerry had predicted, charges were quickly dropped against Danny. Further news revealed that the prostitute and her little girl that lived in the trailer adjoining Danny's had been found several weeks following Cindy's rape and murder. Like his little sister, each had been raped and murdered. And like Cindy, DNA linked their demise to Rafael Gonzales. The reality that another child had been slaughtered was devastating to Danny. He found it impossible to understand the psychological makeup of a psychopath that rapes and kills children and women with no feeling.

CHAPTER 23

BLINDED BY BEAUTY

On a Friday night at a few minutes past 10:00, Danny Murray was stretching by a stone marker. It indicated the start point of the jogging trail circling Memorial Park, a 2.9-mile loop that was the running hub of the nation's fourth largest city. The park was deserted, the sea of runners and walkers that clogged the cinder trail having long gone.

As Murray stretched, he spotted Gabe Seward's black pickup on the asphalt loop road coming toward him. As Seward pulled into the tennis center parking lot just off the trail where Danny was stretching, Murray noticed a female sitting in the passenger seat next to Seward. As Seward killed the engine of his pickup, the female got out of the truck and shut the door. Danny's eyes stayed riveted on her as she approached him with Gabe. She was a dark-haired Hispanic girl, late teens to early 20s, petite, lithe, athletic, and lovely.

"Hello, amigo," Gabe said, his hand extended. As Danny shook Seward's hand, Gabe said, "This is Maria." He turned to Maria. "And this is Danny Murray."

Maria smiled shyly as Danny stood frozen. His instinct to flee was strong, just as it always was when he felt insecure. Gabe had forewarned Danny that he was going to bring the girl out to run with them, and had attempted to assuage his fears. He had told Murray that he had known Maria since her infancy, and that she related to him like family. He characterized her as close-mouthed and smart, with a sense of loyalty that was rock solid.

Besides, he had told Murray that he would reveal nothing about his past to her, letting him tell her what he wanted as he saw fit. But

Murray was still uneasy, having spent so much of his life as a loner fleeing authorities. For years he'd yearned for a relationship with a woman, but had put his and his sister's safety first. Now that he was free, he knew that excuse would no longer fly. To connect with a woman he'd have to face the equally frightening possibility of rejection. Seward understood that fear, having gone through the process time and again on his own. Now into middle age, he still dealt with it, yearning for the one woman that could complete his life.

They started off at a moderate pace, running three abreast, a mode that was unsafe when the trail was crowded. By the half-mile mark, Maria was leading the threesome and pushing the pace. Both Gabe and Danny watched as Maria keyed in on a solitary male runner who was about two hundred yards ahead of them.

Just past the mile mark and Memorial Drive, she had pulled up on the man's shoulder, a muscular figure in his early 30s. Gabe and Danny made eye contact with each other and neither said a word. Their eyes told the whole story. There was a twinkle in Gabe's eyes as there was Danny's, the two running amused as they viewed the unfolding competition just yards in front of them. For the next mile and a quarter Maria and the muscular man battled each other step for step, a study in biomechanics that was as discrepant as black and white. The muscular man struck the ground with his feet like a charging rhino, Maria floating like a butterfly. With a little less than a half-mile to go, the muscular man veered off the trail and ran toward a drinking fountain. As Danny and Gabe caught up with Maria, her breathing was heavy. The three ran as a trio as Maria fought to hang on. With less than a quarter mile to go, they heard heavy breathing coming from behind. Danny and Gabe turned their heads as the muscular man made his way back toward them like an angry bull. He was breathing deeply and loudly, his feet striking the cinder trail with a smacking sound that echoed in the dark forest like nasty slaps.

"Looks like you've got a visitor, Maria," Gabe said softly.

Maria turned her head and spotted the man who was charging toward her. Danny turned his head. In the moonlight Maria's dark eyes flashed like polished stones. His pulse quickened as he keyed in on her eyes. At that moment he experienced a sensation unlike any he had encountered in his life. It was one of such intensity that he could feel his heart kick in his chest, an electric jolt of immeasurable voltage. The dark-haired beauty was a kindred spirit, he realized, an extension of himself with the same tortured soul.

Gabe gently nudged Danny, and as the two eyed each other, they again spoke without speaking. They separated and slowed, allowing Maria and her pursuer to run side by side, the two engaged in a dogfight for the remaining section of the first loop.

"Holy moly," Gabe said softly to Danny, as he watched Maria and the muscular man trade strides on the cinder trail.

"I thought he was finished back at the water fountain," Danny said softly.

"So did I," Gabe said.

"She's feisty," Danny said.

"A very determined young woman."

As Danny watched Maria from behind, he studied her physique and form. She was lean and shapely, about 5'4", 110 pounds, cut fairly evenly in torso and legs. From behind it was difficult for Murray not to stare at her, her rear and legs perfect. She appeared to float as she ran, her gait economical. In contrast to the heavily muscled man running beside her, she did not appear to be working, the economy of movement belying a steady strength that had long-distance potential.

It was apparent to Danny that Maria had talent, but what was more glaringly obvious was her resolute tenacity. The girl ran as if she was purging demons, a condition that Danny understood only too well. As he watched her, he could see every muscle move and flex in her athletic legs, from her long, smooth calves to her peach-shaped rear.

"Want to get up there and run with them?" Gabe asked Danny.

Danny shook his head. "No. Let's let them duke it out on their own. I'd rather watch from back here."

Gabe nodded his head. "We're in agreement on that one."

Maria continued to force the pace, but each time she'd gain a step on the man he'd come back at her. With a quarter of a mile to go, Maria was running at full tilt. Gabe turned his head toward Danny, grinning widely. "Who's your money on?"

"I think they'll tie," Danny said. "That is, if muscleman doesn't die."

"Lordy, I hope not, because I am in no frame of mind to administer c.p.r. this evening."

With 200 yards to go, Maria turned up her speed another notch. She gained several steps on the man as Gabe and Danny gently picked up their pace. They had no desire to be competitive, their increased speed merely a tool to keep them close enough so as not to miss any of the unfolding drama.

The muscular man caught up with Maria again and, just before the stretching area leading to the tennis center parking lot and the finish marker on the trail, she accelerated into a full sprint.

"Look at that!" Gabe said to Danny in a loud whisper.

Danny watched as Maria's knees pumped high in the air, the back of her heels striking her buttocks as she kicked for home. She put several feet on the muscular man but he quickly recaptured them. The two ran neck and neck, finishing at the stone marker where they had started their run in what appeared a dead heat to Murray and Seward.

The man gasped as he finished, bent over double, and then he abruptly moved into the tennis center parking lot. It was apparent that he didn't want Maria to see him, the girl having just turned around, jogging back toward Gabe and Danny. When Gabe and Danny met her at the second driveway of the tennis center, Maria was breathing heavily.

"Okay, Maria?" Gabe asked.

She just nodded.

"Are you sure?"

She nodded again, her breathing heavy.

"Danny and I are going to do another two loops. Will you be okay on your own in the van?"

She nodded again, and Gabe said, "We'll see you soon."

The next loop Danny and Gabe picked up the pace and did a series of half-mile pickups. The third lap Murray took off on his own, his movement gazellelike as he streaked around the cinder path. As Gabe watched him run from behind, he realized he would have to do little if anything to recapture his old form. Seward felt certain Danny could still run record times at any distance from the half-mile to the marathon. Through all his adversity he had continued to run and train at a world-class level.

Danny finished minutes ahead of Gabe, and stood waiting for him at the start marker on the jogging trail fronting the tennis center parking lot. As he stood Maria waited in the van, both shy of each other.

When Gabe finished, Danny said, "I've got to go. I've got to go to work in five hours."

Gabe nodded and extended his hand. "See you tomorrow, amigo."

"With Maria?" Danny asked.

"No, on my own."

"Good," Danny said.

"You don't like her?" Gabe asked.

"No. It's not that."

"What is it?"

"I don't know how much more of that I want to watch. That about wore me out."

Gabe grinned. "I know what you mean."

"Given any more thought about competing again?" Gabe asked.

"No."

"Why?"

"Without Cindy, I don't care."

Gabe eyed Danny for a lengthy period of time. Then he said, "You're angry with the United States Track and Field Federation."

"I think I could get as much satisfaction in suing them as coming back and setting records," Murray said.

"Really? You hate them that much?"

"More."

"They made a bad mistake."

"Mistake? They assumed I was guilty until proven innocent. And they robbed me of a world record that was rightfully mine. You ask me how much I hate them? Let me tell you, Gabe, that the level of contempt that I feel toward them was only exceeded by the rage that I harbored for Rafael Gonzales."

"That's intense," Gabe said.

"That's the truth."

"So you're going to deny yourself the opportunity of setting records and all the money and fame that comes along with it because you're not going to let your anger go?"

"Seward, if I've learned one thing from you, it's that nothing and nobody controls me. No organization and not money. Look at yourself, Gabe. You've never chased the dollar. But look at how many lives you've impacted. And you've always run because you love to. Maybe I'm learning that too, that I love running because of its purity, and the hell with fame and money."

Gabe pushed at his glasses. He scratched his head. "Danny, you have a gift that I never had. All the training and coaching in the world could never have brought me to your level. It's a gift that someday you'll regret not having tapped if you let it slide."

"I don't agree with you. About the gift part, yeah. But not about the rewards of coming back, setting records, and making money. That part is crap. The only person in my life that I truly loved was Cindy. And now that she's gone, grabbing for fame or trying to accumulate money means nothing to me."

"So you're going to write off the rest of your life now that Cindy is gone?"

"Did you write off your life, Gabe? Why did you devote yourself to a career where you knew damn well there was no money to be made? Do you have a martyr complex? Or did you become enlightened early on in life? And come to an understanding that money and things are crap, and mean nothing in the scheme of things? I'd guess the second.

"Maybe with all that I've been through, I'm seeing things in a different light too, and coming to an understanding of things in a different way. Maybe I'd like to become a better person. Maybe I'd like to effectuate some change too. Maybe I can do the same thing that you have and work with kids who have nothing. Touching one of them would mean a lot more to me than any damn world records or money."

Following a lengthy silence Seward said, "Danny, I understand what you're saying and thinking. It's a noble thought. And it's a great compliment you're paying me. But I believe you're doing yourself a terrible disservice by not giving your gift to the world. If you're interested in touching kids, you'll be in a much more powerful position to do that as the world's greatest runner than in the position you're in now."

"Why? You think kids will listen to me any different than they do you?"

"I think you'll be able to reach a larger number."

"Bullshit, Gabe. Look how many lives you've touched over the years in Houston's Hispanic community. You've made an impact on a grass-roots level. You're not some sports star who blows into an auditorium full of kids, gives some b.s. pep talk on why you should never give up, and then goes back to his fancy gated neighborhood not having to sully his hands again with the dirty public until it suits him."

"Who says you'd have to live in a gated neighborhood? And who says you couldn't do grass-roots work?"

Danny rubbed his chin. "Gabe, let it go. I don't want to compete anymore. I don't want to grovel before the United States Track and Field Federation to get reinstated. I don't want to deal with dumb ass track and field writers like Barry Swill. I don't want fame. I don't want wealth. I just want to lead a simple life, do my own thing, and be left alone. If I can help change the life of a kid or two in a positive way, that will be enough. More than that, a bonus. At this point, that's all I want. I think you should respect my wishes and let the running thing die."

Gabe nodded. "Okay. You've got it."

"See you tomorrow," Danny said.

Gabe offered his hand that Danny took.

Murray ran back to his garage apartment, hoping that Gabe understood how much he thought of him. But as the run progressed, his thoughts turned toward Maria. He saw the flash of her eyes and the image of her running from behind. He felt a stirring deep inside. It was both an emotional and physical trigger of an intensity level he'd never experienced. He longed for Maria, knowing he'd spend many sleepless nights thinking of her.

CHAPTER 24

A DOCTOR'S FATEFUL CALL

Gabe got a call from his physician a week following his physical exam.

"Mr. Seward?"

"Yes."

"This is Dr. Baker."

"Hey, Doc. What's up?"

"Mr. Seward, I've got the test results of your physical back, and I'd like to schedule another visit with you. How soon can you come in?"

"I need to come back in? Can't you just tell me over the phone?"

"I'm sorry, but it's not that simple. There are some things on your physical that need some rechecking, so we'll need to schedule another appointment."

"I'm as healthy as a horse, Doc. Running seventy to eighty miles a week, with big old arteries and veins, and a heart that runs like a brand-new Lamborghini. I'm going to live to be 115."

"I hope so, Mr. Seward. But I must tell you that some of your tests are very suspicious, and it would behoove you to come back in as soon as possible so we can determine what's going on."

"You sure there hasn't been a mistake, Doc? You know, I read so many stories about how test results in labs get crossed up."

"That's always a possibility, Mr. Seward, which would give even more reason for you to come back so we can run some tests again to verify the first results."

Following a lengthy silence Gabe said, "Okay. When do you want me back?"

"Please hold on a second and I'll put on my scheduler. She'll take care of that."

"Okay."

...

Two days later Gabe went back to Dr. Glenn Baker's office. After checking Seward the doctor sent him to the lab to repeat blood work.

Four days later Gabe was in Baker's office for a follow-up consultation.

Seward rubbed his hands as he sat on an examining table, Baker sitting in a chair across from him, the physician's head buried in a chart scribbling notes. As he stopped writing, his head came up from the chart. He laid down his pen and lifted off his glasses. His brown eyes showed concern as he said, "Mr. Seward, I've got some bad news for you. There are some very suspicious spots on your lungs. According to your test results, I have a good reason to believe they are cancerous. I would like to schedule you for some more testing at M.D. Anderson, and then we can go from there."

Gabe's face lost its color. "Lung cancer? I don't smoke. I've never smoked. How in the world could I have lung cancer?"

"I don't know. And it's premature to say they are definitely cancerous. But there is a high probability that they are."

"Lung cancer," Seward intoned. "That just doesn't make sense. You're certain that my test results weren't confused with somebody else's?"

"Unfortunately, both sets of tests that you took were almost identical. They are most certainly yours."

"Good gosh," Gabe said. "I can't believe it." He took off his glasses and rubbed his nose. He was 57 years old, and at that moment appeared many years more. He was already so gaunt from the running, that he could easily be mistaken for a cancer patient.

His eyes were wet with tears as he faced the bleakest moment of his life. The organization that he worked for had notified him that its health insurance policy had been canceled. His savings were meager,

195

not nearly the kind that it would take to pay for treatment out-of-pocket.

"Let's not jump the gun on this, Mr. Seward. First, let's determine if indeed you have cancer."

Gabe just nodded. He took a deep breath. "I don't think I have cancer. But if I do, I'm going to kick it."

Baker nodded. "I'll have my staff arrange for appointments with you at Anderson. They'll give you a call when everything is confirmed."

Gabe then stood up. He breathed deep and stuck out his hand. "Thanks for everything, Doc."

"You're quite welcome."

As Seward left, Baker went to his next patient. Cancer was unpredictable, Baker thought. You could be feeling just fine and be totally unaware you had it. It was a medical conundrum that science had made great progress on, but one which would continue to bring untold misery and claim scores of lives for many years to come.

CHAPTER 25

CANCER

The Houston Medical Center is a city within a city, a bustling metropolis of gleaming high-rises, teeming with hospitals and medical professional buildings, including the Universities of Texas and Baylor medical schools. M.D. Anderson is located right in the heart of the Medical Center, a state cancer hospital born by an act of the Texas Legislature in 1941.

The M.D. Anderson Hospital for Cancer Research of the University of Texas started out in temporary headquarters on the Baker estate near downtown Houston, a time when little was known about how cancer started or spread, and only a handful of treatments were available. It was an era when cancer survival rates were no better than one in four. But in the 60-plus years since its inception, Anderson had recorded over a half a million patients through its doors, with survival rates at the turn of the new millennium reaching 60 percent.

The Medical Center was an area that Seward had rarely frequented in his years in Houston. His only visits there were to Ben Taub Hospital, the county hospital known for its superb emergency room facility that cared for the city's poor and indigent.

Now he was facing the possibility of having lung cancer, the leading cancer killer of both men and women in the United States. Seward researched the disease online, and from the American Cancer Society found that in 2000 there were an estimated 156,900 deaths from lung cancer in the U.S. and 164,100 new cases. His study revealed to him that smoking was the number one cause of lung cancer, accounting for about 87 percent of cases. He also learned that secondhand smoke was responsible for another 3,000 lung cancer deaths.

Since he didn't smoke and was only exposed to the secondhand smoke of his parents for a short time as a youth, he assumed that smoking was not the cause of his disease, if indeed he had it. He also learned that the second leading cause of lung cancer in the U.S. was radon, a gas that can come up through the soil under a home or building and enter through gaps and cracks in the foundation or insulation, as well as through pipes, drains, walls, and other openings.

Radon was estimated to cause up to 22,000 lung cancer deaths in the U.S. each year as of the new millennium, the EPA estimating that one out of every 15 homes in the U.S. has radon levels at which homeowners should take action. Radon could be a possible cause if he had cancer, some of the rattraps he had lived in likely places where the gas may have infiltrated.

He learned that another leading cause of cancer was on-the-job exposure to cancer-causing substances, or carcinogens, such as asbestos, uranium, arsenic, and certain petroleum products. Gabe had spent his share of time in the Army working on the brakes of vehicles.

He learned that lung cancer takes many years to develop but that changes in the lung can begin almost as soon as an individual is exposed to cancer-causing substances. Soon after the exposure begins, a few abnormal cells may appear in the lining of the bronchi, and if exposure continues, more cells appear and can become cancerous before forming a tumor. Seward filled out a form which asked if he had chronic cough, hoarseness, coughing up blood, weight loss and loss of appetite, shortness of breath, fever without a known reason, wheezing, repeated bouts of bronchitis or pneumonia, or chest pain. To his knowledge he had none of them, so he answered no.

When he was finally admitted, he saw an oncologist named Dr. Abraham Abramowitz who ordered a CT scan.

When the results of the CT scan came back, Abramowitz spoke to Gabe in an examining room. He breathed deeply, took off his eyeglasses and massaged the bridge of his nose.

"Mr. Seward, I've spotted what appears to be several tumors on your lung. I would like to schedule you an appointment to biopsy them. In this procedure I will insert a small tube called a bronchoscope down your throat to look inside your airways and lungs and take a sample, or biopsy, of what appears to be several tumors."

Gabe nodded. "Okay."

The biopsy procedure was scheduled, and several days later Gabe got a call from Dr. Abramowitz. Seward was sitting at his desk as his phone rang.

" Mr. Seward? Dr. Abramowitz here."

Gabe took a deep breath and grinned. He felt certain his news would be good.

"Hey, Doc. What's up?"

"Mr. Seward, I have some unfortunate news for you. The lesions that I biopsied in your lungs are cancerous. They need immediate attention."

Gabe felt the blood leave his head. His mouth went dry.

"Cancerous?" Seward said in a hushed tone.

"I'm afraid so."

Gabe's pulse raced as he tried to sort out the conflicting thoughts addling his mind.

"Okay, Doc. What now?"

"You mentioned to my nurse that you've had some headaches that tend to be worse in the morning and ease during the day?"

"Sure, Doc. But it's no big deal."

"And that you've had some noticeable vision changes?"

"Yeah. But it's been a while since I've had my glasses checked."

"Mr. Seward, I'd like you to come back in for some more tests."

"What kind?"

"I'd like to order an MRI for your brain."

"You've got to be kidding."

"No. I'm quite serious."

"You think I have brain cancer?"

"Let's not jump to any conclusions. In light of what we've discovered with your lungs, it would be prudent to check your brain also. Mr. Seward, from what I've read in your chart, you were once a top distance runner. Is that correct?"

"I don't know if I'd say 'top,' but I did my share of running."

"I would define a man who went to two Olympic Trials as being 'top' Mr. Seward."

"Thanks, Doc. But what does that have to do with any of this?"

"Mr. Seward, I've done a bit of running myself. Of course nothing like the level that you achieved. But one thing that separates distance runners from the general public is their pain threshold level. Generally, the better the runner, the higher the pain threshold level that he or she possesses."

"Forgive me, Doc, but I'm still not sure where you're going with this."

"Mr. Seward, I would suspect that you probably have an extraordinarily high threshold for pain. And what the average, sedentary man or woman might define as intense pain, you may only regard as a livable discomfort, or perhaps, at best, a niggling annoyance. You're obviously not a complainer, Mr. Seward, which most of us appreciate, but in your case that may have worked against you."

Gabe's body was shaking as he said, "Okay. I'll take whatever tests you suggest. Let's go for it."

Abramowitz said, "I'm going to take good care of you, Mr. Seward. You have worked very hard to keep yourself in good physical health. That will weigh heavily in your favor no matter what we find."

Gabe said, "Thanks", his voice thick, his eyes clouded with water.

...

Gabe was scheduled right back at Anderson where an MRI scan was performed. The procedure would yield detailed pictures of his brain, the images created by a powerful magnet linked to a computer.

It was explained to Seward as a procedure especially useful in diagnosing brain tumors because it can see through the bones of the skull to the tissue underneath.

Several days after the MRI was performed, Abramowitz called back.

"Mr. Seward?"

"Hey, Doc. I'll bet this time you have some good news."

"I wish I did, Mr. Seward. But unfortunately, I do not. The MRI brain scan that was performed on you revealed brain tumors. Mr. Seward, surgery is required, and I would urge you the sooner the better."

Gabe's voice was noticeably shaking as he said, "Good God. Surgery. What does that entail? Actually going into my brain? "

"Yes, it does. A neurosurgeon will have to do the actual surgery. And I can assure you, we have some of the finest neurosurgeons in the world on our staff."

Following a lengthy silence, Gabe said, "And that would be it?"

"Perhaps. But radiation and/or chemotherapy may be required after the surgery, depending on how much of the tumors can be removed without damaging vital brain tissue. I would urge you not to wait on this, Mr. Seward. The sooner we can get to your cancer, the better the likelihood we can cure you. To procrastinate drastically decreases your odds of survival."

At a loss for words, Seward said, "I appreciate everything you've done for me. But right now I'll have to put this thing on hold until I can make other arrangements."

"Why is that, Mr. Seward?"

"Because my company's health policy has been terminated."

Abramowitz gulped. "Mr. Seward, I'm very sorry about your situation. I truly hope you can find a way to tend to this."

"I appreciate that, Doc. Thanks for everything."

As Seward hung up his phone, Maria Alvarez, a receptionist who had worked at the Wellsley House for many years hung up her phone also. She had never been into the process of eavesdropping, but had noticed changes in Gabe Seward that were unlike him in all the years she had known him. Her eyes were full of tears as she hung up, understanding that the man that had devoted his life to disadvantaged kids may now lose that life. She knew that Gabe lived from paycheck to paycheck, and, with his health insurance canceled, would have few options. It was with that in mind that she called Danny Murray; the young man whom she knew Gabe was closest to. Somehow, she thought that Murray could figure out a way to help him.

CHAPTER 26

RUNNING FOR GABE SEWARD'S LIFE

That evening Maria Alvarez met with Danny and told him everything she had learned. Danny was devastated by the news but did little to reveal his emotions. He told Alvarez not to worry, that he had a plan for insuring Gabe's medical care.

The following evening Danny met Gabe at Memorial Park for a run.

"You doing okay?" Danny asked Gabe as the two started around the trail. Danny had cut back the normal pace that the two ran to almost a snail's pace, aware of Gabe's condition and fearful that anything more could tax his friend whose health was hanging by a slender thread.

"Never better," Gabe said. "Healthy as a horse."

"Your physical was okay?"

"Perfect."

Danny nodded. Gabe didn't want to say anything, and that was his business, he thought. And there was no way he would reveal that he knew other, that Maria Alvarez had overheard his conversation with his physician.

"That's good, Gabe, because I was thinking about what I told you a few days ago, and I've changed my mind."

"What's that?"

"I've realized you're right about my running. I can definitely make a bigger impact with disadvantaged kids by competing again than just letting it slide, from both a visibility point of view and a financial one. I'll be able to effectuate immediate change."

Gabe grinned. "That's great. Why the sudden change of heart?"

"I don't know. Sometimes it takes me a while to formulate things and see them in a better light. You've helped enlighten me."

"You're making the right decision. You won't regret it."

"I've contacted an agent, and he's already gotten me into some foreign meets in the Middle East and Europe. There are some very hefty bonuses for records. And they're so damn anxious to have me run, they don't care if I'm a member of United States Track and Field Federation or not. They want gate, Gabe. And they know I can bring it. There are some rabid track and field fans over there, and they haven't forgotten the 5K you saw me run at Hayward. They don't give a damn that USTAFF refused to sanction it.

"And I'm not interested at this point in fighting them. I'm going to rewrite the record books in Europe, Asia, Africa, or wherever they put up the money for me to run. The hell with the s.o.b.'s in USTAFF. They robbed me of what was rightfully mine and convicted me without a trial. It'll be a cold day in hell before I run for a record in this country. If any ass-kissing goes down to get me to run here, I can guarantee you it won't be on my part."

"When are you planning on running?"

"I'll be leaving the country in a few days."

"Don't you need some preparation?"

"Nope. I'm ready. I can run the times I did when I was 17 with my eyes closed. You know that. You've seen me run."

"Why the rush?"

"Why should I wait?"

"Because if you're not in top condition, you could run a race or two and end up injuring yourself."

"I'm not going to get injured. I can handle it."

Gabe stared at Danny. At 21 he had experienced much more than most men would ever in a lifetime. He had survived against overwhelming odds, and it had matured him far beyond his years. Yet in spite of it all, he was still very much the same brash kid that he'd first met as a 17-year-old teenager. Murray had no doubt about his abilities back then, and none now.

"You're sure you're not rushing things?"

"I'm sure."

"Okay then, my friend. Good luck." Gabe stuck out his hand and Danny shook it.

A rushed passport and special arrangements got Danny to Dubai, Saudi Arabia, a week later. It was a place and a country that he loathed, in light of everything that had gone down since the World Trade Center tragedy of Sept. 11, 2001. But the hell with politics, Danny thought. This would be for Gabe, and the money that he'd be taking out of the Persian Gulf would go straight to him. The country he would be running in didn't give a damn about ethics, Danny thought. Their bottom line was oil and money, the second a commodity that Danny would gladly relieve them of.

...

The Dubai mile that Danny was scheduled to run was being dubbed as the greatest mile to ever be contested. It had the current world recordholder from Morocco, and a host of up-and-coming threats from Algeria, Kenya, Ethiopia, Spain, Italy, England, Germany, Ireland, and Portugal.

Danny Murray was the only American entry, the U.S. contingent of current milers and long-distance runners so far removed from where they had once been that many track and field experts were writing off the States as a country that would never again produce great distance runners. But in Danny Murray there was a buzz and excitement created, unlike what any American distance runner had triggered since Frank Shorter's gold medal marathon performance in Munich in 1972.

Though the Saudis had leaped at the prospect of bringing Danny to the desert for a shot at the mile, the smart money said other. London oddsmakers priced him at 40 to 1, the longest shot in a field of 15. The Saudis were offering huge money for the winner, with an equal bonus for a world record. The race was being televised throughout

Europe, in Canada, Australia, and Japan. But the U.S. had no planned television coverage, the networks ho-hum about an event that promised a pathetic viewer share. Their surveys indicated that broadcasting the Dubai meet would capture a viewer share only a mere fraction of what professional wrestling took in.

As Danny lined up for the beginning of the Dubai Mile, he glanced around at his competition that was the best in the world. The current world record holder was running, a Moroccan who had run 3:41.1. But there were a host of other threats too, runners from all over the globe who were capable of testing the current standard or dipping under it.

Three "rabbits" had also been brought in for the affair, men who would be paid healthy sums of cash for leading the field through a lighting quick quarter, half, and possibly even three-quarters if they could maintain, before stepping off the track to let the rest of the field go by. It was a tactic that would insure a quick early pace, making it easier for the rest of the field to trail them and set a record in their wake.

The long plane ride from the States had fatigued Murray, but now was no time to fret over tiredness, he thought. This would be the first leg of five races that would give him world records at the mile, 1,500 meters, 800 meters, 3,000-meter steeplechase, and the 10,000 meters. It would be run over a two-week period, a time he was certain the world of track and field would never forget. He would skip his favorite event, the 5,000 meters, a protest for the record he had already run but had been taken from him by the track federation of his own country.

As the starter called for the runners to come forward to the waterfall start, Danny Murray blocked everything else out of his mind and relaxed. His eyes had the killer look of old as they focused down the track, and he was totally clear as the starter gun went off and he shot forward. The rest of the field would rely on the rabbits to take them through consecutive 55-second quarter miles, giving the lightning fast field a chance for a fast finishing quarter to obliterate the current record.

Murray was oblivious to the rabbits as he smoked an opening quarter mile in 50 seconds, putting him a good thirty to forty yards ahead of the stunned rabbits who dragged the remainder of the field in their wake. A 55-second quarter mile brought him through the half in 1:45, as he maintained his lead.

As the rabbits dropped off the track, Danny increased his pace and lead, his three-quarter-mile split 2:40. He looked behind his shoulder as the gun fired for the final lap. He blotted out the thunderous roar in the stands as the Arabs realized history was being set on their home turf. All Murray needed was a pedestrian final quarter mile of 60 seconds to break the record. But Danny accelerated into another gear and smoked the next 220 in 26 seconds. With only 220 yards to go, his time was 3:06, meaning he could practically jog in with a 34-second 220 for a new world record. But he picked up the pace even more, the rest of the field almost 100 yards back as he approached the finish line. He eyed the digital clock that was at 3:30 as he stopped inches from the finish line. With his hands on his hips standing just inches from the finish line, he turned around. The field was so far behind that he realized nobody could come even close to ruining what he had planned.

A hush came over the stadium as he stood there, just a fraction of an inch from the finish line as precious seconds ticked off the digital clock. At 3:39.8 he moved forward. The digital clock read 3:40.1 as he touched the line. It was a new world record, about a second quicker than the old standard. He had judged it just right, wishing to leave intact the 3:40 range before becoming the first man to dip into the 3:30s.

Murray's expression didn't change as he jogged to his athletic bag where he'd left his warm-ups. As the rest of the field finished, the fans in the stands were still on their feet, screaming and stomping, wild with ecstasy. Murray knew that he had taken the world record, but had left huge room for improvement. It would be his insurance policy for a future of faster miles should he decide to run them.

He made his way under the stands to the locker room and denied the crowd a victory lap. It was his way of sending a message to a land shrouded in veils that he loathed. He had given them what they wanted--a record--and now he would get paid for having run it. The money would be wired back to the States and Gabe would have the first installment of a lot more that would follow to pay for his cancer surgery and treatment.

Reporters swarmed Danny as he made his way off the infield and toward the locker room. The interview that he granted was terse and to the point.

"Why did you stop when you reached just inches from the finish line?" a reporter from England asked.

"Brain went into meltdown," Danny lied. "I'm not used to running in the desert heat."

"My God, mate, you had at least another bloody ten seconds in you," an Aussie reporter said.

Danny shrugged his shoulders. "That's conjecture. Until you do something, what-ifs don't mean a thing."

"Have you been training at altitude?" an Italian reporter asked.

"Nope. Sea level. Houston, Texas."

"That's hard to believe."

"Believe it."

"How do you feel since your sister was murdered?" a French reporter asked.

Danny glared at him. "How would you feel, asshole?"

A hush followed his words. The British reporter whispered in Danny's ear, "Careful, Murray. This isn't the West. They don't take kindly to that kind of behavior here."

"Screw him," Danny said.

"What kind of training did you do in Houston, Texas?" the Italian reporter asked.

"Strictly roadwork and Fartlek."

"No track?"

"Nope."

"That's hard to believe."

"That's your problem."

"What prompted you to run here without having done track work?" a German reporter asked.

"Money."

"To pay your legal bills?"

Danny's fists tightened. "No more questions," he said.

It was the last words that he uttered on Arab soil. After giving urine and blood samples, he took a cab to the airport and caught a flight to London. As his plane streaked across the clear heavens far above the desert, Danny stared out his window thinking of Cindy, Gabe, and Maria. His body was shaking as he went back to the washroom and locked the door. Inside he began sobbing uncontrollably, waves of anger, hurt, and loss engulfing him. He'd taken little pleasure out of his world record run, knowing beforehand it would be that way. Records or money meant nothing to him. The only person that he'd really loved had been taken from him. And now the man that had been his only friend in time of need was on death's bed.

CHAPTER 27

SURGERY

Danny and Maria sat in a waiting room at M.D. Anderson early Monday morning as Gabe underwent brain surgery.

The last two weeks had been a blur. After setting the world record in the mile, he had stunned track and field fans in a two-week blitz of Europe that would likely never be repeated. In that time frame, he had set world records in the metric half-mile, mile, 1,500 meters, 3,000-meter steeplechase, and the 10,000 meters. The only track distance record that he didn't attempt was 5,000 meters, the fated race that he had run preceding Cindy's murder, a legitimate run that had been disallowed by USTAFF officials. Declining to run in a 5,000-meter race in Europe was his way of calling attention to the USTAFF's misdeed.

But Murray had gleaned little joy from his record blitz on foreign soil. His only solace was the fact that the monies earned from his races and records had made him wealthy in a short period of time, money that would be sufficient for Gabe's medical bills and much more. A number of European and Asian athletic concerns were also vying for product endorsements, contracts that would likely guarantee a lifetime of financial security.

Danny thumbed through magazines that were scattered throughout the room, unable to concentrate on any of the articles, disconnected pieces that seemed to run together like a meaningless sea of words and photos. A television quasi-news features show humming from an overhead television did no more to capture his attention. It was like background noise, mind-numbing drivel that mesmerized the American public on a daily basis but held little interest for him. But that morning, even the most captivating novel or work of nonfiction would have had little appeal to Murray. He was, unlike his normal self, nervous and scared. The fearlessness that had enabled him to survive and prosper was gone. In its place was a frightened young man, feeling totally out of control as his best friend lay on an operating table battling for his life. It was unlike running where he had total control, never a doubt in his mind that he could decimate whatever foe lined up next to him.

Murray's only other trip to a hospital had ended in death, the surgeon who had come to tell Danny of Cindy's fate like the Grim Reaper in his psyche. Gabe's surgery was one that Danny had been up all night reading about and studying from medical websites on the Internet.

It was a procedure where the skull was invaded and opened in a way that could be compared to a carpenter working with a high-speed saw. Once a section of the skull was sawed out and removed, the surgeon would then begin the process of searching for cancerous tissue and excising it. A skilled physician would probe the brain with the delicacy of an artist, skilled hands deftly removing select sections of cancerous brain matter with exact precision. Just the slightest of miscalculations—an errant nick or a quiver of the wrist—could spell disaster for the patient, the potential plethora of things that could go wrong from damaging the brain too immense to even begin to list.

In some cases, when tumors were so deeply lodged into areas of the brain that removal would not be safe, Danny had read that those areas would not be removed, future doses of radiation and chemotherapy the only alternatives. He had also learned that following Gabe's brain surgery, chemotherapy would have to be coordinated to attack the tumors that had invaded his lungs.

Statistically, Gabe's chances of long-term survival were slim, his chances of total recovery remote. And even if he did survive, his body would likely never be the same, the ravages of cancer and the therapies to fight it reducing him to a shell of his former self.

As Danny sat, his eyes turned to Maria. Her skin had a sickly pallor and her eyes were sunken from a lack of sleep. Her head turned to Danny and they made eye contact.

"You okay?" Danny asked.

"Scared," Maria said.

Danny nodded. "Me too."

"I didn't think you ever got scared, Danny."

"You're wrong."

"You know, Gabe has known me since I was a little girl. No matter how bad things were at home, he always encouraged me. Always told me I could do things I never thought I was capable of. Without him it would have been a lot harder growing up. I'm not sure I'd be where I am today if it wasn't for him."

Danny nodded. "I understand."

She looked earnestly at Murray. "You know, I know what you did for Gabe. How you went over to Saudi and Europe to run in those meets just to pay for his cancer surgery."

"Who told you that?" Danny asked, the tone of his voice displeased.

"Gabe."

Danny said, "Don't believe everything you hear."

"Why are you so hard on yourself, Danny? How come you have such a problem taking credit for something you did that was good?"

"Maria, what Gabe did for me makes any little thing that I could ever do for him pale in comparison. He literally put his life on the line for me. Do you know what would have happened if he had been caught helping me after I fled my sister's murder and he shielded me from authorities?"

"Yeah. I know. But most people aren't like you. Most don't see beyond themselves. They take what they can and don't care what anybody else has done for them. The people in my family don't give a damn about me. My father is no good. And my own brother has stolen from me. And you know about my mother."

212

Danny nodded.

"You're a good man, Danny. I'll never forget what you did for Gabe."

Danny felt his neck and ears redden. He got up and said, "I'm going to take a walk."

"Okay," Maria said.

Danny took a long walk, and when he got back, Maria was still in the waiting room. "Why don't you get out of here for a while?" Danny said. "It'll do you good."

"Good idea."

Maria left and got back about fifteen minutes later. The two continued taking off and coming back as the surgery continued. When Danny returned, almost three and a half hours had elapsed since the start of the surgery. He walked into the waiting area. As he spotted Maria she began weeping. Danny's heart sank and blood drained from his head. He felt dizzy and nauseous as he realized what had happened.

Maria got up and wrapped her arms around him, squeezing him in a deathlike grip as she wept. Danny's arms gently encircled her as she continued crying. When her sobbing stopped she released him and looked up. As she gazed into his eyes, he was shocked to see her smiling, her face radiant.

"He came out of the surgery okay," Maria said. "His doctor said he's sure he got all the cancer and that the tumors had not invaded nearly as far as they suspected. They think he's going to be fine from the brain surgery. Now it's just a matter of getting to his lungs."

Danny grinned from ear to ear and the two hugged again. Maria looked up at Danny, pushed his red hair out of his eyes, and got up on her toes. She cupped his face in her palms and touched her lips to his. The sensation was overpowering, and he felt drunk with ecstasy.

"Let's go celebrate tonight," she said.

He nodded.

"I know a good Mexican restaurant where I want to take you, and then we'll go to some clubs and Salsa dance," she continued.

"I don't know how to dance," Danny said.

"I'll teach you."

Danny breathed deeply. "Okay," he said.

Maria kissed him again, and the darkness that had shrouded his soul lifted. He felt as if a brilliant sun had ignited a black sky, the radiant warmth breathing new life into his darkened spirit. Gabe was going to make it, he thought. The tough old bird would beat the odds.

...

That night Danny and Maria danced until the wee hours of the morning. At half past 2:00, Maria said, "Are you tired?"

"No."

"Would you be willing to take a drive?"

"Sure."

"Good. I have somewhere I'd like to show you. My uncle has a place in the country that I'd like to take you to."

The two left a club in downtown Houston and headed south on Highway 59. Past Richmond, Texas, they exited, and Maria guided Danny through the country. At a fenced area off a dirt country road, Maria unlocked a gate, and Danny drove onto the property. It was luxuriant land, verdant fields that in the spring were blanketed with blushing wildflowers that dappled the fields with vibrant color. A giant pecan tree shaded the front yard of the property leading to a two-story southern plantation-style home.

"Rich relative?" Danny asked.

"Yes. My uncle Vincente is in the funeral business."

Maria began laughing and so did Danny. "There are a lot of Hispanics in the Houston area," she said. "So Vincente should have good business for generations to come."

Danny killed the engine of his truck, and the two walked toward the house. They walked up a short flight of steps and passed a porch swing. Maria unlocked the front door of the house and led him inside.

She took him on a tour of the home, the wooden floors of rich oak, the furnishings mostly antiques, Hispanic relics from Texas' early past.

"Do you like it?" Maria asked.

"Beats any place I've ever lived in."

Maria nodded. From a downstairs closet she pulled out a thick quilt, two down pillows, and a lantern. She handed the lantern to Danny. "Follow me," she said. "I want to take you to my favorite place."

She led him out the backyard and they walked several hundred yards until they reached an old barn. Maria handed Danny some matches and said, "Please light the lantern."

Danny did, and she led him inside the barn. The barn was free of animal scent, fresh hay laid and stacked throughout. She led him up a ladder to a second-story loft, and there she opened a window that looked out onto a meadow.

"This was my secret place when I was a little girl," she said. "I used to come up here sometimes and sleep. It's really pretty when the sun comes up." She pointed out to the meadow. "It comes up right over there."

"I spent my share of time in barns too, when I was a kid," Danny said.

"You did?"

"Yes."

"You had a rich uncle?"

"No uncles."

"Who had a barn?"

"I don't know."

"How could you not know?"

"I used to sneak into neighbors' barns when I'd run away from home. My parents fought a lot. My dad was an abusive drunk."

"Oh. You had a tough childhood, didn't you?"

"Yes," Danny said.

"Gabe didn't tell me much."

"I don't like to talk about it."

"I understand."

The two sat in silence for a while gazing out into the darkness. And then Danny started to talk. Maria sat and listened as he told her more about his past than he had ever told anybody in his life. By the time he finished, morning was breaking and the sun was rising.

As Danny quieted, Maria's dark eyes locked with his. They remained that way until she stood and faced the window, her back to him. Then she slowly unbuttoned her blouse, slid out of it and laid it neatly on the hay beneath her. The action revealed a gently curved back and long graceful neck. Her white bra was in stark contrast to her nutbrown skin, smooth as satin.

Then she unfastened her skirt, and placed it on top of her blouse. Danny's pulse sped as he viewed her from behind, the slender white thong that separated her shapely legs and peach-shaped rear, an aphrodisiac of immeasurable potency.

She just stood in that position for what seemed to Danny as forever, her beauty and sensuality more fantastic than anything he'd ever fantasized. He felt both aroused and scared, uninitiated to lovemaking and a woman's wants and needs.

As Danny's heart raced, she reached behind her and unfastened her bra, the straps sliding down her smooth shoulders. She lifted the feathery garment off her chest and dropped it on top of the skirt. Then she cupped her breasts with her palms and turned around. In Danny's eyes she could see the want and fear, both the same feelings that she was experiencing in her first encounter with love. She just stood like that for a lengthy time before removing her hands from her chest.

Danny felt like his head was on fire as she stood there, her firm breasts rising and falling with every breath. Her areolas were plum colored, nipples firm and high as they beckoned.

Then she leaned forward and pulled down her thong, stepping out of the garment on the soft hay beneath her bare feet. The action revealed a narrow thatch of dark hair that shielded her femaleness.

She continued watching Danny, his eyes locked to hers, as she made her way forward and knelt on her knees in the hay in front of him. She leaned forward and kissed him gently on the lips, and Danny felt drunk with ecstasy. When the kiss ended, she brought his face forward and buried it between her breasts. Danny kissed them lightly and she shuddered.

As she gently pushed him back she helped him out of his clothes. She studied his body, slender but chiseled. Her eyes traced him from his eyes down, and as they settled between his legs saw him eager and waiting. She wondered if he would hurt her, he being much larger than she had envisioned. And she wondered if he would remain a part of her life when they were finished. Or would he be like other males in her family who were never loyal or left their women whenever it suited them? She wondered how she would feel afterwards, losing the virginity that she'd held out for so long.

Danny cupped her face with his palms and kissed her, and the two fell back into the soft hay, Maria on top. As Danny watched her from beneath, she eased herself down on him, and he could see both the pain and pleasure on her face as he went inside her. It was over quickly, the excitement of the moment more than Danny had bargained for. But just minutes later they were making love again, this time more attuned to their bodies' rhythm and movements.

By afternoon the two were spent, their endless lovemaking a dance they had mastered. As they dressed they had little conversation, the two walking from the barn holding hands as they made their way back toward the house. Danny knew his life had turned around, and felt that in Maria he had found the woman that would become his family. It was truly the beginning of a new life for him, one that would be far removed from the horrors of his past.

CHAPTER 28

HORROR AND HOPE

Danny was not prepared for the sight that met him that afternoon when he visited Gabe in recovery. His head was bandaged and tubes snaked out of his veins.

He was shocked when Gabe opened his eyes and said, "Piece of cake. Doc said they got all the cancer."

Murray fumbled for words. "How long before you can start running?"

"Got to get these tubes out of me."

"Shouldn't be long," Danny said.

"Sooner the better, amigo."

When the bandages were removed from Gabe's head, Murray was again shocked to see the condition of Seward. His scalp was shaved and there was a red scar where it had been laid back like a flap to get to the skull.

As Gabe lay in bed, he gently patted his skull. "Won't have to worry about haircuts for a while. This should save me some money."

"Should make you run faster too. Less wind resistance."

Gabe grinned faintly. "Wasn't that much there before."

Danny stared silently at Seward. Gabe could see the concern in Murray's face. "Do I look that bad?" Seward asked.

"Yeah. But so what else is new?"

Gabe suppressed a laugh and then he started to gag. He pointed to a metal bedpan that Murray grabbed and handed to him. Seward then heaved into the bedpan. When the heaving stopped he looked embarrassed and said to Danny, "Sorry. I feel a little woozy."

"Want me to leave?"

"Don't you have anything better to do than stand here and watch me puke?"

"Nope. I'm a rich man now after all those meets overseas."

Gabe nodded. "You won't be after all these medical bills come in. You know I'm going to repay you, don't you?"

"Shut up, Gabe."

Seward shook his head. "What do people do who can't afford this kind of treatment?" Seward said.

"I'd hate to imagine."

Gabe wiped his eyes that clouded with tears. He didn't answer Murray. He didn't need to.

...

When the chemotherapy treatments for Gabe's lungs began, Danny asked to meet Dr. Abraham Abramowitz, the oncologist who was in charge of Gabe's treatment.

"Gabe told me a lot about you," Abramowitz said. "You are quite a runner."

"Thanks."

"And what you have done for your friend is really unbelievable."

Danny blushed. "Gabe risked his life for me. This is nothing in comparison."

"Humility is the greatest strength a man can exhibit."

"Gabe wrote the book on humility, Dr. Abramowitz. The only thing that I've provided in this equation is money. Money's transitory."

Abramowitz nodded his head. "A profound truth."

"Gabe doesn't have any family. So I guess I'm about as close as he has. Can you tell me what his chances of survival are?" Danny asked.

"Yes. Mr. Seward has instructed me to be frank with you. Frankly, his chances are not good. Remote at best. An infinitesimal percentage of patients survive both brain and lung cancer."

"Gabe will make it," Danny said.

"I hope so."

"No hoping involved. There's not a negative bone in his body."

"And that's a very important part of the recovery process. But Gabe is in for a very trying and lengthy bout. The chemo that we'll give him will practically kill him. It will leave him so devastated and sick that frequently he will wish he were dead. He will be nauseous and dizzy and vomit constantly. He will be vomiting when there is nothing left to vomit. He will feel like he has the worst case of the flu imaginable for hours, and sometimes days and weeks at a time. He will have difficulty drinking or eating. He will lose his lust for every desire we know. His sleep will be a series of nightmares. He will be facing a darkness that is blacker than even the most sinister of torturers could ever conceive of. In short, every fiber of his being will be tested as we attempt to kill his cancer. And that cancer is the most insidious of foes, Mr. Murray. It does not quit, and one can never escape completely from its clutches.

"But with all this darkness I have told you, let me say that in all the years I have practiced medicine, I have never met a patient with a more positive outlook than Gabe Seward. That, and as a 57-year-old man, he has the cardiovascular system of a teenager. If anybody can beat the odds that are stacked against him, he's most certainly a man who can."

Danny nodded. "I appreciate your being so forthright."

"When are you planning on racing again?"

"I'm not."

"Why is that?"

"A lot of reasons."

Abramowitz nodded. "I hope you'll change your mind about that."

"Not likely."

"You have lost your lust to run?"

"Running's fine. It's the hierarchy that controls it that isn't."

Abramowitz nodded his head. "I understand. Just like every institution and organization."

"Running's worse."

"Perhaps. But I wouldn't wager heavily on that. I would be willing to bet that many of the frustrations that you face in the running world are not that far removed from those that I deal with practicing medicine. Life is like that. All institutions have deep systemic flaws."

Danny nodded. "Right. I'm aware of that. But the running hierarchy is particularly bad."

"I've read of Olympic misdeeds."

"Believe them and more," Danny said.

Abramowitz nodded.

"Please get Gabe well," Danny said.

"I will do everything that is within my power."

The two shook hands and Danny left the room. He would spend the afternoon with Gabe, holding his bedpan for him as he threw up bile, doing all the chores that a nurse would do but that he preferred to do on his own. It was his way to let Seward know the deep affection that he felt for him. Gabe had resurrected his life. And he had introduced him to the young lady that he hoped would become his wife. Both she and Gabe were trying to teach him trust. It was a concept that he had difficulty accepting from a life where so many things had gone horribly wrong.

...

On a Saturday afternoon following a run in Memorial Park, Danny and Maria were driving through the Heights when Maria asked Danny to pull over. "I love this old house," she said.

It was a home that had been built probably in the '30s, a wood frame classical structure that needed a lot of work.

An agent was showing the property to some clients, and when they left she spotted Danny and Maria in Danny's truck.

She walked out to the truck.

"I'm Mary Jane Carter. Would you two like to take a look at this home? I'm the agent, and it's just gone on the market."

Danny looked at Maria. Her eyes were wide. "Sure," Danny said.

She took them on the tour of the home, which was in need of many repairs.

"The property value is what makes this home valuable," she said. "The house is basically a teardown, but it's in a very desirable area."

She gave them the price of the home and, after asking a number of questions, left.

"I wouldn't tear down that house if I bought it," Maria said. "I would redo it and live there."

Danny nodded.

Maria turned to Danny. "What do you think about family?" she asked.

"It's what I wanted all my life. I've told you that." He dropped his head and lowered his tone. "It's what I always fantasized for Cindy. But now that that's gone, the dream has changed."

"So you don't want a family now?"

"More now than ever. It's just that the dream has changed. Cindy won't be around to share it."

"I've always lusted for a real family too."

Danny nodded. He reached into his jeans and pulled out a small package wrapped in brown paper. He tore the paper from the package, revealing a black velvet box. He opened the box, and Maria was stunned at its contents. Inside was a round diamond solitaire, set in platinum, its cuts gleaming with shocking clarity ignited by the brilliant overhead sun. Danny lifted out the ring and knelt on his knees. He gazed up at Maria and said, "If you take this ring and be my wife, I'll stay your family as long as you'll have me."

Maria's body shook like a leaf as she helped Danny to his feet and put out her hand. He placed the ring on the ring finger of her left hand and the two hugged intensely. Then they kissed, a long, deep kiss that lasted on and on. When it ended, Danny said, "After we get married, let's have a child."

Maria said, "Let's not wait."

Two days later they flew to Las Vegas and were married, and on return Danny purchased the house in the Heights they had looked at. Six weeks after having moved into their new home Maria tested pregnant.

To those who did not know them, their decisions may have appeared impetuous if not reckless, the heated acts of two young people who had not thought out their actions fully. But life experience and age were not congruent when it came to Danny and Maria, both mature well beyond their years. It was a new beginning for the two of them, a fresh start in two lives where so much in the past had gone wrong. Danny's running had provided them the luxury of financial independence and the security to start the family they had each long dreamt of.

Their new lives could not have started off better. Now it was just a matter of getting Gabe well.

CHAPTER 29

CANCER'S UGLY REALITY

Months passed as Gabe struggled with his chemotherapy. It sapped every bit of strength from him, and in the process Maria saw its effect on Danny. Though Murray tried to remain cheery around Seward, when he was away from him, the bleak reality of his friend's situation deeply depressed him. Gabe's weight was so low that he appeared much like the pictures Danny had seen of concentration camp prisoners in Nazi Germany.

Maria sidled up to Danny in bed on a Tuesday night. She knew he wasn't sleeping, Murray lying on his back staring emptily at the ceiling. She stroked his hair. She kissed his cheek.

"You're worried about Gabe, aren't you?"

"Yes."

"Worrying won't do you any good."

"That's easy to say."

Maria pulled Danny toward her and embraced him. As she stared in his eyes she said, "Gabe is going to die, isn't he?"

She could hear Murray breathe as she waited for his answer.

"He's very weak. The doctors don't give him much of a chance."

"What do you think, Danny?"

"I'm not a doctor."

"You've done everything you could. If he were to die, I know you'd miss him terribly. But I think you'd feel good having known you did everything you could for him."

"Whatever little I've done for Gabe is not enough. He risked his life for me. I need to do something more."

"What else could you do?"

224

"I don't know."

"Why don't you ask him?"

"No. That could be devastating to him. If I were to ask him, it would sound like I were asking him to give me his death wish. The last thing I need is to make him think we've given up."

"Danny, you've gotten to know Gabe very well. I think you know how to ask him."

Danny shook his head. "You don't think it will break his spirit?"

"No."

Following a lengthy silence Danny said, "It's obvious you're a lot more sensitive than me. I've never had a female point of view. Maybe you have an insight into him that I don't. Okay. I'll consider asking him. I just need some time before I decide."

Maria spooned up against Danny as his arm encircled her. He stroked her tummy, the fullness a powerful sensation to his touch. New life was on its way. Life was like that, Danny thought. Life and death were part of an ongoing process. Sometimes there was elation and sometimes heartbreak. Nobody had definite answers as to the riddle's true meaning.

...

Danny sponged Gabe's forehead.

"You look like hell, Gabe."

"But I feel okay," Gabe said.

"I get it. You feel great, but you throw up all day to get sympathy."

"Exactly," Gabe said. He smiled meekly. Then he began retching again as Danny held the bedpan for him. Nothing came up as he retched, his gut empty from the long bouts of vomiting that had drained him.

"Gabe, if you had one last wish, what would it be?"

Gabe looked at Danny with doleful eyes. "I'm not ready to die yet, Danny. This chemo stuff is working and I'll be back running with you before you can blink your eye."

"I'm waiting for the day. And I'll run your ass into the ground once you're back. But you didn't answer my question, Seward. If you could have one last wish, what would it be?"

Gabe stroked his chin. He removed his glasses and massaged his nose. A lengthy silence followed. He put the glasses back on and focused on Danny's eyes.

"I would like to watch you run a 5,000 here on American soil and take down your old record. But I'd want this one to count. You'd have to join USTAFF to put that record in the books."

Danny shook his head. "That's a wish you won't get. I won't lower myself to those bastards. Not after what they've done to me."

Gabe didn't answer.

"Don't just lay there not saying anything, Gabe. Say something. You're laying a guilt trip on me."

"You asked me what I would wish for and I told you."

Danny balled up his fist. It was so tight Seward could see Murray's knuckles protruding like white stones. "Won't happen, Gabe. Forget it."

Seward nodded. "No problem. You asked me what I'd wish for and I told you."

"Won't happen."

Gabe nodded his head. "Okay."

...

Danny and Maria flanked Gabe as they held his elbows, supporting him as they led him up the metal stairway fronting the aircraft. He was as light as a feather, his body having shed almost all vestiges of its former athletic health. It would be a long trip to Oregon.

Gabe was going to get his last wish, Danny thought. Hopefully the trip to Oregon wouldn't kill him. Murray had grudgingly joined the USTAFF and notified the press he would make a record run at the 5,000 meters on American soil. It was what Gabe wanted, and he would not deny him what could likely be his final wish.

226

As the plane lifted off, Gabe to his right, Maria to his left, Danny wondered what kind of reception he'd receive in Eugene. He had been vilified by the USTAFF, along with scathing articles in Barry Swill's Track and Field magazine.

As Danny ruminated, he remembered the previous races he'd run in Eugene. The fans there had treated him exceedingly well. But as he reminisced, he realized this wasn't about how the fans would treat him or how the press would cover him. This was about Gabe and attempting to fulfill a wish for him that may be his last.

...

That night after getting situated in Eugene, Danny and Maria rested in their hotel bed, Gabe staying in an adjoining room. At half past midnight, Murray got up and ambled into the washroom. Maria could hear him as he began retching.

The vomiting continued throughout the night, and Maria felt Danny's forehead that was on fire.

With Danny protesting, she drove him to the emergency room of a local hospital. There he was determined to have picked up a bug, having become dehydrated from the vomiting. He was treated, and the physician strongly advised him to get back to his hotel and into bed. Murray was told not to attempt to run the coming evening, that to do so could end in dire consequences. Danny nodded, and Maria drove him back to the hotel. Murray slept the rest of that day and didn't awake until early that evening. He felt like a worn-out dishrag as he lay.

When he got up out of bed Maria studied his face. It was as white as paste. He showered, and went to his suitcase where he took out his warm-ups and running gear.

"What are you doing?" Maria asked.

"What does it look like?" Danny said. As he spoke, he began getting dressed in his running clothes.

"Danny, you're not going to run tonight. You heard what the doctor told you."

"Doctors aren't gods. I'm running."

Maria remained silent and said, "You're not the only one to think about now. You have me and a child on the way."

Murray continued dressing. "I'll be fine. I know my body."

"Please don't run, Danny."

Danny continued dressing. "I'll be fine."

Maria knew that to say more was a waste. Once Danny made up his mind, that was it.

...

As Murray lined up for the beginning of the 5,000, a wave of emotions that he'd never dealt with previously engulfed him. For the first time in his running career he felt fear. Everything was coming apart.

He realized as he was warming up that he was weaker than he had ever imagined. He rarely got sick and, now that he was, he faced the daunting task of running in a race in which he had brashly predicted a world record. Compounding the pressure was the duty he felt to Gabe who was likely ready to die. Perhaps his final angst was the worst, realizing that his wife had been correct. It was clear to him now that he may be jeopardizing both Maria and their coming child by risking his health. He would be running in a race that a physician had told him could end in disaster.

Intensifying his pressure, Hayward Field had been filled as if it was an Olympic finals run. The stands were packed, and those who could not get into the stadium circled its perimeter. They would visualize the race by imagination, replaying every step in their minds as the track announcer's words colored the event on a loudspeaker sound system.

The noise level inside Hayward field was deafening. The cheering for Murray intensified as his name was announced. He felt overwhelmed. They were rooting for him, a circumstance he was unprepared for. The pressure of being a favorite was infinitely heavier than the underdog status he'd enjoyed when racing here as a 17-year-old. The race had attracted many of the world's best. They all wanted a crack at the man who had rewritten running history. His two-week tour of the Middle East and Europe had culminated in a blitzkrieg of records that would never be forgotten. He'd captured every other distance record from 800 meters to 10,000. Now only the 5,000 remained. If he were successful it would count on the American books, as he was now running as a member of USTAFF.

Danny felt lightheaded and weak as he lined up for the race's start. He could feel his heart running away in his chest. He felt dizzy and everything seemed to be spinning. The track appeared to him as an endless oval, looking infinitely larger than its 400-meter distance.

"Runners set!"

Danny leaned forward. His mouth was dry as cotton.

The crack of the pistol jolted him. He accelerated from the middle of the pack, his plan to run from the front as he always did. A blazing first quarter would put him out in front of everybody, out of harms way. He would be clear of the field and on his way home to his sixth and final record, one that would perhaps have the greatest meaning.

But as he broke for the rail with other runners, he realized that the burst of speed he had relied on was not there. Normally, by the time he broke for the rail, he would already have established a substantial lead on the field. But tonight his effort fell short and he was thrust into the middle of the pack. He was sucked into a sea of flailing elbows and flashing spikes, like a Spaniard on the streets of Pamplona running with the bulls.

He tried to relax, but he couldn't. He was not accustomed to running in a pack. More so he was not accustomed to running with dead legs. A sea of negative thoughts washed his brain as he faced the consequences of failure. He was being humiliated in a way he had never imagined. The bug that he'd picked up had taken more out of him than he had realized. Maria had been right, he thought. He shouldn't be running.

He glanced at the digital clock as he completed the first lap, mired in the middle of a deep pack. The numeral display of a minute and five seconds disheartened him further. A 65-second quarter, he thought, and he was pushing even at that speed.

As he ran the unthinkable happened. He heard the sound of tripping and cursing followed by a hand thrust into the small of his lower back. The action jolted him. A split second later he was down. He hit the tartan track like a brick. He had never been struck from behind in a track race. No one had ever been close enough to him in the beginning of a race to hit him. He was stunned as he pawed at the tartan. By the time he got to his feet, the pack was pulling away from him. Spike wounds had gashed his calf that was bleeding profusely. His knees were bruised and sore. But the physical pain paled to the distress he felt as he watched the field pull away from him.

As he began to run, his opened flesh spurting blood with every step, he visualized his worst nightmare taking shape. The horrors of his past further darkened his vision as black-and-white scenes flashed on his screen in rapid-fire succession.

He saw his father beating his mother. He saw himself shooting his father. He saw the suicide of his mother. He saw the loveless foster homes where he and his sister were victimized. And finally, he saw his sister in their trailer, partially clothed and bleeding, life leaving her tiny body as he screamed into the darkness for the nightmare to end.

As those black-and-white scenes madly flashed, a ray of light halted their action. A gentle wash of colors followed as the shape of Cindy's face sharpened. The scene was of his little sister in the Portland toy store where he'd taken her following his disallowed record run. He saw her smile, her face as radiant as the sun. Her blue eyes looked as large as robin eggs. As she smiled at him, he felt a chill down his spine. Her presence was real as he felt her with him. He felt a surge of energy, the darkness that had enshrouded him lifted. Fresh oxygen filled his lungs as his legs lightened. Then he focused on the field ahead of him and blotted out all else. The hungry cat came to life as Danny Murray stalked the field.

He went through the mile in 4:20, a good fifteen yards behind the leaders. At two miles he caught the pack, his time of 8:22 far off world-record pace. But as Murray began the first lap of his third mile, he threw in a blistering 400 meters of 54 seconds, his running time 9:16. The stunning lap brought the stands to its feet. The noise level was tremendous as he ran, but he heard nothing.

A second 57-second quarter put him at 10:13 with two laps and a tenth of a mile to go. Everyone inside Hayward Field was on its feet screaming. The roar of the fans huddled outside the stadium was thunderous as they heard Murray's splits.

The thunder echoed deep into the heart of the Willamette Valley as Murray separated further from the field. He felt no pain, his body separated from his mind as he ran. A 57-second third quarter put him at 11:10. More madness followed, and the stadium vibrated as Murray followed with a 57-second quarter.

The noise level was so loud that it hurt. Some of the runners held their hands to their ears in an attempt to deflect the screams. But Murray heard nothing, his three-mile time 12:07 as he negotiated his final tenth of a mile.

He had done the unthinkable, throwing in a third mile of 3:45, a time not far removed from his record speed for the distance. It was unfathomable, otherworldly.

As he approached the finish line, everything that had shifted to ecstasy turned to horror. He could feel everything slipping away as his strength left him. He was unaware of the track beneath him, as everything became a blur. And then his legs turned to rubber as his world turned black. He looked like a drunk as he weaved and bobbed. And then he collapsed. He fell like an animal that had been shot by a high-powered rifle. As he struck the tartan track women screamed.

At almost precisely the moment Danny Murray hit the track, Gabe Seward passed out in his seat. The emaciated man lurched forward and struck the concrete floor below him with a thud. As he fell Maria felt a kicking in her gut. She howled as the sea of horrors flooded her with fear and pain.

Medics rushed out onto the field, the prostrate body of Danny Murray attended to by a medical team. A thin ooze of blood leaked from Gabe Seward's lips as he lay on the pavement below Maria's feet. She screamed for help, tears streaming down her eyes as the new life within her kicked frantically. Nobody heard, the noise level in the stadium deafening as they reveled in Danny's run.

It didn't seem to matter to them that Murray was out cold. He had won the race. His finishing time of 12:30, a new world record that had demolished the existing standard, was all they could think about.

CHAPTER 30

STILLWATER, OKLAHOMA
AN UNTIMELY DEATH

"In every life there comes a time when we must choose a path. Sometimes the path chosen leads us to righteousness, and other times to evil. Today we celebrate the life of a man who chose the path of righteousness."

Maria held her infant Gabe Murray in her arms, the baby named after the man that both she and her husband loved so dearly. As they stood, the baby sobbed, and Maria gave the child a bottle that it took eagerly. The baby sucked on the bottle, the offering temporarily satisfying its need, the four-week-old infant content.

Maria and her child stood among a group who had gathered for the funeral--immediate family and friends--the minister fronting a coffin surrounded by pallbearers. They had lifted the heavy wooden casket from the back of a black hearse, the body of their fallen Oklahoma State runner resting inside.

It was the second funeral that Maria Murray had attended in the last month, a time when death and the preciousness of life had taken on new meaning to her. She tried to compose herself as she held her infant, but the moment got the best of her and she began to sob.

Cancer had been the thief of the man's life, 57 years seeming a terribly unfair lifespan for one who richly deserved so many more. It had been a wrenching, long-drawn-out death, the horrors of cancer and its equally brutal treatment, draining both its victim and everyone around him to depths of despair as he suffered.

When his last breath of oxygen was taken, and his chest rose and fell for the final time, those close to him saw it as a blessing, the end to his dreaded ordeal. Those of a religious nature saw it as a new beginning, a time when he would reunite with his maker in a better existence.

"I am not a distance runner," the minister continued. As he spoke the wind whipped across the Oklahoma prairie, ruffling his sandy hair. He pushed the hair back from his forehead and said, "But I have always seen distance running as a metaphor for a path well chosen, one where a man chooses to accept life's most difficult challenges, resistant to taking the shortcuts that lead to shallow gains.

"The distance runner embarks on the most difficult of journeys by taking a single step. And that first step can often be the most daunting, the prospect of endless miles of pain and suffering that lay ahead too frightening for many to ever attempt.

"And once the first step is taken, reality sets in, the jolt to the body a rude awakening that pain will accompany every outing, a constant companion that never leaves. But the distance runner continues on, dedicated to the straight and narrow path, his greatest reward internal, the lure of tangible rewards paling in comparison. The distance runner never quits, perhaps the noblest of his traits in a world where heartbreak and despair suffocate those of us of lesser faith."

The minister paused. A fresh wind whipped across the prairie, ruffling his hair once more. He brushed it away from his forehead and smiled.

"We are blessed to be living in what I feel is the most desirable country in the world. And we are further blessed to be living in what I feel is the most desirable state. Though at times, it can get a little windy."

His words brought some gentle laughter from the funeral-goers. "But the prairie is pure, as are the winds that constantly reshape its face and sweep it clean. The wind is both the distance runner's enemy and friend. Nothing can be more exhausting than running into an unrelenting headwind, while nothing can be more exhilarating than catching the puff of a brisk tailwind. Every distance runner prays for a tailwind. And as we lay our beloved runner into his final place of resting, may he always run with the wind at his back in the heavens above."

The minister signaled to the men surrounding the coffin, the pallbearers all middle-aged men dressed in Oklahoma State running warm-ups, as they picked up the coffin and lowered it into the ground. The minister then said, "Let us read responsively the 23rd Psalm."

Maria remained silent as tears clouded her eyes, and the group chanted King David's psalm.

As the ceremony ended, she waited as the group of Oklahoma State teammates passed on final farewells before the group broke up.

She remained patient as the thinnest man of the group turned and walked toward her. Another slender man who held him by the elbow supported him. The two moved painfully slowly, the older of the duo's bout with chemo and cancer not having finished that long ago. He was almost completely bald, fuzz starting to sprout where there had once been hair. His glasses, though they really hadn't, seemed to have become even larger covering his gaunt face.

The other man's boyish face had matured, and the look of anger that had once etched its edges had now softened. The anger had been replaced by wisdom, the rough edges replaced by kindness.

Gabe Seward had beaten the odds. None of the physicians thought the tough old bird had a real chance, overcoming cancer of the brain and lung a task that few had survived. But Gabe Seward was now part of that fraternity. He had never given up, refusing to be brought down by those who didn't share his bright vision. And Danny Murray had been there every step of the way with him from the time Gabe was diagnosed until just the past week when he had been given a clean bill of health.

Gabe was an amazing man, Maria thought. He had encouraged his friend Douglas Thomson all through his recent bout with cancer, one that he had just days ago lost.

But her husband Danny Murray was incredible also. Like his friend Gabe Seward, he didn't know the meaning of 'quit.'

It was fate that had brought Gabe and Danny together, and fate that had sealed a friendship that would remain eternal.

Just like Gabe Seward, Danny Murray was a survivor.

Slinger Sanchez Running Gun

A NOVEL BY
BRUCE GLIKIN

Slinger Sanchez Running Gun, Bruce Glikin's first novel, became an instant cult classic. The hard driving story of a possessed young man of mixed heritage-Irish American and Hispanic-and his salty Scottish coach, tells of their struggle to make 'Slinger' a world class runner. Praised by both critics and athletes alike, 'Slinger' is a compelling read that's hard to put down.

To order 'Slinger' please send a check or money order of $20.95, which includes shipping, handling, and taxes to:

Amber Fields Publishing
P.O. Box 35746
Houston, Texas 77235

Email: bglikin@houston.rr.com

Slumming Angels

A Trip Chandler Mystery by
Bruce Glikin

Houston based private eye Trip Chandler is a wise
cracking, quick fisted ex-cop, with a penchant
for attracting big time trouble and beautiful
women. When a wealthy Houston oilman is murdered
south of the border, Chandler dives head first
into the fray. The oil man's mistress—a drop dead
gorgeous blonde who's barely legal but has all
the skills-employs Chandler to get her off the
hook. Chandler's warned that the broad's going to
take him down too, but he doesn't listen.

To order 'Slumming Angels' please send a check or
money order of $20.95, which includes shipping,
handling, and taxes to:

Amber Fields Publishing
P.O. Box 35746
Houston, Texas 77235

Email: bglikin@houston.rr.com

To order additional copies of *Distant Runner*, please send a check or money order of $22.95, which includes shipping, handling, and taxes to:
Amber Fields Publishing
P.O. Box 35746
Houston, Texas 77235

Email: bglikin@houston.rr.com

LaVergne, TN USA
12 May 2010
182298LV00004B/224/A